Dance of Hearts

"Are you enjoying Almack's, Lady Selena?" asked the earl, taking Selena's hands in his own and leading her in a sedate circle.

"Yes, it's very nice," said Selena. "Although I must admit that the refreshments are hardly exceptional."

"Indeed, all you'll find here most times is bread and butter. But then there are other things more important. Why, to be seen here is essential to success in Society. You realize there are persons who would sell their own grandmothers to obtain entry to this august establishment?"

Selena laughed. "Isn't it utterly silly? I cannot understand why success in Society is so sought after."

He smiled again. "That is because you are a success. It is human nature to want what one does not have."

"Perhaps," she said, looking into his blue eyes.

The earl, looking down on her, had an almost overpowering urge to kiss her full, inviting lips.

A Royal
Connection

❖

by

Margaret Summerville

A SIGNET BOOK

SIGNET
Published by the Penguin Group
Penguin Putnam Inc., 375 Hudson Street,
New York, New York 10014, U.S.A.
Penguin Books Ltd, 27 Wrights Lane,
London W8 5TZ, England
Penguin Books Australia Ltd, Ringwood,
Victoria, Australia
Penguin Books Canada Ltd, 10 Alcorn Avenue,
Toronto, Ontario, Canada M4V 3B2
Penguin Books (N.Z.) Ltd, 182–190 Wairau Road,
Auckland 10, New Zealand

Penguin Books Ltd, Registered Offices:
Harmondsworth, Middlesex, England

First published by Signet, an imprint of Dutton Signet,
a member of Penguin Putnam Inc.

First Printing, April, 1998
10 9 8 7 6 5 4 3 2 1

1

Lady Selena Paget stood in the ballroom at Verney House surveying the large crush of people around her. The assembled company appeared quite merry, creating a hubbub of talk and laughter that nearly threatened to overtake the orchestra's more sedate tones. Although Selena maintained a polite smile on her face, she wasn't really enjoying herself.

Indeed, she was finding the ball, her first foray into London society, a considerable disappointment. This fact would have astonished most of the other guests, for, after all, the Verney ball was renowned as one of the most important events of the Season. It was attended by the cream of London Society, and many young ladies would have sorely envied Selena's opportunity to appear at such a splendid gathering.

And Selena had succeeded in making quite a splash that evening. It seemed that everyone had been eager to make her acquaintance, and a host of young gentlemen had flocked about her, hoping for a dance.

It wasn't difficult to understand Selena's popularity. Even if she hadn't been one of the loveliest young ladies at the ball, her rank and fortune would have assured her ready acceptance. As the sister of the Duke of Melford, Selena Paget was a lady of considerable consequence and a great prize in the Marriage Mart.

The fact that she was three and twenty and still unmarried was a matter of great interest to Society. After all, at that advanced age, most girls were thought to be on the shelf. What was even more curious was the fact that this was Selena's first London Season, for until now, she had lived with her father, the late duke, on the family's estate in Northumberland.

Of course, it hadn't been Selena's choice to stay away from London. Since the time she had been a little girl, she had often dreamed of the great city, imagining the glittering company that would abound in London and wishing that she could be a part of it.

Unfortunately, Selena's late father had not shared her enthusiasm for town. In truth, the Seventh Duke of Melford had heartily detested the city. Apparently the duke had formed his distaste for London as a young man, and he had often referred to it as a place of "jackanapes and humbugs." Indeed, the late duke avoided London at all costs, only coming to town when his lofty position made an appearance there necessary.

Over the years Selena had often asked her father when she might go to London, but the duke had steadfastly refused to take her there. After all, his grace hadn't wanted his only daughter exposed to the questionable morals of town. And he hadn't been eager to have Selena marry and leave Melford Castle. As he had often declared, if she needed suitors, she could choose among the local gentry and stay close at hand.

And so Selena had remained at home with her widowed father, associating only with the county families. During the past few years, her father had grown ill, and Selena had been very much occupied with his care.

Following the duke's death more than a year ago, Selena had remained in Northumberland. Then, with her period of mourning over, she had been persuaded by her brother and sister-in-law to come to London and stay with them in town for the Season.

Having arrived in London just two days prior to the ball, Selena had been quite thrilled to be in the great metropolis at last. She had eagerly looked forward to her introduction to London Society at the Verney ball.

Yet, now as she stood trying to appear interested in what one loquacious matron was telling her, Selena was tired and bored. She found herself reflecting that her feet hurt and she wished to go home. She also wished that a certain stout young gentleman named Sir Ronald Witherington hadn't apparently become enamored of her. He was beside her now, eyeing her like a devoted puppy.

Yet, one could well understand Sir Ronald's interest. Selena was exceptionally attractive. Tall and statuesque, she had a voluptuous figure that elicited considerable masculine attention. And, although her striking red hair was scarcely in vogue, it caused more than one dark-haired lady to wish she had Selena's flamboyant tresses. Selena was also blessed with fine classical features and lovely sea-green eyes.

Attired in a magnificent white silk gown with a low-cut bodice and tiny puffed sleeves, her red hair festooned with dainty white flowers, Selena had been an instant sensation. Gentlemen had swarmed about her like bees around a hive and she had soon been engaged for every dance.

While most young ladies would have been flattered at commanding such attention, Selena was quickly becoming disillusioned with her high expectations of Society. She had always thought that such functions would be filled with fascinating people who would entertain one with stimulating conversation and witty repartee. However, Selena was quickly finding that the Verney Ball was much like those she had attended in Northumberland.

The topics for discussion were exactly like those in her old neighborhood. The ladies spoke chiefly of the weather and a host of ailments suffered by themselves or their relations. The gentlemen, if they spoke at all, seemed to focus primarily on horse racing and fox hunting.

Suppressing a sigh, Selena tapped her elegant fan absently against her gloved hand. Avoiding Sir Ronald's gaze, she nodded to the talkative lady standing with her. The evening she had so looked forward to now seemed to stretch out endlessly before her.

"There you are, Selena," said a dark-haired lady, coming up to her. "I see you are enjoying yourself."

Selena managed a smile. "Oh, yes, Hetty." She was relieved to have her sister-in-law join them.

Henrietta, Duchess of Melford, was having a wonderful time. She was particularly delighted with the reception that Selena was receiving. She smiled brightly at Selena and the others.

At five and twenty years of age, Henrietta was an exceedingly pretty woman. Petite and what was called "pleasingly plump," the duchess had sparkling brown eyes and black ringlets framing her round face. Although she was known in Society to be something of a featherhead, Henrietta's good heart and generous nature made her quite popular.

"I fear I must take Selena away from you, Lady Braxton. There are so many others dying to meet her."

Allowing Lady Braxton and Sir Ronald no opportunity to protest, she took Selena by the arm and steered her away.

"Thank you for rescuing me, Hetty," said Selena.

"I thought you needed rescuing, my dear. Lady Braxton is such a bore and it is clear Sir Ronald has a *tendre* for you. And while he is a nice boy, he isn't very dashing and he has little money. Poor lad. You mustn't lose your heart to him, Selena."

Selena laughed. "I assure you there is no danger of that."

Henrietta smiled in reply. "Isn't it a splendid ball, Selena? And you have had such a triumph! Why, I have scarcely had an opportunity to speak with you all evening with all the gentlemen clamoring about you."

Selena cast a sardonic glance at her sister-in-law. "It is easy to have a triumph, as you call it, when one is the sister of a duke with the prospect of a rich dowry."

The duchess shook her head, causing her dark curls to bob up and down. "What nonsense, Selena! It's obvious that you are very much admired. Why, I daresay even if you were the sister of a chimney sweep you'd still be the most sought-after girl at the ball tonight."

Selena laughed. "You are quite ridiculous, Hetty. A chimney sweep's sister at the Verney ball?"

Henrietta looked slightly befuddled. "I suppose it would be extremely unlikely. But I only meant to say that you must cease thinking that every gentleman is a fortune hunter. Now that you are in town you will have all manner of suitors to choose from. We will make a splendid match for you."

Selena rolled her eyes heavenward. "I beg you not to play the role of matchmaker. If I choose to marry, I shall prefer to find my own husband."

This remark appeared to disturb Selena's sister-in-law. "Choose to marry? You cannot choose otherwise."

"Indeed I can. I shall remain as I am unless I find a man whom I wish to marry. Thus far, I haven't met him."

"Of course, you haven't. Why, you've only just come to town. There were so few suitable gentlemen in Northumberland, but now that you're here, you'll find no shortage of handsome, eligible suitors." She paused and regarded her sister-in-law hopefully. "Haven't you found any of the gentlemen to your liking?"

Selena was about to reply negatively to this, but she was interrupted by the appearance of her brother, a tall, handsome man with red hair of a shade somewhat lighter than his sister's. The Duke of Melford smiled as he stopped before the two ladies.

"Wonderful ball, don't you think? And Selena is creating quite a stir. I saw you dancing with the Marquess of Woodbury's son. You should encourage him, Selena."

Selena directed a pained look at her brother. "You, too, James? I was just telling Hetty that I shall choose my own husband, if, indeed, I choose to marry at all."

The duke smiled as he turned to his wife. "My sister is the most stubborn female imaginable, Hetty. I imagine we had best leave the choice of suitors to her."

"Perhaps you are right, my dear," returned the duchess. She smiled at Selena. "You'll be far more interested in marriage when you meet the right gentleman. I only hope you are as fortunate as I have been." The duchess looked up adoringly at her husband.

Selena shook her head. "I fear I may disappoint you, Hetty. I'm not in the least romantic, you know. I've never acted the moonling over any man and I'm firmly convinced that I never shall." She turned to her brother. "But I will say, James, you must be an excellent husband. It appears your wife thinks so highly of matrimony that she is eager to push me into it." Selena paused, a mischievous gleam appearing in her green eyes. "Or, perhaps, it is only as the proverb says, Misery loves company."

Henrietta laughed. "I should only hope you will know such misery, my dear," she said, exchanging a fond glance with her husband.

"Oh, I'm well aware that you two are deliriously happy," said Selena. "Though knowing James as well as I do, I must admit I find it difficult to comprehend." Her brother gave her a mock look of indignation and they all laughed.

The duke's smiling expression changed abruptly to a look of displeasure as his glance fell upon a gentleman who had just entered the ballroom. "One might expect him to arrive at such a late hour," he muttered.

Both Selena and Henrietta looked at the object of the duke's disapproval. He was a tall, elegantly dressed gentleman, who was languidly walking across the room. Selena studied the stranger with great interest. The offending gentleman had an athletic build that did much credit to his well-cut evening clothes. He had curly dark hair and even from her distant gaze, Selena could see that he was extremely handsome. "Who is he?" she asked, keeping her eyes fixed upon the gentleman.

The duke frowned. "The Earl of Heathfield," he replied in icy tones.

"That is the Earl of Heathfield?" said Selena, eyeing him in surprise. She had heard a great deal about the earl, for her brother loathed him and had often complained of his infamous conduct. Over the years, she had formed a picture of the Earl of Heathfield that rather resembled a drawing of a grinning satyr that she had in one of her favorite schoolbooks.

"Yes, that is Heathfield," said the duke, frowning. "There is no more detestable fellow in all of London. When I think of him buying my Titian, I am furious."

"Your Titian?" asked Selena, raising her eyebrows.

"You must remember. I wrote you about it."

"Oh, yes. The painting you wanted so badly."

James nodded. "Heathfield was well aware that I wanted that picture. He snatched it up before I could even make an offer on it."

Henrietta nodded sympathetically. "It really was bad of him. James had his heart set upon that painting."

Selena managed to suppress a smile. She and her brother shared an interest in art, but James's passion was of a more acquisitive bent. An almost obsessive collector of paintings, the duke had spent a goodly sum on his hobby. As a result, he now boasted one of the premier collections of the Venetian school of Renaissance art in the kingdom. "It seems Heathfield had his heart set upon it as well."

"Nonsense," he replied testily. "Heathfield just bought it because he knew I wanted it. The fellow finds sport in annoying me."

"Well, at least he has managed to save you a good deal of money," said Selena with a smile.

Her brother's expression made it clear that he was not amused by the remark. Selena glanced back toward the earl. She found that he was now surrounded by a large group of people, all looking exceedingly pleased to be in his company. "It seems that not everyone shares your opinion of Lord Heathfield," she said. "He appears to be quite popular."

"I never said he wasn't popular," said the duke, watching the earl with a disgusted look. "He's dashed popular with the ladies. In fact, that's how he got my Titian."

"Indeed?" asked Selena, very much interested. "Pray tell me what you mean."

Her brother nodded. "The painting was owned by a Mrs. Raleigh, who was recently widowed—a woman far removed from her youth, I might add. I believed we had an agreement that she would sell me the painting. Heathfield somehow had gotten wind of it and, apparently, he charmed the painting right out of her hands." He paused and shook his head. "I fear the poor woman was misled by Heathfield's . . . shall I say, attentions to her."

"Good heavens, James," said Selena. "You mean that the earl seduced this Mrs. Raleigh only to get her painting?"

"I should not be surprised if he did," replied the duke. "He is a rake and a scoundrel. No woman is safe from him."

Henrietta nodded. "James is right, Selena. You must be on your guard if you should ever meet him. He is so very charming . . ." Henrietta stopped abruptly as she noted her husband's eyes upon her. "Or, I should say, many ladies find him so."

Selena laughed. "Well, you have no need to fear that I shall be a victim of his charm."

"We will take care that you never make his acquaintance," said the duke.

She laughed again. "So I must be protected from him? Really, James, don't be ridiculous."

"I'm not being ridiculous. And you know that he is my greatest enemy. Ever since I was at school with him, he has done everything he could to make my life miserable. I shouldn't be surprised if he does attempt to charm you once he finds you are my sister. He'd find it very amusing to break your heart, my girl. I can't imagine anyone introducing you to him, but if you do have the misfortune to meet him in society, you must snub him. I won't have you even exchanging a civil word with the man."

Henrietta was about to launch into a firmer warning against the earl, but the appearance of a young blond gentleman prevented her. Bowing to them, he turned to the duke. "I do beg your pardon, your grace, but Lady Selena has promised me the next dance."

"Of course, Huntley," said Selena's brother. Selena, who was quite disappointed with the interruption, managed to smile at the young gentleman. She then proceeded with him toward the dancers.

*   *   *

As she went through the rather intricate steps of a country dance, Selena wondered how much longer the ball would last. The hour was growing quite late, but there was no indication that the festivities would be ending any time soon. In fact, some of the guests seemed to be getting livelier as the evening progressed, which was undoubtedly the result of their overindulgence at the punch bowl.

After her conversation with her brother and sister-in-law, Selena had danced with Mr. Huntley and several other gentlemen. Her current partner was an amiable middle-aged baronet with lamentable dancing skill. Although Selena managed to smile as they danced, she was growing quite weary with the effort of trying to be charming. She found herself wishing that she could leave.

Glancing around the ballroom, Selena spied her sister-in-law talking to two ladies. Henrietta was laughing and appeared to be in high spirits. Selena suppressed a sigh as she looked back at her partner. Then taking his hand, she proceeded with him and the other dancers in a circle around the floor.

Once again scanning the room, her eye fell upon the Earl of Heathfield. He was standing at the far end of the ballroom, surrounded by an eager throng of females who appeared to be hanging onto his every word. It appeared that her brother was right about the man, she thought. Heathfield did seem to be quite popular with the fair sex.

As the dance continued, her partner took a misstep and clumsily trod upon Selena's foot. He stopped abruptly and regarded her with a stricken look. "My dear Lady Selena, I'm so very sorry. I do hope I haven't hurt you."

Smiling stoically, Selena assured him that it was nothing. However, she was quite relieved when the music ended and the embarrassed baronet escorted her back to where Henrietta was standing with the other ladies.

After conversing for some time, the two ladies took their leave. Relieved to finally be alone with her sister-in-law, Selena sighed. "Hetty, I am so tired, and my feet hurt so terribly. Couldn't we go home now?"

The duchess's pretty face took on a look of surprise. "But no one has left yet."

"Well, someone has to be the first to leave," said Selena with a smile. "Can't it be us?"

Henrietta shook her head. "Oh, no, Selena. That wouldn't do. One must never arrive first or leave first." She looked closely at her sister-in-law. "But I thought you were enjoying the ball."

"It isn't that, Hetty. It's just that I'm growing rather tired."

"My poor dear. I daresay, it has been an exciting night for you and you must be exhausted with all your dancing. Yes, perhaps we could go home." She looked around the ballroom in search of her husband. "Oh, dear, James is talking to Lord Barclay and he wouldn't want to be interrupted. Lord Barclay has a Madonna by Bellini and James is determined to get him to sell it to him."

"Oh, dear," said Selena. "A Bellini. We could be here all night."

Before Henrietta could reply, they were joined by several ladies who were eager to supply them with their opinions of the ball. Selena listened politely for a time, but found her attention wandering. Glancing around the ballroom, she saw that her brother was still talking to Lord Barclay and that gentleman had a rather intransigent look upon his face. Suddenly realizing that her sister-in -law was speaking to her, she turned and looked at her. "I beg your pardon, Hetty. What were you saying?"

"I just said that there is Lady Sutherland. I haven't even spoken to her this evening."

"Neither have I," chimed in one of the other ladies. "Let us go and see her."

The other ladies nodded and quickly went off. Henrietta turned to Selena. "Aren't you coming?"

Selena smiled and shook her head. "You go ahead, Hetty. I confess I prefer to find an inconspicuous chair somewhere and rest my feet."

"Yes, that is a good idea, my dear," said Henrietta. "I shan't be long." Hesitating a moment, Henrietta then followed the ladies.

Feeling a need to escape from the crowded ballroom for a few moments, Selena made her way toward one of the doors in the vast room. Slipping out the door, she began walking down a long hallway. Surely, she thought, there would be a nice quiet room where she could sit undisturbed for a time.

At the end of the hall, Selena saw that a door to a room was partially open. Stopping before it, she glanced inside and found it was empty. In the dim glow cast by the flickering fire from the fireplace inside, Selena thought she could discern bookshelves and the outlines of a chair. Deciding that she had happened upon the library, Selena pushed the door a trifle wider and walked inside.

Suddenly, someone appeared in the darkness behind her. "So you're here at last," said a masculine voice, pushing the door so it shut behind them. Before Selena could protest, the man grabbed her in a firm embrace and fastened his lips upon hers.

Selena was too startled to react at first. However, she quickly came to her senses. "Let me go!" she cried, putting her hands against his chest, and shoving him away. This unexpected action caused the man to nearly fall backward.

"What the devil are you doing, Louisa?" he said, after recovering his balance.

Selena mustered all of her dignity. "You have mistaken me for another lady, sir," she said stiffly.

There was a momentary silence and then the man laughed. "By God, so I have. But seeing how dashed pretty you are, I must say I don't regret my error."

Selena bristled at his insolence. Becoming more adjusted to the darkness, she stared up at him. To her astonishment she realized that the man before her was none other than the Earl of Heathfield. "You are Lord Heathfield!"

He bowed. "At your service, madam. I fear I'm at a disadvantage. I don't believe we've met."

Selena frowned at him. Remembering her brother's admonition about not speaking with Heathfield, she hesitated before replying in a cool voice. "I am Lady Selena Paget."

"Lady Selena Paget?" said Heathfield. "Good God! You are the Duke of Melford's sister!"

"I am."

Heathfield grinned. "I'd heard you'd come to town. I know your brother well, but I must admit that we aren't friends. Indeed, his grace isn't in the least fond of me."

"If you will excuse me, Lord Heathfield . . ." said Selena, turning to go.

He reached out and took her arm. "Do stay, Lady Selena."

Snatching her arm away, she frowned at him. "Do not forget you are expecting someone."

"Expecting someone?"

"Louisa."

"Oh, yes, of course. But she's late and I do hate tardiness." He smiled. "Verney has a good many other rooms we might try."

Selena regarded him indignantly. "It appears that your reputation is well deserved, my lord."

Heathfield lifted his dark eyebrows. "My dear young lady, I can't imagine what you mean."

"My brother has told me all about you."

"So Melford's been slandering me, has he? You mustn't believe everything he says. He is just angry with me because we were rivals for the same lady and I won her."

Selena's eyes opened wide in shock. "What? How dare you say such a thing! My brother would not . . ."

Heathfield smiled. "I was referring to a lady in a painting. A Titian. You really must see it. It's magnificent." After pausing for a brief moment, he continued in a low voice. "And she has beautiful red hair very much like yours. Indeed, I can scarcely blame Melford for getting his back up about it."

Selena was rather disconcerted by the earl's reference to her beautiful red hair. She started to retreat toward the door when it suddenly opened and a lady hurried inside. "Heathfield," said the newcomer in a throaty whisper. The lady stopped abruptly as she saw two figures in the room. "What?" she said in some bewilderment.

"Louisa," began the earl, but that lady, on discerning that the figure with him was another female, gave an indignant cry and rushed out of the room.

"Good heavens!" said Selena. "That was Lady Verney!" She was quite amazed to realize that the hostess of the ball was the person having the assignation with the earl. Staring up at him, she shook her head. "It is clear that what my brother said about you is true."

"You mustn't listen to slander," he said with an amused look.

"It is hardly slander if it's the truth. It is very clear to me that you are a despicable rake, sir."

Heathfield only grinned at this aspersion to his character. "Come, come, Lady Selena, don't be so dramatic. Despicable rake? It sounds like a line from a play. I do apologize if I have shocked you. I imagine that a lady such as yourself who has been living sheltered away in the country might be rather surprised by what is considered quite ordinary in town."

Selena bristled at this remark. So he thought she was some sort of country bumpkin, did he? "I'm sure there are few living in London who consider your conduct 'ordinary.' "

He smiled again. "It seems I've put the wrong foot forward, Lady Selena, but I'm really not so bad. I'm kind to children and animals. Indeed, my dog finds me a capital fellow."

Selena regarded him disapprovingly. "Your dog is probably the only one to do so," she said, fixing a disgusted look on his handsome countenance. Then she turned and walked swiftly from the room.

Heathfield followed her into the hallway. "Won't you allow me to escort you back to the ballroom?"

Turning to look at him, her green eyes grew wide in surprise. "You cannot think I'd wish to be seen with you." Before he could reply, she hurried away. Returning to the ballroom, she quickly sought out her sister-in-law, who was still talking with Lady Sutherland and the other ladies.

Seeing Selena motioning to her, Henrietta excused herself and went over to her. "Why, Selena, is something the matter?"

Selena nodded. "I fear I have the most dreadful headache, Hetty. I want to go home at once."

"Oh, you poor thing," said her sister-in-law, eyeing her sympathetically. "You should have said so before. I will drag James away from Lord Barclay and we will go home immediately." Selena smiled gratefully and the ladies went off to fetch the duke.

2

The following morning Charles Augustus Hastings, the fifth Earl of Heathfield, sat eating breakfast at an elegant cherry table in the dining room of his London townhouse. A large Scottish deerhound sat at his feet staring up at him with pleading brown eyes.

Looking down at the dog, he smiled. "Oh, very well, my lad, but this is the last one you get." Taking a plump sausage from his plate, the earl tossed it to the deerhound, who immediately gobbled it down.

"There, you see, Duncan," said Heathfield with a grin, "I provide you with sausages and you think me an admirable fellow. Perhaps if I'd offered Lady Selena Paget some sausages, she might have thought better of me."

Smiling again, the earl continued to eat his breakfast. Since his encounter with Selena the previous evening, he had thought about her a great deal. Indeed, he found he could scarcely think of anything else. Remembering Selena's lovely face, Heathfield shook his head. For some reason, it greatly bothered him that Selena seemed to hold him in such contempt.

He found himself reliving their meeting. How shocked she must have been to come into the room and be kissed by a strange man. And Melford would be outraged when he heard of it. "He'll probably call me out, Duncan," he said, addressing the dog. "I shouldn't like to have to shoot him. No, indeed, it won't do, shooting a duke." Heathfield picked up a piece of buttered toast. "Well, perhaps he won't call me out. He knows I'm a crack shot, after all."

The deerhound listened to his master's words with a solemn expression. Amused, the earl tossed him another sausage.

"Excuse me, my lord." Heathfield's butler, a balding middle-aged man with a solemn demeanor, had entered the room. "Mr. Percy Hastings is here to see you."

This announcement seemed to please the earl. A broad smile appeared on his face. "Send him in, Preston."

The butler left, returning a moment later with a very dapper looking gentleman at his heels. The honorable Percy Hastings was well known in society for his sartorial splendor, and his appearance that morning wouldn't have disappointed anyone. Dressed in a splendid olive coat and spotless ivory pantaloons, a pair of sparkling Hessian boots on his feet, Percy looked every inch the dandy. Of medium height with light brown hair that was cut in the popular Corinthian style, he was quite good looking, although not nearly as handsome as the earl.

The appearance of the visitor sparked some interest in the deerhound, who gave an excited bark and made his way over to him. Percy dutifully patted the large canine's head. "Good day to you, Duncan," he said. "You're a handsome beast, aren't you?" The dog opened his mouth in a canine grin and wagged his tail.

Heathfield smiled. "This is a surprise, Percy. I thought you were in Brighton."

"I was, Cousin," replied Percy in a languid voice, "but I was summoned back to town by my tyrannical father. Or perhaps commanded would be a more appropriate word."

The earl regarded Percy with an amused expression. "Don't tell me you've incurred the parental wrath once again."

Percy took a chair next to his cousin. "Gad, no. Although I do hope Father doesn't hear of my ill luck at cards while I was in Brighton. No, I was called home on pressing family business."

Heathfield raised his dark eyebrows curiously. "Pressing family business?"

Percy nodded. "That's why I'm here. I'm hopeful of enlisting your aid in Father's scheme."

The earl eyed him skeptically. "Good God, not another one of Uncle's crack-brained schemes?"

Percy nodded. "I fear you may think so, Charles."

"And you don't?"

His cousin leaned back in the chair. "I don't know. I have to confess at first I thought it ridiculous, but the more I ponder the matter, I think it may be a good idea."

"Well, then, I'm eager to hear it," said Heathfield. "But do you want some breakfast?"

"I would, indeed," said Percy. "I find myself quite famished."

After summoning the butler to have a plate brought for his cousin, the earl turned back and regarded Percy with a questioning look. "So, what is this scheme that my uncle has cooked up and what the devil does it have to do with the family?"

"You are aware of our Great-Aunt Eustacia and how she married that foreign prince?"

Heathfield nodded. "Yes, of course. He was the prince of some insignificant principality. I forget the name of it."

Percy appeared slightly offended. "The principality of Brunconia might be insignificant, Cousin, but it still links our family to royalty."

The earl laughed. "Brunconia! Good God, how could I forget that?" He regarded his cousin with an amused look. "So, we are related to the royal Brunconians through Great-Aunt Eustacia. How extremely interesting, Percy."

"Why, it is dashed interesting. You see, our great-aunt has a grandson, Maximilian—Prince Maximilian von Stauffenburg. He would be our second cousin or some such thing. Father has recently received a letter from him. Prince Maximilian has just turned one and twenty and is anxious to come to London."

"Is he? I can't say that I'm surprised that one would be eager to get away from Brunconia."

Percy frowned slightly. "I fear it is a rather frightful, mountainous sort of place with a large number of goats. But to get back to our mutual cousin—you see, Prince Maximilian has a purpose for coming here, and my father wishes me to assist him in achieving his mission. Father thinks the prince's success could mean a great deal to the entire family." Percy paused.

"Pray, do not keep me in suspense," said Heathfield. "What is our cousin's great purpose in coming to town?"

"He wishes to marry Princess Charlotte."

The earl was so startled he was temporarily speechless. "Good God!" he said finally. "Princess Charlotte!"

Percy nodded. "You know the gossip that Charlotte refuses to marry the Prince of Orange? That leaves the field open to other royal gentlemen such as our Cousin Max."

"Our Cousin Max?" repeated Heathfield. He stared incredulously at Percy for a moment and then threw back his head and roared with laughter. "A prince of Brunconia marry the heir to the British throne? Of all the beetle-headed notions! Do you really think that the Prince Regent would even consider such a ridiculous match for his daughter?"

Percy shrugged. "Perhaps it's not so ridiculous, Cousin. Certainly Brunconia wouldn't be an illustrious alliance, but our cousin is a prince, after all. And if Princess Charlotte were to favor him among her other royal suitors . . ."

"That is all very well, Percy, but I doubt if our cousin will get near the princess. You know she is kept closeted away from people, only seeing those gentlemen whom her father wishes her to meet."

"Yes, that's a problem," agreed Percy. "But I thought if you used your influence with the Prince . . . He is fond of you and your father was one of his dearest friends."

"So you expect me to try to foist this royal cousin of ours on Prinny as a future son-in-law? The Prince would doubtlessly have me thrown into the Tower for such effrontery. Why don't you use *your* influence with His Royal Highness, Percy?"

"You know very well that I'm not in the Prince's good graces at the moment," said Percy, taking a snuffbox from inside his coat. He delicately took a sniff and then returned the box to his pocket. "As you recall, I made the mistake of telling Lady Congreve that I thought Prinny's waistcoat an abomination. I never suspected that she was such a tattlemonger. Lady Congreve repeated my remark to the Marchioness of Bellingham, who reported it to Colonel Foster who, of course, told Prinny. HRH is still quite furious with me. Fortunately, he doesn't hold your being my cousin against you."

At that moment, a footman placed a plate filled with food in front of Percy. That gentleman immediately took up a fork and stabbed a sausage. The earl watched him, a mischievous look in his blue eyes. "I really think you are serious about this absurd scheme."

His cousin nodded. "I am serious, Cousin. Why just think of the advantages of such a family connection. I'm certain Prince Max would be most grateful to us and would shower us with royal favors. I might get some sort of lucrative appointment at court."

Heathfield made a ludicrous face. "Lucrative appointment? Then this whole business is about money?"

Percy swallowed a forkful of sausage and then turned back to his cousin. "Of course, it's about money. Oh, I know you don't care about blunt, Charles, since you're as rich as Croesus already. But I have to rely on Father's generosity, and you know what a tight fist he is."

Heathfield didn't reply. While he was well aware that his uncle was a frugal man, the earl could hardly blame him for not handing over great sums of money to his son. After all, Percy was addicted to gambling and was quite profligate in his spending. Indeed, Heathfield had often bailed his cousin out from his debts. While he was very fond of Percy, the earl often wished that the young man was more sensible about his finances.

Percy took up a piece of toast and began to slather marmalade on it. He looked over at his cousin. "Come, Charles, you must say you will help me. Father will be very displeased if I'm not able to assist our Cousin Max."

"But we have never even met the fellow, Percy. The whole thing is utterly absurd."

"I don't know. Perhaps this foreign cousin of ours is a romantic looking fellow who will sweep Princess Charlotte off her feet." He paused and grinned. "Perhaps he's very much like you, Charles. I've never known a female who did not succumb to your famous charm."

The earl smiled. "I hate to disillusion you, Percy, but not every lady falls at my feet upon first acquaintance."

"What? Modesty from you? Tut, tut, Charles. We all know that no female can resist you."

"Well, I believe I have found one who can resist me. Indeed, I met a lady last night at the Verney ball who thoroughly detested me."

Percy put on a mock look of astonishment. "By heavens, you astound me, Cousin. Who was this lady with such poor judgment?"

"Lady Selena Paget."

"Lady Selena? You can't mean you met her! Indeed, I so wanted to be introduced to her. She is such a beauty. And they say she'll have at least thirty thousand when she marries."

"Then you must make her an offer."

Percy, who had begun to chew on a piece of sausage, nearly choked.

Heathfield laughed again. "Yes, there's a rich wife for you, Percy."

"Don't believe I wouldn't want to marry such a girl," said Percy, "but the Duke of Melford dislikes me nearly as much as he dislikes you. I can imagine what he would say if I displayed an interest in her. But tell me of your meeting with Lady Selena."

"Last night in Verney's parlor. I was waiting for another lady, you see."

"You rogue, Charles," said Percy in an admiring tone.

"Well, I was waiting for someone else and in came Lady Selena Paget. I thought she was the other lady and so I kissed her."

"Good God!" cried Percy, very much astonished.

"I fear she thought me a bold fellow. She said I was a despicable rake."

"Well, it must have been rather shocking for a lady to be kissed like that."

"I suppose so," said Heathfield. "I imagine she didn't enjoy it nearly as much as I did. By all the gods, she is dashed beautiful."

"And then what happened?"

"We had a brief conversation and then she took her leave."

"Well, Melford will be furious."

"I suppose he will," said the earl in a tone that implied it was a matter of complete indifference to him.

"I shouldn't wish to offend him any more," said Percy. "He is a duke, you know."

"What is that to me?" said Heathfield. "Isn't my cousin a prince?"

This remark caused both cousins to break into hearty laughter. Finally Percy spoke. "We must return to the matter of our royal cousin."

"I thought we'd discussed that enough."

"Now, Charles, you must help me in this. You must say the idea of our own cousin marrying the Princess is quite appealing. Where is your sporting blood, old man? The odds are very long, I know, but wouldn't it be great fun to attempt it?"

A slight smile appeared on the earl's face. "Perhaps it would be diverting at that."

His cousin beamed and clapped him on the back. "Capital! Cousin Max said that he is arriving in at the beginning of next week, so we must come up with some sort of plan by then."

As he finished his breakfast, Percy continued to discuss their royal cousin's upcoming visit. Although Heathfield pretended to show interest, he found himself thinking again about Lady Selena Paget.

3

A week after the Verney ball, Selena sat at a desk in the stylish drawing room of her brother's house, writing a letter to one of her friends in Northumberland. A small red and white King Charles spaniel lay sleeping at her feet.

Dipping her quill pen into ink, Selena quickly wrote a postscript at the bottom of the page. Then, after allowing the ink to dry, she carefully folded the paper.

Henrietta, who had been half-heartedly stitching on an embroidery of purple pansies, looked over at her sister-in-law. "Have you finished your letter, Selena?" she asked hopefully.

Selena smiled. "Yes, I've told my friend Fanny all about my adventures thus far." In truth, Selena hadn't revealed all of her escapades in town to her friend. She had prudently left out the episode in which the Earl of Heathfield had kissed her.

In fact, Selena hadn't told anyone of the incident with the earl. Knowing of her brother's dislike for Heathfield, she had had no wish to upset him by telling him of the earl's infamous behavior toward her at the ball. Selena was also well aware that she could scarcely tell Henrietta the story without her sister-in-law's repeating it to her husband.

Henrietta gratefully pushed her embroidery away. "I'm certain your friend will be very glad to hear from you. Why don't we post your letter on our way to the park?"

"That is an excellent idea," said Selena, turning back to the desk to affix a wax seal on the letter. When she had completed this task, she looked down at the dog sleeping at her feet. "Come, Fluff, we're going to the park." The toy spaniel's head darted up and the little dog gazed up eagerly at her mistress.

Henrietta laughed. "I think Fluff looks forward to our daily outings."

"As do I," said Selena. "And it is such marvelous weather today. The park should be quite lovely."

Her sister-in-law nodded and, getting up from their seats, the two ladies went upstairs to their rooms to put on their pelisses and bonnets.

A short time later, Selena and Henrietta made their way down the stairs, Fluff scampering happily at their heels. When they reached the landing there was suddenly a mournful cry behind them. "Mama!"

Both Selena and Henrietta turned around to find Henrietta's little daughter staring piteously at them from the top of the stairs. At five years of age, the child was a charming miniature of her mother, with Henrietta's round face and large brown eyes. "Sophie!" said her mother, hurrying up the stairs, "What is the matter?"

"Nanny says I must take a nap and I don't want to! I would rather go to the park with you and Aunt Selena!"

At that moment, the girl's nanny appeared, looking quite dismayed. "I'm so sorry, your grace," she said apologetically. "I was putting Lord Hillsborough to bed and didn't realize Lady Sophie was out here."

"That is all right, Walters," said Henrietta. She looked down at her daughter. "Come, Sophie," she said, making a vain attempt to sound strict, "you must do as Nanny tells you."

Sophie hung her head down. "I know, Mama, but I don't need a nap. I'm not a baby like Harold. Can't I go to the park? Aunt Selena said there were some ducks on the pond."

"Oh, dear," said Selena with a smile. "I did tell her about the ducks, Hetty." She glanced over at the nanny. "Perhaps Sophie might accompany us this time?"

Nanny Walters, an amiable, stout woman of middle years, smiled and looked at the duchess. "If your grace would allow it."

Henrietta paused a moment. "I suppose it would be all right. But you must promise you will obey Nanny in the future, Sophie."

"Oh, I will, Mama!" said the little girl.

"Very well," said Henrietta. "Now go with Nanny and she will get your bonnet."

Sophie nodded excitedly and hurried off with the older woman. She returned shortly, a pink and white bonnet perched upon her dark curls and a broad smile on her face. "Oh, Fluff," she cried, seeing the little dog, "I'm going with you to the park today!" The spaniel barked as if she was glad to hear this announcement, and Sophie laughed.

It didn't take long for them to all be seated in the duke's open carriage. Henrietta and her daughter sat on one side while Selena took the opposite seat, her spaniel Fluff in her lap. The groom urged the horses on and they were soon on their way.

Since the park was several blocks from the ducal residence, Sophie had ample opportunity to prattle on about Fluff and the ducks and a number of other topics that the five-year-old found equally fascinating. Selena listened with considerable amusement to her niece, exchanging a smile every so often with her sister-in-law.

As the carriage pulled past the wrought-iron gates into the green confines of the park, Sophie clapped her hands. "Oh, we are here, Mama! Now we must see the ducks. I do hope the babies are there, Aunt Selena."

They traveled along the tree-lined road until they came to a glistening pond where willow trees arched gracefully over the water. Selena gazed out appreciatively at the scenic view before her. Sophie was eager to scramble out of the carriage and could hardly wait for the driver to lift her down.

When they were all on the ground, Sophie took her mother's hand. "Come, Mama," she said. However, just as Henrietta was about to accompany her daughter to the pond, a rider on a large black horse appeared on the road before them. Running along after the horse was a large dog.

Selena was startled when she recognized the horseman as the Earl of Heathfield. Pulling his horse up beside them, the earl tipped his tall beaver hat. Smiling, he dismounted. "Duchess, Lady Selena," he said, bowing politely to each lady.

Sophie's eyes widened as she looked at the enormous deerhound standing beside the earl. Fluff had never seen a dog of Duncan's size either. The appearance of the giant canine threw the spaniel into a frenzy. The little dog barked and ran behind Selena for protection. Then, getting up her courage, Fluff ventured out from behind her mistress's skirt to bark again. The deerhound just regarded the little dog with a perplexed expression.

Heathfield, who had witnessed Fluff's behavior, smiled. "It appears, Lady Selena, that your little friend is wary of us."

Scooping up the spaniel into her arms, Selena frowned at him. "She has good reason to be wary."

Heathfield laughed. "What great good fortune to find you here."

Actually, the earl's meeting Lady Selena was no coincidence. Since their brief meeting at the ball, he had continued to think about her, knowing he wished to see her again. Finally, he had sent one of his servants to discreetly investigate Selena's activities. Having learned that the lady was in the habit of going to the park at approximately the same time every afternoon, Heathfield had set off to find her.

Selena glanced sideways at Henrietta. She could see that her sister-in-law was quite dumbfounded that Heathfield was acquainted with her. "I met Lord Heathfield at the Verney ball," she said in explanation.

Henrietta regarded the earl with an amazed look.

The earl, although surprised to realize that Selena hadn't mentioned their meeting to her sister-in-law, smiled at Henrietta. "Your grace, how wonderful to see you again."

Henrietta managed to murmur a polite reply before casting a quizzical look from the earl to Selena. Selena was well aware that her sister-in-law was thinking it very odd that she hadn't mentioned the matter.

"I must tell you, Duchess, how much I enjoyed meeting your charming sister-in-law at the Verney ball," continued Heathfield, glancing at Selena with a meaningful look.

Selena feared she was blushing. She was glad when the earl's attention was drawn to her niece. Looking down at the little girl, he smiled. "And who might this lovely young lady be?"

Sophie, who had been watching Heathfield and his deerhound with great interest, spoke before her mother or aunt could reply. "I am Lady Sophie Paget," she said in her childish voice, making a curtsy. She stared up curiously at the tall earl.

Heathfield made an exaggerated bow. "I am the Earl of Heathfield, Lady Sophie, and I'm delighted to make your acquaintance."

Very impressed by the handsome earl, Sophie smiled up at him. "You have a very large dog, Lord Heathfield," she said.

"Yes, Duncan is a rather tall fellow," he said. "Would you like to pet him?"

Sophie nodded eagerly and, stepping up to the canine, she

reached up to pat him on his muzzle. "Do be careful, Sophie," said Henrietta, somewhat alarmed to see her daughter next to the formidable looking dog. "Do not fear, your grace," said Heathfield, "Duncan is as gentle as a lamb."

Fluff, watching Sophie pet the dog, gave an outraged sounding bark and squirmed in Selena's arms. "Mind your manners, Fluff," said Selena.

"Ah, so that is your name, is it?" said the earl, taking a step closer to Selena and the little dog. "How do you do, Fluff?" He made another sweeping bow and Fluff responded with an excited, high-pitched bark.

Sophie was finding the earl quite amusing. Looking up at him, she grinned. "Will you come and see the ducks with us?"

Selena cut in before Heathfield could reply. "I'm certain that his lordship is too busy for that, Sophie." She fixed her green eyes upon him. "Indeed, we should not keep you, Lord Heathfield."

The earl smiled back at her, a mischievous gleam in his blue eyes. "Nonsense, Lady Selena. I assure you, I have no other business and I should like nothing better." He tied his horse to a hitching post nearby and then returned to them. "I am ready to meet the ducks."

"And will you bow to the ducks, too?" asked Sophie, grinning up at him again.

The earl nodded. "One should be civil to feathered creatures as well, don't you think?"

The little girl giggled. "That is silly!" she cried delightedly.

"Well, let us see these ducks of yours, Lady Sophie," said Heathfield. "Why don't you and your mother lead the way?"

Henrietta gave Selena a strange look, but since Sophie was eagerly pulling her hand, she went off toward the pond with her daughter. Duncan, sensing some adventure ahead, loped off after them.

Casting a suspicious glance at the earl, Selena then hurried after Henrietta and Sophie, still carrying Fluff in her arms. With his long strides, Heathfield soon caught up to her. "Must you walk so quickly?" he asked. "It is such a splendid day, one should take a more leisurely stroll to appreciate it."

"My appreciation of the day has suddenly seemed to desert me," said Selena, frowning over at him.

Smiling, he shook his head. "You don't appear pleased to see me."

"Indeed, I'm not," she said.

"I do wish you wouldn't hold our first meeting against me," said Heathfield. "I'm very sorry that I offended you."

Before she could reply, Sophie was running back to them, calling out, "Aunt Selena! The baby ducks are here!" Fluff barked at this exciting news and once more squirmed in her mistress's arms. Selena and the earl exchanged a glance and then followed off after the little girl to view the ducklings.

After viewing the ducks for a time, Heathfield escorted the ladies back to their carriage. Heathfield first helped Henrietta and her daughter up into the vehicle. He then took Fluff from Selena and handed the dog up to Sophie. Finally, he extended his hand to Selena, who, after taking it with seeming reluctance, climbed up into the carriage.

"I have had a most delightful time, ladies," he said, tipping his hat to them.

Henrietta merely nodded while Sophie waved happily at him. "Good-bye, Lord Heathfield! Good-bye, Duncan!" Selena met the earl's smiling gaze and then she looked away.

The driver directed the horses out onto the road and they were soon on their way home. Glancing back, Selena saw that the earl was still standing there watching them.

"Oh, Mama," said Sophie, "wasn't Lord Heathfield the nicest gentleman? And Duncan was a very good dog." The little girl looked down at the spaniel in her lap and stroked her silky ears. "Of course, he is not as good a dog as you, Fluff." The dog snuggled up in Sophie's lap, content to take a nap after the afternoon's adventure.

Sophie continued to chatter on for a time as they rode through the streets of London. Apparently she had found the earl and his deerhound even more interesting than the duck family. However, all the excitement soon took its toll and Sophie fell fast asleep on the carriage seat.

Selena looked over and smiled at the charming picture of her niece cuddled next to Fluff, both of them sleeping peacefully. "Do they not look sweet, Hetty?" she said.

Henrietta smiled over at her little daughter and the dog, but then fixed a questioning look at her sister-in-law. "I am very much astounded to find that you met Heathfield and didn't mention the fact to me."

Selena frowned. "I am sorry, Hetty, but I found it a matter of

such little significance. We only exchanged a few words. And
knowing how James feels about him . . . I didn't wish to upset
him. And that's why I didn't mention it to you."

"I do wish you had told me," said Henrietta. "He seemed quite
interested in you."

"I don't know about that, Hetty."

"Oh, Selena, you must be careful. I know Heathfield is very
charming, but he can't be trusted. You mustn't lose your head
over him."

Selena frowned. "Don't be absurd, Hetty. I don't find the man
charming in the least." However, even as she spoke these words,
Selena knew that they weren't true. She was finding that the
handsome earl had an undeniable appeal.

Although Henrietta was somewhat relieved by this declaration,
she still regarded Selena with a worried expression. "I imagine
James will be upset when he hears of our meeting Heathfield.
And I feel I must tell him, Selena."

"Of course, tell him by all means. But really, Hetty, you are
making too much of this," said Selena. "There is no reason for
James to fly into the boughs over such a trifling thing."

Henrietta didn't appear convinced, but she nodded as the carriage continued on its way through the fashionable streets of the
city.

4

After meeting Selena in the park, Heathfield returned to his house to find his cousin Percy's high-perch phaeton parked at the curb. Leaving his horse with a groom, the earl hastened inside, his deerhound at his heels.

"Good afternoon, Preston," said Heathfield cheerfully as his butler took his hat. "What a marvelous day it is."

The servant nodded. "It would appear so, my lord," he said soberly. He paused a moment. "Mr. Percy Hastings arrived some time ago and is in the drawing room."

"Thank you, Preston," said the earl, smiling. "Come, Duncan," he said, and the dog followed along after him. Opening the door to the drawing room, Heathfield found his cousin in a recumbent position on his elegant French sofa, a glass of wine in his hand. "I'm glad you've made yourself comfortable," said Charles, regarding Percy with an amused look.

"So, you have finally returned," said his cousin, sitting up. "I was getting deuced bored waiting for you."

"You could have had Preston fetch you a book from the library," suggested the earl.

"Good heavens, Heathfield, I wasn't that desperate," said Percy.

The earl laughed and took a chair next to the sofa. Duncan stretched out on the floor at his master's feet. After resting his huge brown eyes for a moment on Percy, the canine put his head down for a nap. "It appears Duncan is exhausted," said Percy. "Where the devil have you been all afternoon anyway?"

Heathfield leaned back in his chair, a satisfied look upon his handsome face. "I've been to the park, Percy. Did you know there are some adorable ducklings on the pond there?"

His cousin regarded him as if he were addle-pated. "Adorable ducklings? Gad, Cousin, you can't mean that you spent the day gaping at such things?"

The earl smiled. "Actually, although I did enjoy seeing the creatures, I was far more interested in gazing upon the fair lady who accompanied me."

Percy grinned. "You sly devil, Heathfield. I should have known you were with a lady. So who was this nature-loving female?"

"Lady Selena Paget."

His cousin regarded him with an astonished look. "By God, you can't mean to say you were romping about the park with her?"

"I shouldn't exactly call it romping," said the earl sardonically. "I just happened to meet the lady there."

"You just *happened* to meet her there? I'll wager chance had little to do with it."

Heathfield shrugged. "I did learn beforehand that the lady is fond of taking afternoon rides in the park. It was not difficult to take advantage of such information."

Percy shook his head. "You told me that Lady Selena detested you."

"She does. Or, at least, she thinks she does. But I do see a glimmer of hope in that regard." The earl had glimpsed Selena smiling a couple of times as he had talked to her little niece by the pond. And he had not failed to note the faint blush that had appeared on her cheeks as he had helped her into the carriage. He thought that such signs were most encouraging.

Percy was regarding the earl with a concerned expression. "I don't think it wise of you to pursue Lady Selena."

"I'm not pursuing her. Well, perhaps I am, but she is a deuced attractive female. She has the loveliest green eyes." He paused. "And there is something about her . . ."

Percy eyed him in surprise. "Something about her?"

Unfortunately, Heathfield elaborated no further. "She is a very attractive lady."

"Well, I advise you to stay away from her. My dear Charles, in addition to the unfortunate fact that she is Melford's sister, she is also a respectable maiden lady. One doesn't have dalliances with girls like that. One marries them."

Heathfield looked thoughtful. "Perhaps that would be the thing to do."

"What!" exclaimed Percy. "Marry Melford's sister! You must be joking."

"I don't know," said the earl. "I never thought seriously of marriage before, but I confess the idea of having a wife like Selena Paget has its appeal."

"By my honor, I never thought I'd see this day," said Percy. "Imagine you falling in love, and with Melford's sister."

"I didn't say I'd fallen in love," said Heathfield defensively.

"Well, it sounds as though you have," said his cousin with a frown. "I must say, it's dashed inconvenient for you to fall in love now."

"What do you mean?" asked Heathfield, raising his dark eyebrows.

"I mean, this mad passion you have for Lady Selena may distract you from more pressing matters."

"More pressing matters?"

"Our Cousin Max, of course! You do remember that he is arriving the day after tomorrow "

The earl gave his cousin a long-suffering look. "How could I forget such a momentous event, Percy? You have scarcely spoken of anything else for the past few days."

"I just wish you would be a little more enthusiastic, Heathfield. Events have already been set into motion. I have told scores of people about our royal cousin's visit. I even paid a visit to Lady Brayburn and told her all about Prince Max. Her daughter knows Miss Elphinstone very well and Miss Elphinstone is an intimate friend of Princess Charlotte. I don't doubt that Her Royal Highness has already been informed of our cousin's imminent arrival and that she is in a state of eager anticipation."

Heathfield grinned. "I daresay the whole of London is awaiting him with bated breath."

Missing the sarcasm of his cousin's remark, Percy nodded his head vigorously. He reached into his pocket and took out his snuffbox. Taking up a pinch, he glanced up at the earl. "Oh, there was something I forgot to mention to you, Heathfield."

"Yes, what is it?"

"As you know, our cousin will be arriving at Dover. We will need to go and meet him there."

"What the devil for? Surely our cousin can make his own way to London."

Percy took a sniff and then put his snuffbox back into his coat. "Well, you see, Heathfield, I fear our Cousin Max is not a wealthy man. He wrote that he would be taking the mail coach to town."

"So? What of it?"

"Why, a prince can't arrive in town in a *mail coach!* What if someone should see him? No, he must ride in a vehicle that is fitting to his consequence. I thought your new traveling coach would be just the thing."

"Oh, did you?" said Heathfield with a ludicrous expression. He regarded Percy for a moment. "I begin to think that our royal cousin may be a considerable pull upon my pursestrings. I hope you don't think I'm going to pay for his stay here."

"Certainly not," insisted Percy, although that is precisely what he intended. "I only thought you might agree to bring him to town in your traveling coach. It is not so very much to ask. After all, my father has offered to have Prince Max stay with him." Percy hesitated and then plunged ahead. "Of course, it would be much better if our cousin could stay here at Heathfield House."

"What?" cried the earl.

"Well, you must admit that Father's house is not in a very stylish neighborhood. I should think people would find it odd having the prince stay with his poor relations."

Heathfield shook his head. "Poor relations? Don't be ridiculous. My uncle lives very well. And it sounds as if our Cousin Max is the pauper in this family. I should think he will find accommodations at your father's house quite satisfactory."

Percy frowned. "Satisfactory, perhaps, but my father's residence can scarcely compare to yours, Cousin."

"I don't want the fellow hanging about me all the time," said the earl in some annoyance.

"Oh, he won't, Charles," said Percy, smiling brightly. "I shall take on the main responsibility of showing him about town. But you are the Earl of Heathfield and the head of the family. He will need your patronage if he is to succeed. Do say you will go to Dover tomorrow."

Heathfield looked at his cousin for a moment and then he nodded. "Oh, very well, we will go to Dover tomorrow. And I will let our royal cousin stay here, but only for a short time. I don't wish to be saddled with this Max as a permanent house guest."

Percy smiled. "You needn't worry about that, Cousin. I'm certain that our cousin will soon be making his residence in one of the royal palaces with Princess Charlotte."

"You are either a great optimist, Percy, or a great fool," said Heathfield with a smile. His cousin didn't take offense at this remark since he was now convinced that his plan for introducing Prince Maximilian into society would be a great success.

Two days later, Heathfield stood on the dock at Dover, watching the commotion around him. It was a bustling place with crowds of people hurrying about and workmen depositing cargo of all shapes and sizes.

The earl and his cousin had arrived in the busy port city the previous evening. After spending the night in a seaside inn, the two men had made their way to the wharf to await the arrival of their cousin, Prince Maximilian.

Glancing out at the harbor, the earl couldn't help but appreciate the impressive sight of the scores of ships out on the water. The famous chalk hills rose up from the shore around them, their white cliffs sparkling against the bright blue sky.

Heathfield found himself daydreaming. He pictured Selena by his side as they set off for a long voyage. He imagined the two of them in a cabin at night with the moon shining down and the ship gently rocking. However, his pleasant fantasy was interrupted by his cousin's voice.

"I say, Charles," said Percy, who was standing next to him, looking at the ships. "I believe that's it. Yes, *Valiant Lady*—that one over there."

Heathfield looked in the direction that his cousin was indicating. A ship had put down a long gangplank and it appeared the passengers on board were getting ready to disembark. "Well, we'd best go and meet it," said the earl. "We shouldn't want to miss our royal cousin."

"Indeed, we should not," said Percy.

Making their way through the milling mob on the dock, the two cousins stopped beside the ship's gangplank. There they stood watching the passengers leave the ship. An elderly gentleman with a cane and an attractive young lady were the first ones to walk toward them. Percy smiled at the lady and then craned his head to view the passengers walking behind them.

"How are we to know this Prince Max?" asked Heathfield. "Do you know what he looks like?"

Percy glanced back at him. "Gad, Charles, he is a prince, after all. I shouldn't think he would be so difficult to identify."

The earl shook his head. "So you expect him to be wearing a

crown then, Cousin? Or perhaps you expect him to have a royal
retinue trailing behind him?"

"Don't be ridiculous," said Percy. "I only meant that there is a
certain air of royalty that is unmistakable."

Heathfield crossed his arms in front of him and continued to
watch as people made their way down the gangplank. As his eye
alighted on one of the passengers, a broad smile suddenly appeared on his face. "I believe I see him, Percy. And you are very
right. Royal Max does have a certain air about him."

Percy followed his cousin's glance and his expression turned to
one of horror. "Good God!" he said. "That can't be him!"

The gentleman who had so appalled Percy was drawing the attention of many in the crowd. Attired in a shabby peacock-blue
uniform with a motley array of ribbons, the young man had a
huge blue military hat adorned with feathers perched on top of his
head. Heathfield found himself thinking that he looked like a figure from a comic opera.

Certainly Prince Maximilian von Stauffenburg, for that was indeed who the gentleman was, exhibited a rather unprepossessing
appearance. Tall, broad-shouldered, and inclined to stoutness, the
prince had curly blond hair that appeared in unruly fluffs from
under his hat, long bushy sideburns, and a mustache. He had inherited the von Stauffenburg nose, which, although considered a
mark of distinction in his country, was a bit too prominent.

Yet, while the prince had never been considered handsome, he
possessed a pair of bright blue eyes, an affable smile, and an amiable personality that made him immensely popular in his native
land. As he walked down the gangplank, he boisterously called
out farewells to several of his fellow passengers.

He then scanned the crowd, looking for the cousin who was to
meet him. When his eye fell upon the earl and Percy, Maximilian
grinned as Percy lifted his hand to wave to him. "Ah!" he cried,
hurrying up to them, "you are my Cousin Percy, I think."

That gentleman made a formal bow. "Yes, your highness, I'm
your cousin, Percy Hastings."

"*Ja, ja,* I would have known you anywhere, my dear cousin,"
said the prince in a strong accent that a person unfamiliar with the
cadences of Brunconian speech would have mistaken for Austrian. "You look so very much like my grandmother."

While Percy wasn't too pleased at being told he looked like
anyone's grandmother, he smiled politely.

"It is with much pleasure I meet you, Cousin Percy!" With that, the young man grabbed him in a bearlike hug and then kissed Percy on both cheeks. Heathfield nearly laughed at the expression on Percy's face as he endured this effusive greeting.

Percy attempted to regain his dignity as he stepped back from the prince. He made another bow. "Welcome to England, your highness," he said.

Prince Maximilian shook his head. "No, no, you must call me Cousin or Max," he insisted. He fixed a questioning stare upon Heathfield and Percy quickly made the introduction.

"Your high—that is to say, Cousin Max, this is your other cousin, the Earl of Heathfield."

"Heathfield!" cried the prince. "Yes, of course!"

The earl bowed gracefully and extended his hand. However, before he could speak. Prince Maximilian had also engulfed him in an exuberant embrace. After kissing Heathfield on both cheeks, the prince grinned at him.

Unlike Percy, the earl was quite amused by his royal cousin. "I do hope you had an enjoyable journey, Cousin Max," he said.

Maximilian made a face and rolled his eyes. "Ah, it was, as you English say, wretched. Yes, wretched, that is it. The waves, they were very high and the boat it rocked up and down. I was very sick. Seasick, yes, that is the word."

"I'm sorry to hear that," said Heathfield. "I'm afraid the crossing can be rough."

"Oh, yes," repeated the young prince, nodding his head. "A very rough crossing. I could not eat a thing. I tried, but it would not stay down and I must go to the side of the ship—"

Percy, who did not relish a more graphic description of his cousin's seasickness, rapidly jumped in. "How dashed unpleasant for you, to be sure, Cousin. But I daresay, you are anxious to be off to London."

Maximilian's face brightened. "Oh, yes, I very much wish to see this great city of the English."

"Yes, well," said Percy, exchanging a glance with the earl, "let us get your luggage to Heathfield's carriage."

"Ah, yes, of course," said Maximilian. He looked around them and spying a sailor from his ship, he turned to his cousins. "That fellow should help, I think. I shall talk to him." Without another word, he hurried over to the man, calling out loudly to him.

Percy watched him go and then turned to the earl. "My God,

Heathfield, this is a disaster! What will everyone think of us, introducing such a fellow to Society? And the very idea of him marrying Princess Charlotte! I do wish I'd been told what he was like."

"Why, I find our royal cousin rather engaging," said the earl. "There are no princely airs about him, to be sure. And while he isn't the dashing fellow you had hoped he might be, he does have a certain rough-hewn charm."

"Rough-hewn charm? You are being charitable, Cousin." Percy shook his head. "Whatever will we do with him? Can you imagine taking him to Almack's?"

"Come, come, Percy," said Heathfield. "Don't be so melodramatic. I'm certain that Prince Max will be quite a sensation at that august assembly." The earl paused and smiled. "Almack's is always so accursedly dull, I should think everyone there would be eager for some diversion."

Percy frowned. "Yes, I don't doubt that Prince Max will provide considerable entertainment. But have you forgotten? He is supposed to be a candidate for royal bridegroom. Now that I have met him, I see the idea is laughable."

Heathfield shrugged. "One can't be sure. After all, it's said Princess Charlotte takes after her mother and it is well known that lady prefers gentlemen of a . . ." The earl stopped and grinned. "A rough-hewn charm."

Percy, whose eyes were still fixed on Prince Maximilian, appeared to think this over. "Yes, that's true. But I can't imagine that the Prince Regent would be impressed with our cousin."

"Oh, I don't know," said Heathfield, his eyes twinkling. "Our royal cousin appears to share Prinny's love of military uniforms."

A slight smile appeared on Percy's face. "It appears poor Max's uniform has done duty in several Brunconian wars. And that horrible mustache!"

The earl grinned again. They both noted that their royal cousin was now laughing uproariously and gesticulating wildly to the sailor. "Good God," muttered Percy.

Heathfield clapped his cousin on the back. "Buck up, Percy. We have some time until Max makes his grand appearance at Almack's. We should be able to apply a bit of polish to him by then." Percy didn't appear encouraged by this remark, but continued to watch Maximilian with a gloomy expression.

After the prince finished his discussion with the sailor, he hurried back toward them. "The fellow says my luggage should be over there," he said, pointing to an area on the dock.

The three of them walked to the designated location and Maximilian soon spotted his luggage amid the pile of trunks and crates piled there. The prince's large, well-worn trunk with the royal seal of Brunconia was then carted over to Heathfield's waiting traveling coach.

After making a great fuss over the carriage and its magnificent team of horses, Maximilian climbed inside, followed by the earl and Percy. The three cousins then began the journey back to London.

5

Selena sat at her dressing table as her maid diligently worked upon her hair. After making sure that every curl was in place, the servant stepped back and studied her mistress's attractive red tresses with satisfaction.

"Thank you, Betty," said Selena, smiling into the mirror at the young woman's reflection. "You have done a fine job."

"Oh, you do look lovely, my lady," said the maid. "There is none who could hold a candle to you in that dress."

"Such bosh," said Selena, although she had to admit that she appeared to good advantage that evening. Attired in a magnificent gown of sea-green silk that matched the color of her eyes, Selena was quite pleased with her appearance.

"Would your ladyship wish to wear your emerald necklace?" asked Betty, well aware that the jewelry would add the crowning touch to the splendid dress. Selena nodded and the maid quickly fetched the necklace and fastened it around her neck.

Selena looked in the mirror, noting the emeralds with a slight smile. The necklace had been a favorite of her mother's and she never wore it without thinking of her. "Yes, that will do very nicely, Betty," she said.

The toy spaniel Fluff was perched on Selena's large canopied bed, intent upon watching her mistress's preparations. When Selena got up from her chair, the dog gave a sudden bark. Apparently realizing that her mistress was about to leave the room, Fluff eagerly jumped off the bed and regarded her expectantly.

Selena glanced down at the small dog with a rueful smile. "My dear Fluff, I don't know if our guests would appreciate your company at the dinner table this evening."

"Fluff so hates being parted from your ladyship," said Betty.

Scooping the dog up into her arms, Selena handed Fluff to her. "You'd best see to her, Betty."

The servant nodded. "Don't worry, Fluff. I'll take you to the kitchen where Cook will give you a bit of the beef," she said in an apparent attempt to spare the little animal too much disappointment.

Leaving her room, Selena then made her way to the drawing room where the duke and duchess stood awaiting their guests. Glancing over to see Selena enter the room, Henrietta gave a little cry. "Oh, Selena, what a beautiful dress! You look splendid!"

"Thank you, Hetty," said Selena, walking across the stylishly appointed room to join the duchess. "It appears we both look grand this evening. That gown suits you very well. What a lovely color." Henrietta did appear quite pretty in her peach-colored dress, her dark hair entwined with ribbons.

"I don't hear anyone remarking on my appearance," said Selena's brother sulkily. Standing next to the mantel, the duke was dressed in elegant black dinner clothes that fit his tall frame to perfection.

"My dear brother," said Selena, fixing her eye on the duke's excellently tailored form, "you are a sartorial wonder."

The duke nodded at this compliment. "That is better."

"I expect your guests will arrive very soon," said Selena.

Henrietta nodded. "I am so looking forward to this evening. I do love such intimate little dinner parties. I know you'll adore Count von Gessler and his sister. You and Lady Blackstone will get on famously, I'm sure."

Selena smiled. Her sister-in-law had been singing the praises of Lady Blackstone for days. The duke had been no less enthusiastic about Count von Gessler, who was a friend and fellow art collector.

The count's sister, Lady Blackstone, had married a wealthy baron who was nearly thirty years her senior. Lord Blackstone was a fond, indulgent husband whose ample fortune enabled his wife to entertain extravagantly.

A cosmopolitan woman who had lived in Paris and Brussels as well as a number of other European cities, the former Theresa von Gessler, was very fond of art and literature. Her London salon was a gathering place for artists and writers as well as those members of society who appreciated the arts.

"Oh, I can't say enough about the count," said Henrietta. "He is a remarkable man, so very handsome and so intelligent!"

"And he is a first-rate collector of art as well," supplied

Melford. "In fact, he has just informed me of a painting that is being put up for sale by a certain Prussian gentleman—a Tintoretto!" The duke rubbed his hands together, a look of anticipation on his face. "The count thinks the man would be agreeable to selling me the painting."

Selena shook her head. "It isn't difficult to see why you are so fond of our guest," she said with a smile.

Henrietta nodded her head. "Yes, James thinks the count a fine gentleman."

"Yes," agreed the duke, "Von Gessler is a capital fellow. Dashed pity that he's not an Englishman."

"That is a serious failing, indeed," said Selena, casting an amused look at her brother.

"Yes, it is rather," said Henrietta with a serious expression. "But Count von Gessler is very distinguished. He is an intimate friend of Prince Augustus of Prussia. There are those who think it is Prince Augustus who will win Princess Charlotte's hand in marriage."

"I sincerely doubt that," said the duke. "I've heard that the Prince Regent was very displeased with Prince Augustus for his shameful conduct. The young man got horribly drunk at a dinner and behaved in a disgraceful manner."

"Indeed?" said Selena, very much interested.

"Poor Princess Charlotte," said Henrietta. "It must be rather tiresome being a princess and having so few gentlemen from which to choose. You must consider yourself fortunate, Selena, with so many suitors."

"I pray you don't mention my suitors," said Selena, raising her eyes heavenward. Since the Verney ball, she had been besieged with masculine visitors, all eager to impress her. "You know very well I don't care three straws for any of those fortune-hunting popinjays who have been calling here."

"Now, Selena," began the duchess, but she was cut short by the appearance of the butler, who announced that their guests had arrived.

"Lord and Lady Blackstone and Count von Gessler," announced the servant.

Selena looked expectantly at the three figures now entering the room. Catching sight of Lady Blackstone, Selena realized that her sister-in-law hadn't exaggerated when she had proclaimed her one of the great beauties of society. Lady Blackstone, a slim, elegant creature in a white silk gown, very pale with blond hair and light blue eyes, was exceptionally lovely.

Lord Blackstone was a short, stout man with stooped shoulders who looked considerably older than his sixty-one years. Plagued by gout, he had difficulty walking.

In contrast, Count von Gessler was tall and thin and extremely good looking. Like his sister, von Gessler had light blue eyes and aristocratic features. He was, however, somewhat darker in complexion than Lady Blackstone, and he had curly brown hair, arranged in the fashionable Corinthian style. With his striking looks and continental manners, the count was adjudged to be quite dashing.

Both gentlemen were very well dressed, although the count was more splendidly attired than his brother-in-law. Von Gessler was considered to be one of the best-dressed men in society, and his well-cut evening clothes fit him to perfection.

The guests approached their host and hostess. Lady Blackstone made an elegant curtsy.

"Ah, your grace," said von Gessler, bowing to the duke. "What a pleasure to be here." Turning to Henrietta, he bowed again. "And how lovely you look this evening, your grace."

The duchess beamed at this compliment, which was delivered by the count in a charming foreign accent. "Good evening, Count, I'm so glad you could join us." She then smiled at his sister. "Lady Blackstone, how good of you to come. Good evening, Lord Blackstone."

"May I present my sister?" said James, eager to introduce Selena. "Lady Blackstone, Lord Blackstone, and Count von Gessler—my sister, Lady Selena."

Selena smiled and curtsied to the guests, who bowed and curtsied in reply. The duchess did not fail to note that Count von Gessler was regarding her sister-in-law with great interest.

The count's sister smiled warmly at Selena. "I have so wished to meet you, Lady Selena. We have heard so much of your beauty and accomplishments." Like her brother, Theresa, Lady Blackstone, spoke with a slight Germanic accent.

"You are too kind, Lady Blackstone," said Selena, who was well accustomed to receiving such remarks.

The ladies and Lord Blackstone took seats in the drawing room while James took von Gessler by the elbow and steered him away for some private conversation. Henrietta looked over at the duke, who appeared to be engaged in a serious discussion with his guest. "Oh dear, it appears my husband and your brother are talking about pictures. I do hope he won't monopolize the count."

"My brother loves nothing better than to talk of art," said Theresa. "Indeed, I adore the subject myself."

"Art is all very well," said Henrietta, "but what I don't understand is my husband's need to collect every picture he takes a fancy to. We have so many paintings that I don't think we need any others. Why, there is hardly an empty space on any wall in any of our houses." She gestured toward the wall across from where they were sitting. "See how many paintings there are."

Theresa, who was as much a connoisseur of art as her brother, fixed an appreciative eye on the pictures hanging there. "My dear duchess, one cannot have too many paintings when they are as fine as those."

"Perhaps you're right, Lady Blackstone," said Henrietta. "I must confess that one painting is very much the same as another to me. My husband and Selena are the art fanciers in the family."

"You share the duke's love of paintings, Lady Selena?" said Theresa.

"Oh, yes," replied Selena. "Although I'm not the expert that James is. And while he loves Italian Renaissance painting best, I prefer modern works."

"Then we are much alike," said Theresa, smiling brightly. "You must attend my salon. Every Thursday I have the most delightful people. Artists and authors. Some are quite brilliant. You would enjoy meeting them."

"Indeed I would," said Selena.

While Henrietta thought Theresa Blackstone an admirable lady, she wasn't entirely sure that Selena should be encouraged to attend her salon. After all, while artistic people could be very amusing, they weren't the sort to provide what her sister-in-law needed most, a husband. Indeed, Selena would be better off avoiding Lady Blackstone's salon, where she might meet unsuitable gentlemen.

"Then you must come on Thursday," said Theresa. "I shall introduce you to Travers."

"Henry Travers?" said Selena.

"Yes, of course. And he is a charming man as well as a splendid poet."

"I would love to meet him," said Selena eagerly. "He is one of my favorite poets. I adored his 'Ode to a Summer's Night.'"

"Oh, yes, that is quite wonderful, is it not?" said Theresa.

"Pray, don't talk of poetry," said Lord Blackstone, speaking for the first time. "I can't abide it. Nothing but unmitigated drivel."

Selena raised her eyebrows at the baron, but Theresa only laughed. "My husband is a terrible Philistine," she said. "Can you imagine anyone hating poetry?"

"Drivel," repeated Blackstone, "drivel of the worst sort."

"Do ignore him, Lady Selena," said the baroness. "Everyone does."

"And I won't have that fellow Byron in my house," said Blackstone.

"Lord Byron is abroad, my dear," said Theresa, smiling indulgently at her husband.

"He'd best stay abroad," muttered the baron.

Theresa laughed again. "My husband is convinced that Byron is in love with me. It is so very amusing."

Selena noted that Lord Blackstone didn't seem in the least amused. He scowled, but said nothing further.

"Did you hear that Carolyn Montjoy is engaged to marry Sir Arthur Simpson?" said Henrietta, thinking it best to change the subject. "She is such a nice girl." Henrietta then launched into a long monologue about the young lady and her prospective groom.

By the time she was finished, they were joined by the duke and von Gessler. "Well, I have the Tintoretto!" exclaimed James, rubbing his hands together with apparent glee. "And I have von Gessler to thank for it. He used his influence with the Prussian gentleman, who agreed to sell it to me for a very good price."

"What very good news," said Henrietta, trying to sound enthusiastic.

"Yes, isn't it?" said her husband, smiling broadly. "Now do sit down, my dear count. You must have a glass of wine."

Von Gessler smiled urbanely as he took a place on the sofa where Selena was sitting. The count thought Selena a very lovely and desirable young lady. He was quite impressed with her red hair and remarkable green eyes. Von Gessler also very much appreciated the enticing charms displayed by her décolletage.

A bachelor who was in search of a wealthy wife, von Gessler found himself wondering whether the Duke of Melford might consider him for a brother-in-law. He was glad that he had acted on his behalf in the matter of the painting.

Selena, who had accepted a glass of wine from a silver tray presented by a footman, took a sip. "It seems you have my brother's eternal gratitude, Count von Gessler. He was quite enamored of this Tintoretto."

"I am only too happy to be of service to his grace," said the count. "It is a wonderful painting." He fixed what he hoped would be regarded as a charming smile on Selena. "You said you are fond of modern works, Lady Selena. You must go to the Royal Academy exhibition. There are some excellent paintings there. I know you would appreciate them."

"Rubbish," said Lord Blackstone, "all rubbish."

His wife laughed delightedly. "My husband is a very severe art critic."

"Rubbish," repeated Blackstone. "All of it."

The count cheerfully ignored his brother-in-law. "Yes, there are many fine paintings. We must all go together.

"That is a good idea," said the duke, turning to Selena. "Von Gessler is such a good judge of art."

At that moment, there was a diversion as Fluff ran into the room. The little dog rushed across the room to Selena, wagging her tail furiously.

Arriving at the sofa she hopped up into Selena's lap. "Fluff!" cried Selena. "What are you doing here?"

Von Gessler eyed the dog with disapproval. He didn't like dogs, especially tiny lap dogs, considering them "little yapping creatures."

Fluff, who had been looking up at her mistress, turned suddenly toward the count. After eyeing him for a moment, she emitted a surprisingly ferocious growl. "Fluff!" cried Selena sternly. "Behave yourself!"

Von Gessler pulled back at the dog's belligerent display. Fluff then erupted into a fit of barking. She started to lunge toward the count, but Selena held her fast.

"Good God!" cried the duke. "What has gotten into her?"

Selena rose quickly from the sofa. "I'm so sorry. Fluff, you bad dog! Do be quiet!" Ignoring her mistress's pleas, the toy spaniel continued to bark at von Gessler. "Do excuse me. I shall rid us of this little fiend." Selena hurried from the drawing room, the dog still barking in her arms.

Arriving in the hallway, she frowned at the dog, who had finally quieted down. "Whatever is the matter, Fluff? You've never behaved in such a reprehensible fashion before. And why don't you like Count von Gessler? He seems like an amiable gentleman."

Betty appeared in the corridor. "Oh, there she is! I'm so very sorry, my lady. She slipped away from me."

Selena handed Fluff to her maid. "She misbehaved dreadfully, Betty. She was barking at one of the gentlemen in a frightful manner. Now, do keep her away from the company. The duke will have my head if we see her again."

"Of course, my lady," said Betty, bobbing a curtsy and taking the dog away.

Selena turned to reenter the drawing room. Fluff had acted in a very peculiar manner. While she was sometimes reserved with strangers, she had never reacted so fiercely.

Coming back into the room, Selena apologized for the interruption. The count assured her that the incident was only a trifling one and that she should think no more about it. Lady Blackstone began to talk about her latest meeting with the Prince Regent, a topic that occupied the company until the butler arrived to announce that dinner was served.

The ladies and gentlemen made a small procession to the dining room, with Selena on von Gessler's arm. With only six at table, it was an unusually small and intimate dinner party. Selena found herself seated next to the count, who seemed only too pleased to find himself with such a lovely and charming dinner companion.

Since the Duke of Melford had an excellent cook, von Gessler's attention was somewhat distracted from Selena by the delectable food placed before him. A gourmet who was often disappointed at English tables, he was very pleased by such delicious fare.

Lady Blackstone seemed likewise pleased with the excellent food. She complimented every dish and, despite her slim frame, ate heartily.

"I must say, Duchess," said Theresa, "I have never had such a fine dinner in London. No indeed, not since leaving Paris have I eaten so well. I must congratulate you on your chef."

Henrietta beamed at the praise. Compliments from Lady Blackstone were compliments indeed, for that lady was renowned for her sophistication and taste.

Selena found herself enjoying the dinner party. Count von Gessler and his sister were both interesting conversationalists, who told many amusing anecdotes about European courts. When she listened to Theresa talk of Paris and Brussels and von Gessler mention Vienna and Rome, Selena felt very provincial. She found herself wishing that she might visit all the interesting places they mentioned. She asked numerous questions about the Continent, which the count and his sister were very pleased to answer.

Henrietta, on the other hand, wasn't enjoying the conversation as much as her sister-in-law. A loquacious individual, the duchess found that her guests and sister-in-law weren't affording her enough opportunity to speak. She wasn't happy to find herself remaining quiet during most of the dinner while Theresa and the count chattered merrily on.

When the opportunity finally presented itself, Henrietta hurried to enter the conversation. "I've heard the most interesting news from Lady Carrington today," she said. "It seems an interesting young gentleman has arrived in town, a foreign prince. His name is Prince Maximilian. No one has seen him yet."

"Prince Maximilian?" said the duke. "Never heard of him."

"Lady Carrington said he is from . . ." Henrietta hesitated. "Oh, dear, I can never remember the name of the place."

Von Gessler regarded her with a grim expression. "Brunconia, your grace?"

Henrietta's face lit up. "Brunconia! That's it!" She turned and smiled at the count. "I'd never even heard of Brunconia. But then you would know all about such places, wouldn't you, Count?"

"He would indeed," said Theresa with a slight smile. "You see, your grace, we are Brunconian."

The duchess regarded her in some astonishment. "You are Brunconian?"

The count nodded.

"The devil you are," said James. "I thought you were Prussian."

"I have been attached to the Prussian court, but I am Brunconian," replied von Gessler.

"Brunconia?" said Lord Blackstone, speaking for the first time since sitting down at the table. He looked at his wife. "You said you were Austrian."

Theresa raised her eyes heavenward. "I have told you countless times that I was born in Brunconia, my dear. I left there when I was a small child and don't remember much about it."

"Isn't that interesting?" said Henrietta. "To think you are from Brunconia. And until today I'd never heard of the place."

"It is a very small country," said the count.

"We must find it in the atlas after dinner," said the duke. "Indeed, I should like to see where it is. So you must know this prince my wife is talking of, eh, von Gessler?"

"No, your grace," said the count. "I have not made his acquaintance." He paused. "Nor would I wish to do so."

Selena looked over at von Gessler. "What do you mean, sir?"

"I mean that I have no wish to meet this prince nor any of the royal family of Brunconia."

Selena and the others regarded their guest with considerable interest, but the count said nothing further. His sister felt it necessary to step in. "You must forgive my brother and myself if we are reluctant to discuss the von Stauffenburg dynasty. It brings up very painful memories."

"Oh, dear," said Henrietta. "I shouldn't have mentioned it. It was only that Lady Carrington made much of the story. She said that Prince Maximilian was staying with the Earl of Heathfield, who is his cousin."

"Heathfield!" cried the duke. "If he is Heathfield's cousin, I wouldn't be surprised if he's a scoundrel."

"If you don't wish to speak of this, Count von Gessler, we will certainly change the subject," said Henrietta.

"No, I shall speak of it," said the count. "But I must ask you to say nothing to anyone about what I will tell you."

"Of course, we wouldn't say a word," said Henrietta, dying of curiosity. "You may have confidence in our complete discretion, Count."

"I have lived for many years in Prussia," said the count, beginning his tale, "but my family is one of the oldest and noblest

families of Brunconia. My father served the Grand Duke of
Brunconia loyally for many years. He was a well-respected offi-
cial who was much beloved by the Brunconian people.

"The grand duke was jealous of his subjects' regard for my
father. Like most of the von Stauffenburg line, he was a bit mad.
The grand duke came to think that my father was plotting
against him, so he had some outrageous charges trumped up
against him. Orders were issued to arrest my father, but, fortunately, he was warned of this treacherous plot and we fled from
the country. I was a child of twelve at the time and my sister
only seven. Penniless and friendless, we were forced to wander
about from place to place. Finally, we sought asylum in the
court of the King of Prussia. My father found new employment
in the king's service and my family once again prospered."

"Oh, I am glad of that," said Henrietta, "but it must have been
very dreadful for your family, having to leave the home you had
known for so long."

"It was indeed," said Theresa. "My poor mother was quite
devastated. She was always melancholy thinking of her old life
and the friends she had left behind. Now you will understand
why neither my brother nor myself would wish to meet any
prince of Brunconia."

"Yes," said the count, nodding solemnly, "Grand Duke Wilhelm is a cruel, ruthless, tyrannical ruler and I don't doubt that
his son is very much like him."

"Cruel and ruthless," said the duke, regarding the count with
great interest, "a most unpleasant combination."

"Indeed it is, your grace," said von Gessler. "My father was
lucky to escape from Brunconia with his life. We later learned
that the grand duke planned to have him executed."

"Oh, dear!" cried Henrietta.

"Yes, your grace," said the count, "and heaven knows what
would have happened to the rest of us."

The duke resolutely put down his fork. "I'm glad you told us
of this, Count. We will certainly have nothing to do with this
Prince Maximilian."

"Indeed not," said Henrietta, "and I should think that everyone in Society should know what sort of man this prince's father
is. Do give us leave to tell your story, Count von Gessler."

"No, your grace, I must beg you to keep silent on the matter.
It will serve no purpose to open old wounds."

"We will do as you wish," said Melford, "but I do hope that I never cross paths with the fellow. I shan't be civil to him if I do."

"You can be sure that we will snub him," said Henrietta resolutely, and then she changed the subject.

6

·→·ᵉᵉᶜᵉᵉ·ᵗ·

The morning following his arrival in London, Prince Maximilian woke up in one of the spacious guest bedrooms of Heathfield House. Sitting up in the large canopied bed, the young man gave a great yawn and then he looked around him.

Maximilian was quite pleased with his accommodations, noting the fine cherry dresser, ornate chairs, and pleasant landscape paintings that decorated the room. The prince wasn't used to luxury and he felt himself most fortunate to be staying at his cousin's splendid residence.

Maximilian had been quite overwhelmed by the grandeur of Heathfield's house. Awed by the elegantly furnished rooms, he was equally astonished with the great number of books in the earl's library and the superb art collection that graced the residence's walls.

Heathfield House was quite a contrast to Maximilian's home in Brunconia. While it was true that Maximilian had grown up in a palace, the residence of the Brunconian royal family was by no means luxurious.

Hard times had taken a toll on the ancestral dwelling of the rulers of Brunconia. Its once-splendid rooms were now shabby and threadbare, with moth-eaten tapestries hanging on the walls. The palace was in great need of repair, but there was no money in the royal treasury for such expenses. In the winter, the wind howled through its drafty, cavernous rooms, making it a most unpleasant place to live.

Getting out of the bed, Maximilian walked over to the windows and pulled open the draperies to look out at the fashionable street of brick townhouses. Gazing out at the London street, he wondered what his parents were doing at that moment. Doubtless his father was attending some dreary meeting with his ministers discussing where some money might be found to pay Brunconia's tiny army. His mother and sisters were probably diligently working on their sewing. And his brothers Fritz and Wilhelm were probably at work with their tutor, the humorless Herr Gruber.

Yes, he missed his family already, but he missed Frederica most of all. Maximilian frowned. He had always thought that he would marry Frederica. They were very much in love. It had been so painful accepting the fact that she would never become his bride.

His frown deepened as he remembered the conversation with his father in which the grand duke had said he must give up Frederica. Yes, his father had said, Frederica was a princess and a member of one of the noblest families of Brunconia, but she was very poor. It was essential that Maximilian marry for money. His bride must be a very wealthy woman.

While Maximilian had protested violently at first, he was a dutiful son and he had known that his father was right. When the grand duke had said he must try to win the hand of Princess Charlotte, the heir to the British throne, he had reluctantly agreed. After all, he could not argue with the notion that such an alliance would be the answer to his country's prayers.

He pondered the matter. He had promised to do all he could to charm the Princess. He would have to be very strong and put aside his feelings for Frederica, for he knew that his duty came before his personal happiness.

Maximilian folded his arms as he continued to stare out the window. He must stop being forlorn. One must accept things as they were. And wasn't it grand to be in London, staying with his rich cousin in a fine house. And if he were successful, he would marry the Princess Charlotte and help restore his country's fortunes.

He knew that winning Princess Charlotte's hand was a formidable task. After all, he knew many other princes were eager for the honor of becoming her husband. And he also knew that he wasn't particularly handsome or dashing. Yet, he would do his best, and now that he had met his two English cousins, Maximilian was sure that they would assist him in his matrimonial mission.

Maximilian's frown disappeared as he thought of Heathfield and Percy. His two cousins had been quite kind to him and he thought them both splendid fellows. He especially admired the earl, who, with his dark good looks, charming manner, and wealth, seemed to have everything that Maximilian lacked.

There was a tap on the door and the prince turned away from the window. "Do come in," he called. The door opened and the earl and Percy entered the room.

Heathfield suppressed a smile at the sight of his Brunconian cousin. Maximilian was attired in a large striped nightshirt, a ludicrous-looking nightcap perched on his head.

"Good morning, Cousin Max," said the earl.

"Ah, cousins," said the young man, smiling at them, "Good morning to you!"

Heathfield noted with amusement that Percy was eyeing the prince's nighttime attire with an appalled expression. He smiled. "Did you sleep well?"

"Oh, yes," said Maximilian, nodding his head emphatically. "I have never had so good a bed. I slept like a Brunconian bear in winter."

"I'm glad to hear it," said Heathfield. "Percy and I thought we might take you to our tailor this morning."

"We thought you should like to have some new attire for meeting Society," said Percy.

The prince suddenly looked sheepish. "Oh, I would like new clothes but the money is, how do you say, difficult."

"Don't worry, Max," said Percy, smiling for the first time. "Our cousin Heathfield is a dashed generous fellow. He's never happier than when he's spending his blunt on others. He'll be pleased to buy you an entire wardrobe."

Maximilian shook his head in wonderment. "You are too good, Cousin," he said.

The earl exchanged an ironic glance with Percy. "It is nothing, I assure you," he said. "Well, I shall have my man come to assist you in dressing. Then we shall have breakfast and be off to the tailor."

The prince seemed happy with this plan and within a short time, the three cousins were once again inside a carriage. After making its way through several residential neighborhoods, the vehicle pulled into the main business district of the city.

As the carriage pulled up in front of the tailor's establishment, Heathfield glanced over at his royal cousin. He suspected that Lydcott, a tailor of renown, would have quite a challenge in making his royal cousin into a man of fashion.

As they entered the shop, a clerk who had witnessed Heathfield's carriage arriving, hurried up to them. "May I be of assistance, m'lord?" he said.

The earl nodded. "We need to see Mr. Lydcott."

The clerk hurried off, returning a moment later with a short, balding man in spectacles. "My lord," said the tailor, making a bow.

"Good day, Lydcott," said the earl, smiling amiably. "Mr. Hastings and I have a new client for you."

"Very good, my lord," said the tailor. He looked over at Percy and nodded. "Good day, Mr. Hastings."

"Good day, Lydcott," returned Percy. "And this is your new client."

Lydcott's gaze then fell on Maximilian. The tailor needed all his self-control not to show how appalled he was by that gentleman's attire. Maximilian, who was dressed in his shabby military uniform from the previous day, presented a most unpromising appearance.

"Lydcott, may I present his highness, Prince Maximilian von Stauffenburg of Brunconia," said the earl.

The tailor could not hide his astonishment at this announcement. He seemed dumbfounded for a moment, but then managed to regain his professional manner and bowed low. "Your highness's humble servant," he said.

Maximilian waved his hand cheerfully. "I'm pleased to meet you, sir. My cousins tell me you are a most excellent tailor." He grinned. "As you see, I am in need of your services."

Lydcott murmured a polite reply and then glanced through his spectacles at the earl. "I am only too pleased to be of assistance to his highness, Lord Heathfield."

"Prince Maximilian requires a complete wardrobe," said Heathfield. "And I shall pay all the expenses."

The tailor, instantly calibrating the bill for such a large order, suddenly smiled. The Earl of Heathfield was one of his best customers, for not only did his lordship look exceedingly well in his clothes, but he settled his accounts quickly. "Very good, my lord," said Lydcott. "Do come with me, your highness." Leading Maximilian to a back room, he immediately set about taking the prince's measurements.

After a considerable length of time had passed, the three cousins exited the tailor's shop. The prince seemed quite exhausted by all the measuring and fussing about, and was happy to have finally escaped.

"Well, Cousin Max," said Percy with a smile, "Lydcott has assured us that he will have a suit of evening clothes ready for you within a week. We must return in a couple of days for your final fitting."

Maximilian's face fell. "A fitting? Not again?" he asked.

"I fear so," said the earl with an amused look.

"Yes," said Percy, "one must be willing to suffer for fashion, you know."

"If that is what you are saying, Cousin Percy," said Maximilian skeptically, "I shall submit to your opinion."

"Yes, in matters of fashion, one should submit to Percy's opinion. It is the one subject in which he has some degree of competence. And there is no one who can tie a cravat better, I assure you."

While Percy didn't appreciate the earl's remarks, he only raised his eyebrows in an exasperated fashion. "I do think we should return home. It won't do for Max to go about town without his new clothes."

"Shame on you, Percy," said Heathfield with an amused look. " 'A man's a man for a' that.' "

"What?" said Percy.

"You know, Robert Burns, the poet?"

"I have no idea what you're talking about, Charles," replied Percy. "But I feel it best that Maximilian stay out of public view until Lydcott has worked his wonders."

"Well, I shan't argue. But I should like to stop in at the bookstore across the street for a moment."

"What, another book?" Percy shook his head and then he looked over at Maximilian. "Our cousin Heathfield is a great reader. It is one of his peculiarities."

"Ah," said the prince, nodding again.

"Well, I daresay a book shop is safe enough," said Percy. "I don't think I'll find any of my friends there."

Heathfield laughed, and the three of them proceeded across the street. They entered the small shop, which was a cluttered place filled with tall shelves stacked with books. The place was crowded with customers and a clerk was perched on a rather perilous looking ladder, retrieving several volumes from a high shelf.

Maximilian looked about at all the people crowded into the

bookstore. They seemed to be either intently perusing books on the shelves or deeply engrossed in the volumes they held in their hands. The prince continued to glance about when his eye suddenly alighted on a lady standing in the corner of the shop, her eyes cast down upon a book before her. Maximilian gave an exclamation in his native tongue and then he turned excitedly to Percy. "Cousin," he said, "is that not a most beautiful lady?"

Percy looked over in the direction of his cousin's gaze, recognizing the lady at once. It was Lady Selena Paget. While he hadn't yet been introduced to her, he had seen her at the Verney ball. She was very well dressed in a sky-blue pelisse and matching bonnet. The lady's bright red curls peeked out from beneath the bonnet. "Why, that is Lady Selena Paget," he said.

Heathfield, who had been looking at a travel book on Arabia, looked up with a startled look. "Where?"

"There in the corner."

"Good God!" said Heathfield as he caught sight of her. "I can't believe it. It must be fate. Do excuse me for a moment, cousins," he said, handing his book over to Percy. "I must have a word with that lady. I'll return shortly." The earl then made his way down the crowded aisle toward her.

Selena, intent upon the first page of a novel, had not seen Heathfield and his cousins. Turning the page, she eagerly continued reading.

"That must be a fascinating book, Lady Selena," said a voice, and she looked up in astonishment to see the earl smiling down at her.

"Lord Heathfield!"

He bowed. "Your ladyship's most devoted servant. What a happy chance to meet you again. Doesn't it seem that the fates are throwing us in each other's path?"

Selena, who had managed to recover her composure, shook her head. "Indeed, the fates can be cruel," she said with a sardonic smile.

The earl laughed. "Not as cruel as you, Lady Selena." He looked again at the book in her hands. The volume had *Waverly* emblazoned in gilt letters on the cover. "That really is a deuced good book," said Heathfield, glancing back at her. "And the whole of London is in a lather over the identity of the author."

Selena nodded. "I must confess I'm eager to read it."

Heathfield noticed that Selena also had two books set down on the shelf before her. "So you've made other selections as well," he said. He picked up a thin volume and glanced down at it. "So, you like poetry, Lady Selena. A work by Henry Travers. I fear I find Mr. Travers a bit . . ." He paused. "Too much for me."

"I don't know what you mean by that."

"You don't think his style a trifle overdone?"

"Overdone?" said Selena.

"You know, overblown metaphors and the like."

"Why, no, not in the least," said Selena. "I think his work is quite wonderful."

"Well, perhaps he is more to a lady's taste," said the earl.

Selena bristled at the remark. "Perhaps Mr. Travers's work is more to the taste of sensitive individuals."

The earl arched his dark eyebrows and smiled. Then, taking up the other book, he read the title, *The Curse of Orlando*. Shaking his head, he met her glance. "I fear you shouldn't strain your lovely eyes on this book. It is utter rubbish."

Selena frowned slightly. "My sister-in-law recommended it very highly."

"I fear I must disagree with the duchess," he said, still smiling. "The plot is totally ludicrous, with ghosts clunking about and people being cast into castle dungeons. And the heroine is a complete ninny who is always swooning over the most trifling things."

"Then you read it?"

"I confess I did, but it was only that I was staying at my uncle's country house and it was the only book my cousin Percy could provide me with. He thought it a veritable masterpiece. Since my cousin Percy has scarcely ever read a book in his life, I must say I was intrigued." He paused. "My cousin is a very good fellow, but he is a wretched judge of literature."

Selena appeared skeptical. "And you consider yourself a worthy critic, Lord Heathfield?"

"I don't wish to appear immodest, ma'am, but I do think myself a fair judge of literature. And I assure you that this book is not worth your money." With that, the earl unceremoniously tossed the volume down. Selena frowned and indignantly picked it up.

"Really, sir, I'm quite capable of choosing my own books." Looking down at the volume, she hesitated for a moment and then she glanced back up at him. "The heroine is a complete ninny?" she asked.

Heathfield grinned. "Indeed, she is."

Selena put the book back on the shelf. "Perhaps I shall look for another. I also wanted a collection of Mr. Wordsworth's poems. Of course, you probably don't approve of him either. I warn you, my lord, he is my favorite poet and I won't take kindly to hearing his work criticized."

"As he is my favorite as well, Lady Selena, I shall only sing his praises," said the earl, smiling his devastating smile at her.

Meeting his gaze for a moment, Selena quickly looked away, alarmed at the disturbing sensations the earl was provoking in her. Trying to appear nonchalant, she glanced toward the door of the shop. "You must excuse me, Lord Heathfield. My sister-in-law should be here at any moment and I did wish to find another book. The duchess was just stopping a moment at the linen draper's, and she will be very impatient to be off."

"Well, I certainly don't mind if the duchess takes her time," said Heathfield. He paused. "I do hope she and the duke are well."

Selena nodded. "They are very well, thank you."

"And how is your charming little niece, Sophie? I so enjoyed meeting her the other day at the park."

Selena smiled in spite of herself. "Sophie is fine. She still speaks of your dog, Duncan. She was very much enamored of him even though she doesn't like to say so in front of Fluff."

The earl laughed. "Yes, it wouldn't do to make Fluff jealous."

"No, that isn't wise," agreed Selena.

Heathfield, gazing down at Selena's lovely face, felt an almost overpowering urge to kiss her. It took a good deal of self-control to refrain from doing so.

"Cousin," said Percy, coming up beside him. He bowed politely to Selena. "Madam," he said, before turning to look expectantly at the earl.

Although his lordship wasn't happy at the interruption, he made the introduction. "Lady Selena," said Heathfield, "may I present my cousin, Mr. Percy Hastings? Percy, this is Lady Selena Paget."

Percy bowed. "I'm frightfully honored to meet you, Lady Selena. I didn't have the pleasure of doing so at the Verney ball."

"How do you do, Mr. Hastings?"

"I'm very well, indeed, Lady Selena," replied Percy.

Maximilian, who had been following Percy, had been waylaid

by an elderly man whose slow passage across the aisle had delayed his joining his cousins. When he finally stood beside Percy, he smiled at the attractive young lady who was commanding his cousins' attention.

Selena looked inquiringly at Maximilian, noting his mustache and comical blue military coat. Although Percy wasn't too eager to introduce Maximilian to anyone in Society before Lydcott had transformed him into a presentable young man, Percy realized that he had no choice. "Allow me to present my cousin, Prince Maximilian von Stauffenburg of Brunconia. Maximilian, this is Lady Selena Paget."

Selena tried hard to hide her amazement. The rather ungainly looking young man standing before her in the faded military uniform seemed decidedly unprincely. He certainly didn't appear to be very prosperous, she thought. Remembering Count von Gessler's words at last night's dinner party, she marveled to think that this awkward gentleman was one of the evil von Stauffenburgs. It seemed quite absurd.

Smiling broadly at her, Maximilian stepped forward and bowed in the formal style of European courts. "My Lady Selena," he said, taking her hand and bringing it to his lips as was the custom in Brunconia, "it is a great pleasure to meet you."

Selena made a graceful curtsy. "Your highness," she said.

"Our cousin has just arrived in town, Lady Selena," said Percy.

Selena smiled at Maximilian. "Then we are both newcomers to town, sir," she said. "I haven't been in London very long myself, having only just arrived from the country. I do hope you enjoy your stay here."

"You are very kind, madam," said Maximilian, who thought Selena very charming. Indeed, there was something about her that reminded him of his dear Frederica.

At that moment, Henrietta entered the shop followed by her lady's maid, who was carrying a parcel. The duchess glanced about. Then, catching sight of Selena, she noted with surprise that her sister-in-law was speaking with a young man in a strange military uniform. Then Henrietta saw Heathfield.

As always, the sight of the handsome earl caused the duchess's pulse to quicken a bit. Whatever was he doing there, she wondered. How very odd that he appeared again with Selena. Frowning slightly, Henrietta made her way to where Selena was standing. "Selena," she said.

"Henrietta," said Selena, turning to smile at her sister-in-law. "See who is here. Lord Heathfield and Mr. Hastings."

The duchess nodded gravely to the gentlemen. "Your grace," said Percy, bowing.

"Duchess," said the earl, smiling and bowing as well. "How do you do, ma'am?"

"Well enough, Lord Heathfield," said Henrietta with uncharacteristic coolness.

"Do permit me to introduce my cousin," said Heathfield. "This is Prince Maximilian von Stauffenburg of Brunconia. Maximilian, I have the honor to present her grace, the Duchess of Melford."

At hearing the young man's name, Henrietta was rather taken aback. Here was the man she had promised to snub.

Maximilian was happily unaware of the duchess's displeasure. Very pleased at meeting a lady of such august rank, he came to attention, clicked his heels together, and bowed smartly. "A very great honor, madam," he said.

Henrietta wasn't sure how to respond. Surely it wouldn't do to be polite to such a man after what she knew of his family. After staring at him awkwardly for a moment, she nodded again. "How do you do, sir?" Then turning to Selena, she said, "We really must go. It grows very late."

"Very well, but I must pay for my books," said Selena, holding up her two volumes.

Taking the books from her hand, the duchess handed them to her maid. "Adams will see to that, my dear. Place these on my account and join us in the carriage, Adams."

"Yes, your grace," replied the servant, going off to obey the duchess's orders. Henrietta then took Selena firmly by the arm. "You gentlemen must excuse us. Good day to you."

Selena could only nod to Heathfield and his cousins as Henrietta propelled her from the shop.

Heathfield, who had been very disappointed at seeing Selena depart so hastily, watched her go. A carriage was waiting outside and through the shop window, the earl saw a liveried servant assist Henrietta and Selena up into it.

"What a pity the ladies rushed off so quickly," said Maximilian.

"Well, I fear that the duchess didn't wish to be seen with me," said Heathfield.

"But why?" said Maximilian, regarding his cousin in surprise.

"My dear Max," said the earl, "I am not on the best of terms with the duchess's husband. Indeed, the Duke of Melford detests me."

"Detests you?" said Maximilian, looking puzzled. "But how is that possible?"

Heathfield laughed. "It is hard to imagine, isn't it? But Melford and I haven't gotten on since we were boys at Eton. I can't resist besting him whenever I have a chance. He collects paintings, you see. Whenever I find a picture I know he'd want, I have to buy it. And then I have to let him know about it. It's such great fun to see him fuss and fume."

"And Lady Selena is the Duke of Melford's sister," said Percy.

"His sister?" said Maximilian, mulling over this information. He thought Selena very lovely and she had a wonderful smile. Yes, it was a smile very much like Frederica's.

"Yes, it's dashed peculiar that Melford would have such a charming sister," said the earl.

"She is charming," said Maximilian, gazing out the window at Selena and Henrietta, who were sitting in the open carriage waiting for the duchess's maid. In a few moments, the servant completed her mission and made her way from the bookstore to the street. Once she was in the vehicle, the carriage drove away.

"I have another book to find," said the earl, trying to appear unaffected by seeing Selena once again. "I won't be long." Then, turning away from his cousins, he started to once again peruse the bookshelves.

As the carriage made its way down the cobblestoned street, Selena turned to Henrietta. "I don't know why you had to be rude, Hetty."

"I wasn't rude," replied the duchess.

"Indeed, you were rude. Why, you hardly said a word to Prince Maximilian. And then you hurried me off before I could even politely take my leave."

"And I cannot believe that you spoke to that man. Have you forgotten what Count von Gessler said about him?"

"Well, how do we know whether he spoke the truth? I don't know very much about the count. I remember that James said that he hasn't been in England very long."

"I think we know him well enough to trust what he says. And this Prince Maximilian didn't look very respectable to me. Indeed, I could scarcely believe that horrid uniform he was wearing. It was quite shabby."

"Perhaps he hasn't money for new things."

"Hasn't money What nonsense. He is a prince, isn't he? I think it more likely that he is simply careless and slovenly. A man who doesn't care for his appearance isn't to be trusted."

"Well, he seemed a pleasant gentleman to me," said Selena.

"He may seem pleasant, but that doesn't mean what Count von Gessler said is untrue. And in any case, you know what my husband thinks of Heathfield."

Not wanting to say anything else in front of her sister-in-law's lady's maid, Selena made no reply. She thought that Henrietta had acted very badly, and she was vexed with her.

Turning away from the duchess, Selena looked out at the activity on the busy street as the carriage rounded a corner. Of course, Henrietta was right that her brother wouldn't want her to speak to Heathfield. Selena suppressed a sigh. The earl was so terribly charming and handsome, but she knew that losing her heart to such a man was sheer folly.

When they arrived home, Selena went to her room to change her clothes. She then retired to her sitting room to write a letter, accompanied by Fluff, who was very glad to see her mistress again. Selena had scarcely begun her letter when she was interrupted by Henrietta.

"I'm sorry to disturb you, Selena," said the duchess, entering the room and seating herself in an armchair, "but I must talk with you."

Putting down her quill pen, Selena regarded her sister-in-law expectantly. "Yes, Hetty?"

"Did you arrange to meet Lord Heathfield in the book shop?"

"Arrange to meet him?" Selena regarded her sister-in-law incredulously. "Certainly not."

"Well, what was I to think when we meet him a second time in such an unlikely place."

"I don't think it so unlikely. Really, Hetty, you're being ridiculous. Upon my word of honor, I didn't contrive to meet Heathfield. It was simply a coincidence that he was there."

"Oh, I am glad," said Henrietta, clearly relieved. "I was rather worried."

"Worried?"

"That you've fallen in love with him. You know that James would never approve."

"I've met Heathfield but three times in my life," said Selena. "I assure you I have no intention of running off with him."

"That is a relief," said Henrietta. "It would sorely distress your brother if you did."

Selena laughed. "What a goose you are, Hetty. The very idea."

"You may laugh, but I know that a man like Heathfield can make a lady quite forget herself."

"I promise I shall endeavor to keep my wits about me," said Selena. She laughed again, but then remembering the way the earl looked at her that morning, she wondered if she'd be able to keep her promise.

7

The next few days passed quickly for Heathfield, since he was kept very busy making Maximilian fit for society. The earl had taken a great liking to his princely cousin, and he wanted to do all he could to assure his success.

Of course, his lordship had no illusions that Maximilian would be taken seriously as a match for Princess Charlotte. No, Brunconia was far too insignificant and Maximilian far too poor to suit the heir to the British throne. Still, the earl thought that he would enjoy squiring his cousin about London.

While Percy had little hope that Maximilian could be transformed into a fashionable gentleman, Heathfield had no doubts on that score. He saw in his cousin a diamond in the rough who needed only a bit of polishing to be acceptable in London society.

The earl called in his barber to cut Maximilian's unruly blond locks. The prince was well pleased with his new English haircut, but he was less happy when Heathfield told him that his Brunconian mustache must go. It wasn't the English fashion to wear a mustache, the earl insisted. Percy backed him up very strongly on this point.

With his cousins determined he shave the mustache, Maximilian reluctantly submitted to the razor. He wasn't at all pleased to do so for it hadn't been easy to grow the mustache and he had been very proud of it. And besides that, all gentlemen in Brunconia wore mustaches.

Yet when the deed had been done, the young prince had stared into the mirror in some trepidation. Both Heathfield and Percy had proclaimed that he looked like a handsome English gentleman, and Maximilian had had to admit that perhaps he didn't look too ridiculous after all.

When they had returned to Mr. Lydcott's establishment for

Maximilian's final fitting, Percy and Heathfield had been well pleased with the tailor's handiwork. A flurry of activity among Lydcott's associates had produced a fine wardrobe worthy of a prince.

Two days after the second visit to Lydcott, Maximilian's clothes were delivered to Heathfield House. The earl assigned his valet to do his best and Maximilian was given over to his lordship's capable servant.

When the prince joined Percy and the earl in the drawing room, he was beaming with pleasure. "What do you think?" said Maximilian. "Do I not look like a handsome English gentleman?"

"By my faith!" said Percy, staring at his cousin. "You look a veritable Corinthian."

"That is good, yes?" said Maximilian.

"It is exceedingly good," said the earl, smiling at the prince. The young man had certainly undergone a remarkable transformation since they had first seen him in Dover. Now attired in a well-fitting coat of charcoal-gray superfine, buff-colored pantaloons and gleaming Hessian boots, Maximilian looked splendid. His new haircut and lack of mustache completed the picture.

And while nature hadn't favored the prince with Heathfield's classically handsome features, he wasn't at all bad looking. And his new clothes made him seem slimmer, taller, and more dignified.

Percy stood smiling at the prince. Certainly, no one could fault his appearance now, thought Percy. Why, he looked almost handsome. Princess Charlotte wouldn't be ashamed to stand up with Maximilian. "Well, Charles, now that our cousin is turned out in prime style, why don't we go somewhere to show him off?"

"That is exactly what I'm thinking," said Heathfield. "I believe it's time to call at Carlton House. Come, gentlemen, let us fetch our hats and be off."

"But wait a moment," cried Percy. "Carlton House? You cannot mean to call on the Prince Regent?"

"Why, yes, of course," replied Heathfield.

"The Prince Regent?" said Maximilian in surprise. "Now? *Nein*, I had not thought to meet him so soon."

"My dear Max," said Heathfield, "it is customary that a visiting prince pay a courtesy call to our sovereign. It would be rude to delay it any longer." He smiled. "And besides, we are expected."

"Expected?" exclaimed Percy.

"Yes, I wrote the Prince asking if we might bring Max. He sent the most charming reply and invited us to tea."

"Tea?" said Maximilian. "That is very good, no?"

"It is indeed," said Percy. "Yes, this is marvelous, but why didn't you tell me until now?"

"I didn't want you to worry and have a sleepless night."

"But I would have worn my new coat had I known," said Percy. "Will we have time to stop at my house so I might change?"

"Certainly not," said Heathfield. "The Prince Regent must take you as you are. And you don't want to outshine our princely cousin, do you? Now come along, we don't want to be late."

Soon the three cousins were on their way to the Prince Regent's residence in Heathfield's carriage. Percy seemed nervous. A good deal was riding on this visit. If the Prince Regent disliked Maximilian, he would have no chance with Princess Charlotte. "Now remember, Max," he said, "don't ask after the Princess of Wales."

"Our cousin isn't a simpleton, Percy," said Heathfield, leaning back against the leather seat and seeming totally unperturbed about their upcoming interview with the first gentleman of the land. "Everyone in Europe knows that our prince despises his wife."

Ja, it is known even in Brunconia," said Maximilian.

"Well, it doesn't hurt to be certain," said Percy. "Now, Max, don't speak to His Royal Highness unless addressed."

"Good God, Percy, Maximilian is familiar with etiquette. Need I remind you that his father is the Grand Duke of Brunconia?"

"Yes, of course," said Percy, although that fact did little to lessen his misgivings. Brunconia wasn't England and what was suitable for Brunconians might give offense elsewhere.

They arrived at Carlton House, the Regent's splendid London residence, a short time later and were soon escorted into the royal presence. Royal George was seated on a chair in the magnificent drawing room. Two of his aides were also present, Colonel Lyon and Sir Geoffrey Caruthers.

Heathfield was well acquainted with the Regent for the earl's father had been an intimate friend of the Prince. The Prince of Wales was now more than fifty years of age and time and His Royal Highness's fondness for high living had taken their toll on his once-famed good looks. While the Regent's face was still handsome, he had grown very stout and his great girth was corseted beneath his fine clothes.

The Prince suffered from gout and digestive disorders, and he was often moody and irritable. His marital difficulties and his unpopularity with the people also caused him a great deal of distress.

When the Earl of Heathfield and his cousins were announced, the Prince Regent appeared pleased to see them. His Royal Highness had always liked Heathfield, who shared the Prince's love of art and his good taste. And since the Prince Regent had been very fond of Heathfield's father, he was always happy to receive the earl.

The three gentlemen approached the Prince and bowed politely. "Ah, Heathfield," said the Prince Regent. "Good of you to come."

"Your Royal Highness was very kind to invite us," said the earl.

The Prince of Wales looked at Percy. "Hastings," he said, nodding a bit coolly to that gentleman.

"Your Royal Highness," said Percy, bowing again.

"And this must be your cousin from Brunconia, Heathfield," said His Royal Highness.

"Yes, sir," replied the earl. "May I present Prince Maximilian von Stauffenburg of Brunconia?"

Maximilian executed a stiff Brunconian style bow. "Your Royal Highness."

"You are most welcome to England, sir," said the Prince Regent. "Now do sit down, gentlemen. We'll have tea at once for I confess I'm damned hungry. Come, come, do sit down."

The gentlemen obeyed the royal command with alacrity. "Hastings," said the Prince Regent, once they were all seated. "How do you like my waistcoat?"

Percy colored at the remark, an obvious reference to his uncomplimentary judgment that had been reported back to the royal gentleman, who had been quite vexed with the impudent Mr. Hastings. "By my faith, sir," said Percy. "I like it exceedingly well."

The Prince seemed pleased at Percy's discomfiture. He grinned. "Good," he said. He then turned his attention to Maximilian.

"And what brings you to England, Prince Maximilian?"

"I have longed to come, Royal Highness," said Maximilian. "To see London. Yes, the great city of the English. And it is truly grand. So many things I wish to see here. And do forgive me, sir, if my English is not so good."

His Royal Highness smiled graciously. "You are doing very well, sir." And then he switched to German. Fluent in that language, the Prince Regent was proud of his linguistic skills.

Heathfield listened with a smile on his face. He didn't understand a word of German, but he knew that His Royal Highness enjoyed speaking it.

Percy relaxed a bit as Maximilian conversed with the Prince Regent. It seemed that they were getting on famously. His Royal Highness was smiling happily, and Percy was hopeful that he would forget all about waistcoats as the visit wore on. Smiling, Percy began to enjoy himself.

The following day Selena set off on a walk to the park with Henrietta and Sophie. Fluff, eager as always for her afternoon walk, pulled at the leash as the ladies made their way along the sidewalk.

Sophie held on to her aunt's hand. "Aunt Selena."

"Yes, dear?" said Selena looking down at the little girl.

"Will we see Duncan today?"

Selena laughed. Each day since their meeting with Heathfield and his dog in the park, Sophie had asked the same question. "I don't know, Sophie."

"I do wish we'd see him," said the girl. "I think Duncan was wonderful. And I know Fluff would like to see him, too."

"I should think Fluff would be happier without Duncan," said Selena.

"Indeed, yes," said Henrietta.

"I believe she would like to see him," said Sophie, tightening her grip on Selena's hand. They walked on for a short time in silence, before Sophie spoke again. "Won't Lord Heathfield be in the park?"

"I told you that I didn't know, Sophie," said Selena.

"I did like Lord Heathfield," said Sophie. A thoughtful expression appeared on her face. Then, looking up at Selena, she said, "Why don't you marry Lord Heathfield, Aunt Selena?"

This unexpected question caused Selena to burst into laughter.

"Sophie," said Henrietta, "don't speak such nonsense. Selena has no intention of marrying Lord Heathfield."

"I wish she would marry him," said Sophie.

"Good heavens, child," said Henrietta in some frustration. "Whyever would you say that?"

"Because he is very handsome and he has Duncan," returned the girl.

Selena smiled at her sister-in-law. "Well, those are very good reasons, Hetty," she said.

Henrietta smiled a little, but she didn't like joking about Selena's marrying Heathfield. "Do stop your silly prattle, Sophie," said the duchess. "I want to hear no more about Lord Heathfield and Duncan."

When they arrived at the park, Selena was as disappointed as her niece to find no sign of the earl. Since meeting him at the book shop, Selena had thought of him constantly, and she wanted very much to see him again.

Although the day was cloudy and threatened rain, it was pleasantly warm. Sophie ran happily across the green to the duck pond, where she stood watching the birds.

Selena and Henrietta proceeded after the little girl. When they arrived at the edge of the pond, they remained there admiring a pair of swans which glided over the smooth surface of the water.

Finally, with Fluff and Sophie in tow, they left the pond and started back across the park. "Oh, I do believe that is Mrs. Sinclair," said Henrietta, catching sight of two well-dressed ladies and a little boy who were coming toward them. "And Lady Richardson and young Georgie." The duchess smiled. Both ladies were well known to her, and Mrs. Sinclair was an old and dear friend. The boy, who had just turned seven, was Mrs. Sinclair's son. Henrietta turned to Sophie who was following behind them. "Look, my dear, it's Georgie."

Sophie's face lit up. She didn't have many playfellows in London, and the sight of another child was wonderful.

"My dear Hetty," said Mrs. Sinclair, coming forward to greet the duchess with a kiss on the cheek. She was a petite, attractive woman with dark hair and eyes, who wore a plum-colored pelisse and bonnet.

"Dolly, how wonderful to find you here," said Henrietta, smiling delightedly at her good fortune in meeting her friend in the park. "Good day, Lady Richardson."

Lady Richardson, a plump middle-aged woman who was Mrs. Sinclair's aunt, curtsied. "How do you do, Duchess?"

"I am quite well, thank you. I do believe you know my sister-in-law, Lady Selena Paget?"

"Of course," said both ladies.

Selena nodded to them. "How very good to see you both."

"Your daughter is such a darling little girl, your grace," said Lady Richardson, eyeing Sophie who was standing beside her mother.

"Yes, she's lovelier each time I see her," said Mrs. Sinclair.

Henrietta beamed with maternal pride. "And Georgie is growing so tall, isn't he? And he is so handsome."

"Do say hello to Lady Sophie, Georgie," said Mrs. Sinclair, pushing her son forward.

"Hello," he said shyly.

"Would you like to see the ducks?" said Sophie.

"Indeed, I would," replied Georgie. He glanced up at his mother. "May I, Mother?"

"Yes, but don't go too near the water. I won't have you falling in, Georgie."

The children hurried off together, with Sophie chattering happily to the boy. The ladies started after them at a slower pace. "Yes, your Sophie is a dear," said Mrs. Sinclair. "And I do hope that darling boy of yours is doing well."

Henrietta launched into a rapturous description of little Harold. Selena listened indulgently as the ladies compared notes on their children. As she walked along, she watched Sophie and her newfound friend while her mind wandered to thoughts of Heathfield.

Selena was brought out of her reverie by hearing Mrs. Sinclair say the words, "Prince Maximilian. Yes, that is his name, Prince Maximilian von Stauffenburg of Brunconia," she said.

"He had tea with the Prince Regent yesterday, and Mrs. Lyon told us that His Royal Highness was quite taken with him. The colonel said that the two of them spoke in German for more than three quarters of an hour."

"Everyone is very eager to meet him," said Lady Richardson. "He sounds like a most accomplished young gentleman."

"Well, I have met him," said Henrietta with a frown, "and having done so, I cannot imagine what the fuss is about."

"You met him?" said Mrs. Sinclair.

While the duchess hadn't wished to speak with Prince Maximilian, she was very pleased that she had been the first of her friends to see him. She nodded. "Selena and I were introduced to him a few days ago in a book shop. He was there with Lord Heathfield and Mr. Percy Hastings."

"Yes, they are his cousins," said Lady Richardson. "I'd quite forgotten that Lady Eustacia Hastings had married that foreign prince. It was rather before my time. Lady Eustacia would be Prince Maximilian's grandmother."

"What was the prince like?" said Mrs. Sinclair. "Did you find him handsome?"

"Handsome?" said Henrietta. "Not in the least. He was rather stout and he had an unfortunate mustache. And he wore the most dreadful uniform."

"He seemed very pleasant," said Selena, entering the conversation.

"Yes, Colonel Lyon thought him very amiable as well," said Mrs. Sinclair. "His Royal Highness must have liked him for he made a point of suggesting Prince Maximilian call at Warwick House."

"Did he?" said Selena, very much interested, for Warwick House was the residence of the Regent's daughter.

"It is well known that Princess Charlotte does not wish to marry the Prince of Orange," said Mrs. Sinclair. "Perhaps Prince Maximilian would be more to her liking."

"What nonsense," replied Henrietta. "One has never heard of this Brunc9onia before. Why . . ." The duchess was about to tell her friend what Count von Gessler had told them about Prince Maximilian's father, but she remembered that the count had asked that they not repeat his words. "Count von Gessler is Brunc-onian by birth. We must consult him on the matter."

"Count von Gessler is Brunconian?" said Mrs. Sinclair. "I thought he was Prussian."

"I was sure that someone told me he was Swiss," said Lady Richardson.

"No, he is Brunconian," said Henrietta.

Mrs. Sinclair declared that she would mention this interesting fact to her husband. They were then distracted by the children, who had begun to chase each other around the pond. Both Mrs. Sinclair and the duchess smiled indulgently and once again the conversation turned to their high-spirited offspring.

8

The library at Heathfield House was a large, richly decorated room, its walls lined with heavily filled bookshelves. That afternoon, while Selena walked in the park, the earl sat at his desk in the library, a thoughtful expression on his handsome face. Before him on the desk were two volumes, one of which he opened to stare at the flyleaf. After a time, Heathfield took up his pen, dipped it into the ink, and inscribed a few words in the book.

"There you are, Charles," said Percy, coming into the library. "I hope you don't mind my showing myself in."

"Good afternoon, Percy."

The earl's friend sat down in an armchair near the desk. "But where is Maximilian?"

"He's taken Duncan for a walk, but I expect him back soon. He and Duncan get on famously."

"Well, I hope he gets on as well with Princess Charlotte," said Percy, taking out his snuffbox and taking a pinch. "My father was overjoyed at hearing how Prinny seemed to take a fancy to Max. I said that we should hasten to Warwick House and present our royal cousin at once, but my dear mama has heard from Miss Elphinstone that the Princess has a cold. I fear we'll have to wait a few days."

Heathfield shut the cover of the book that had been lying open on his desk. "What a shame," he said, casting an ironical gaze at his cousin. "And to think that Her Royal Highness might have met her future husband this very day."

Percy smiled. "I know you still think it impossible for Max to marry Princess Charlotte, but why is it so unlikely? The Prince Regent wishes to see her married, and if the Princess likes our cousin, I don't see why His Royal Highness would object."

The earl shrugged. "Well, I imagine odder things have happened in the world, but I still wouldn't wager much on Max's prospects if I were you, Percy."

"I shan't allow you to discourage me," said Percy. "No, indeed, I expect a royal wedding is imminent."

Heathfield only lifted his dark eyebrows at the remark. At that moment, Duncan bounded into the room, followed by Maximilian, who looked ruddy-faced and cheerful.

"My dear cousins, what a fine walk had I with Duncan. The weather is very good. The sun shines and the flowers bloom. *Ja*, it is a very fine day. You should have come with me."

"Indeed, we should have done so," said Heathfield, rising from his chair. A footman entered the library. "Your carriage is ready, m'lord."

"Very good, Robert."

"Your carriage?" said Percy. "Where are you going?"

"I must pay a call," said his lordship, taking up a book from the desk.

"Pay a call?" cried Percy, frowning at him. "But I thought we'd go to see Major Cummings about that horse of his. I wanted you to tell me if the creature is a right one. You know I'm such a bad judge of horses."

"Yes, I know," said the earl with a smile. "But there is time for that later," said the earl. "One must fulfill one's social obligations, you know. You may accompany me if you wish, Percy, and you, too, Max."

"Oh, I should like that," said Maximilian.

"Oh, very well," said Percy. "Where are we going?"

"To call on the Lady Selena Paget."

"What a good idea," said Maximilian, remembering Selena from the bookstore. She had made a very considerable impression on him.

"Lady Selena?" said Percy. "Is that wise? Have you forgotten that her brother the duke despises you?"

Heathfield laughed. "But hang the Duke of Melford! It's his sister I wish to see. Now come along, we can't keep my carriage waiting."

"Oh, very well," said Percy. He and Maximilian then followed the earl from the room.

When they returned from the park, Selena and Henrietta retired to the drawing room where the duchess had been working on a guest list for a large dinner party. A reluctant Sophie had been sent to join her governess in the schoolroom.

Sitting down at a fine mahogany desk, the duchess took up the guest list and studied it. "I don't know what to do," she said. "I'd like to invite Lady Dugdale, but if I do so, I'd have to ask her sister, Mrs. Billington. And if I invite the Billingtons, how could I not ask Sir John and Lady Wentworth? And if the Wentworths will be there, the Marquess of Brookhaven will be very upset. He simply detests Sir John."

Selena, who was seated nearby on a chaise longue with Fluff curled up beside her, laughed. "My dear Henrietta, this is far too confusing for me. Why don't you simply invite anyone you wish?"

Henrietta regarded her sister-in-law as if this were an extraordinary idea. Before she could reply, the butler appeared to announce the arrival of visitors. "Three gentlemen are here, your grace. Prince Maximilian von Stauffenburg, Lord Heathfield, and Mr. Percy Hastings."

Very much surprised at this announcement, the duchess turned to Selena. "Can you imagine the audacity of Heathfield to call on us? Surely he couldn't hope to be admitted."

"Then you won't see him?" said Selena, trying to appear indifferent.

"Of course not," replied Henrietta. "James would be furious if I did so."

"I suppose you're right," said Selena, languidly stroking Fluff, "but I do wonder if it's wise."

"Wise?" said Henrietta. "Whatever can you mean?"

"Oh, I don't mean about Lord Heathfield. It is Prince Maximilian. Is it prudent to snub him?"

"I don't know that I'm snubbing him."

"Oh, I shouldn't be surprised if the prince would think it a snub," said Selena.

"Even so, what does that signify?" said Henrietta. "You mustn't forget what Count von Gessler said about this Prince Maximilian."

"Yes, I know what he said, but I was thinking of what Mrs. Sinclair told us in the park. Prince Maximilian got on very well with the Prince Regent. One never knows. What if he did marry Princess Charlotte?"

"You cannot be serious!" exclaimed the duchess.

"I'm sure it isn't at all likely," said Selena, suppressing a mischievous smile, "but sometimes unlikely things do happen. And it does seem a good idea not to offend him. I mean to say that it might be very awkward later on."

Henrietta pondered this for a moment. "I'm sure the idea of Princess Charlotte marrying this prince is utterly ridiculous."

Selena nodded in agreement. "Yes, but wouldn't it be a good idea to see Prince Maximilian? We'll be able to tell everyone about it. Don't forget how eager the ladies we met in the park were to hear that we'd already been introduced to Prince Maximilian."

"Yes, that is true," said Henrietta thoughtfully. "Well, perhaps it wouldn't hurt to receive them. But I shall say it was your idea, Selena."

"Do so by all means," said Selena.

"Show the gentlemen in," said the duchess, addressing the butler, who had stood patiently waiting for his instructions.

"Very good, your grace," replied Walker, bowing again before exiting the room.

Selena looked expectantly toward the doorway. While she would have never mentioned it to her sister-in-law, she was quite excited at the prospect of seeing Heathfield again.

In a few moments the visitors entered the room. Selena's attention was first focused on the earl, who looked infuriatingly handsome in a splendid coat of dark-gray superfine, pale ivory pantaloons, and gleaming Hessian boots. She noted that he was carrying a book under his arm. Seeing her, the earl smiled brightly.

The duchess had moved from the desk to take a seat in an armchair. She nodded to the callers as they made their bows.

Prince Maximilian made his obeisance over the duchess's hand. "How excellent to see your grace," he said.

Selena regarded the prince with keen interest. He had changed quite dramatically from the day they had met him at the book shop. That day he had appeared a rather odd figure in his peculiar military uniform with his mustache and bushy sideburns. Now his mustache was gone and his hair and sideburns much shorter.

The military uniform had been replaced by a splendid suit of clothes that even the most critical dandy couldn't fault. The young prince now looked like a fashionable English gentleman.

The duchess was very surprised at Maximilian's appearance.

Having thought him a comical, unattractive figure, she found his transformation quite remarkable. "How do you do, Prince Maximilian?" she managed to say.

"Very well, madam," returned the prince, smiling brightly.

"Do sit down, gentlemen," said Henrietta.

They obediently took their seats, with Heathfield sitting down beside Selena on the chaise longue. Fluff appeared quite delighted to see him. Wagging her well-feathered tail, she left her mistress's side to jump into the earl's lap.

"Fluff!" cried Selena, mortified by her pet's behavior. "Oh, I am sorry, Lord Heathfield."

The earl only grinned. "Oh, I don't mind in the least," he said, scratching the dog behind the ears.

"I fear Fluff isn't the most well behaved of dogs," said Selena. "I spoil her so dreadfully."

"One cannot help to spoil dogs and children," said Maximilian. "Yes, I am very fond of dogs too. I adore them. My cousin Heathfield has a wonderful dog."

"The ladies have met Duncan, Max," said the earl.

"Yes," said the duchess, "my daughter Sophie talks of him constantly."

"And how is Lady Sophie?" said Heathfield.

"She is very well," returned Henrietta. "She is having her lessons, which I fear she does not enjoy."

"I never enjoyed my lessons," said Percy. "All that dull arithmetic and Latin verbs. Indeed, I shudder at the thought. Of course, Heathfield here was always a bookish sort of fellow. He never minded the schoolroom."

Selena turned her green eyes on the earl with an interested look. "You, a bookish fellow, Lord Heathfield?"

"Indeed, I was a prodigious scholar," said his lordship with an ironical smile.

"Yes, he was always reading," said Percy. "He even brings a book when making calls."

"Oh, this is for Lady Selena," said the earl, handing the book, a slim, vellum-bound volume, to her. "I don't believe you had the opportunity to find that collection of Wordsworth's poems you said you wanted."

"That is very good of you, Lord Heathfield," said Selena, taking the book and looking down at it. "Thank you."

Henrietta directed a disapproving look at Heathfield. She considered it highly improper for him to give Selena a gift. The duke would be extremely vexed to hear of it.

"We have some very great poets in my country," said Maximilian, eager to enter the conversation. "Otto Kirchgraber is the most famous."

"I fear I haven't heard of him," said Selena, smiling at the prince. "We know so little of the poets of other countries."

"What a pity," said Maximilian. "He is very good." Clearing his throat, he recited a few stanzas of poetry in a dramatic fashion. Since the poem was in German, his listeners had considerable difficulty in appreciating it.

"You recited that so well, Prince Maximilian," said Selena. "I do wish I spoke German."

"Oh, you don't speak any German?" said Maximilian, rather disappointed.

"Not a word," confessed Selena.

"Well, Maximilian had the opportunity to speak German with His Royal Highness," said Percy, eager to impress the ladies. "My cousin and HRH spoke for the longest time. They got on quite famously."

"And what is the prince like, sir?" said Selena, smiling at Maximilian. "I have never met him."

"You have not met him?" said Maximilian, very much surprised. "What a shame for the Prince not having met such a beautiful young lady as you. But he is a charming man. So courteous and, what is the word? Oh, yes, gracious. I liked him extremely well."

"Yes, I always find His Royal Highness very pleasant," said Henrietta.

"And how are you enjoying your visit in England?" said Selena, smiling at Maximilian again.

"Oh, very much," said Maximilian. "Everyone has been so kind to me here. And I cannot say how wonderful it is to be with my dear cousins. They are so good to me."

Selena was about to ask Maximilian another question when her brother James entered the room. Since the duke spent most afternoons at his club, his arrival was quite unexpected.

His grace hadn't been at all pleased to hear that Heathfield and his cousins were ensconced in his drawing room. The duke's expression was grave as he came toward them.

The gentlemen rose to their feet. "Melford," said Heathfield, smiling slightly, "what an unexpected pleasure. May I present my cousin, Prince Maximilian von Stauffenburg of Brunconia? This gentleman is the Duke of Melford."

Maximilian made a low bow as was customary in Brunconia. "It is a great honor to meet your grace," he said.

James nodded stiffly in reply. He then directed a disapproving look at his wife. Noting her husband's displeasure, Henrietta frowned.

"I fear we must be going, Melford," said the earl. "I'm sorry we cannot stay."

While the duke was only too happy to see a man whom he considered to be a rival and enemy quit his house, he seemed to have a sudden thought. "Heathfield, before you go, perhaps you'd like to see my new Tintoretto. It has just arrived."

"I would indeed," said his lordship.

"It has just been hung," said the duke, eager to impress Heathfield with his new acquisition. "It's quite splendid." He was very proud of the painting and he knew that the earl would be very envious to see it.

The ladies rose from their chairs and everyone left the drawing room to go to what was known as the green parlor. There the duke displayed a number of paintings from his collection.

James led them across the room to the painting. "There it is. Isn't it wonderful?"

They all stood before the painting. It was a large work depicting Adam and Eve being driven from the Garden of Eden. "That is quite splendid, your grace," said Percy, who really didn't like the painting. He knew very little about art, but he didn't think Eve had a good enough figure. He also didn't like the look of the serpent who had, in Percy's opinion, far too prominent a place in the composition.

"It is very good," said Maximilian, studying the picture solemnly.

"And what do you think, Heathfield?" said James. When the earl frowned, he grinned triumphantly. "Yes, I believe this is the finest Tintoretto in England."

Heathfield made no reply. Folding his arms across his chest, he stood studying the picture.

"Well?" said the duke, rather irritated by his lordship's lack of response.

Selena watched Heathfield intently. He seemed to be mulling over what he would say.

"Come, come, Heathfield, why don't you admit it?" said James looking very smug. "I have you now, don't I? You don't have a Tintoretto that can match this one, do you?"

The earl turned to James. "At least mine are true Tintorettos," he said.

"What?" said the duke, eyeing him with astonishment.

"I hate to be the one to tell you, Melford, but this is clearly a forgery."

James stared at him as if he hadn't heard correctly. Then he burst into laughter. "Good God! You amaze me, Heathfield. Your envy has made you take leave of your senses."

"I wish it were authentic," said the earl, "but I fear there is no mistake. But it is a very good forgery. Only an expert could tell the difference."

This remark only further infuriated the duke, whose face was reddening dangerously.

"Are you certain, Lord Heathfield?" said Selena.

He nodded gravely.

"Nonsense," sputtered James. "Utter nonsense! I suggest you leave my house, sir!"

The earl bowed to the ladies before turning and exiting from the room. Percy and Max hastily followed suit.

When they had gone, the duchess tried to soothe her husband. "I'm sorry, my dear. Surely there is some mistake."

"The mistake was your admitting that man to our house."

"It was my fault," said Selena. "I persuaded Henrietta to see Lord Heathfield and the other gentlemen. You mustn't blame Hetty."

"He is never to be admitted here again," said James hotly. "Is that understood?"

"Yes, of course, my dear," said Henrietta meekly, and the two ladies followed the duke from the room.

As Heathfield's carriage pulled away from the Duke of Melford's residence, Percy frowned at his cousin. "I daresay, Charles, I wish you hadn't told the duke about his painting. And you *are* sure you're right, aren't you?"

"My dear Percy, I'm damned sure of it."

"Well, you are the expert on these things. I hated it anyway. I don't like snakes in paintings, do you?"

The earl grinned. "Not particularly."

"The Duke of Melford was very angry," said Maximilian.

"I don't doubt he paid a fortune for that painting," said Heathfield. "And I can imagine how he felt to hear me say it wasn't authentic. But you must both promise not to say a word about this painting to anyone," said the earl. "I don't wish to cause any further embarrassment to Melford."

"I shall say nothing," said Maximilian.

"Nor shall I," said Percy. "Although I'd think you'd be happy to spread this about. It would make Melford look a fool."

"I have no wish to make him look foolish," said Heathfield.

"Now that is a change," said Percy, "since in the past you've liked nothing better. But now that we have paid your call, do you think we might go see Major Cummings about that horse?"

"Yes, I suppose we could," said the earl.

"Good," said Percy, who began to talk about horses. Heathfield pretended to listen, but soon found himself thinking about Selena.

9

The Duke of Melford was in an exceedingly foul mood after Heathfield and his cousins left his house. He retired to his library, saying he didn't wish to be disturbed.

After a while, Selena and Henrietta sat down to tea in the drawing room. "I do wish I'd never admitted Heathfield," said the duchess, pouring the tea into blue and white china teacups. "Your brother is so terribly vexed with me."

"I shouldn't worry, Hetty," said Selena, taking up her cup and saucer. "You know James comes out of these bouts of ill temper very quickly."

"Well, I do hope that Heathfield is wrong about the painting. James loved it so. Although, by my faith, I thought it quite dreadful."

Selena laughed. "I didn't like it either. But I doubt Heathfield would have said what he did if he wasn't certain."

Henrietta nodded. "I fear you're right, my dear. I do hope that Heathfield won't bandy it about town that James bought a forgery."

"I'm sure he won't say anything about it," said Selena.

"And I don't approve of his giving you the book. Perhaps you should send it back to him. But in any case, we won't tell James about it. I do hope you haven't lost your heart to Heathfield, Selena."

"Don't be silly, Hetty," said Selena. "I scarcely know him."

"Well, he isn't at all suitable. He is a devil with the ladies, for one thing, and that doesn't bode well in a husband."

"Yes," said Selena thoughtfully.

"And besides that, your brother detests Heathfield. No, my dear Selena, we must find you someone else."

"I pray we don't get on the subject of my suitors again."

"Well, I don't know of a more important topic to discuss.

But very well, I shan't say any more." The duchess took a sip of tea and then nibbled on a biscuit. "I must admit that I was very much surprised to see Prince Maximilian looking so changed. When I saw him in the bookshop he seemed so unattractive. He did have horrible mustachios, did he not?"

"Yes, I believe he did. And he obviously improved his tailor."

"Yes, wasn't he wearing a strange uniform of some sort?"

Selena nodded.

"He isn't at all bad looking now," said the duchess. "Indeed, perhaps it isn't such an absurd idea that he marry Princess Charlotte. He does seem to be a good-natured young man. If I hadn't heard about his family from Count von Gessler, I should think him quite likeable."

"As I have said before, Hetty, one cannot take what the count says as gospel. I shouldn't doubt that there is more to the story than what von Gessler has told us."

"Perhaps you are right," said Henrietta. "I do hope Princess Charlotte marries a nice young man. I do wish her happiness, the poor girl. I daresay it isn't easy being the heir to the throne."

"Indeed not," said Selena. "I don't envy her that in the least."

They discussed the princess for a while. Then the conversation turned to Henrietta's children, a topic that could occupy the duchess for hours.

After breakfast the following morning, Selena sat in an armchair reading the book of poetry Heathfield had given her, her spaniel Fluff sleeping contentedly at her feet. Every so often, she'd turn to the flyleaf, where the earl had inscribed a brief message. "To Lady Selena, from a man who admires Wordsworth nearly as much as he admires you. H."

When she had first read this, she had been rather taken aback. Then later that evening when she had returned to her room after a dinner party, she had studied it again. Heathfield undoubtedly sent such things to ladies on a routine basis. It was folly to make too much of it, she told herself. No, one had to be sensible. Still, thinking of him, Selena reflected that might be far easier said than done.

Across from her, seated on the sofa, Henrietta was thumbing through the latest issue of her favorite fashion magazine. "I don't like these hats, do you?" she said, holding up the magazine.

"What?" said Selena, looking up from her book.

"These hats."

"Oh, they're very nice."

Frowning, the duchess decided that it was best to leave her sister-in-law to her book. After gazing down at one particular drawing of a new ball gown for a time, Henrietta sighed and tossed the magazine aside.

The door suddenly opened and the butler entered the room carrying a silver salver. "The post has arrived, your grace," he said.

Glad for any diversion, Henrietta eagerly took up the stack of letters. "Thank you, Walker," she said and the servant nodded and retreated from the room. Quickly scanning through the pile, Henrietta picked up one envelope and glanced over at Selena. "It is from Lady Blackstone," she said.

Selena closed her book and regarded Henrietta with considerable interest as her sister-in-law proceeded to open the letter and read it. "Lady Blackstone says that she and her brother were enchanted with you," said Henrietta, smiling over at Selena and then returning her gaze to the paper before her. A slight frown suddenly appeared on her face. "Oh, dear," she said.

"What is it, Hetty?" asked Selena.

Henrietta looked up. "It is only that Lady Blackstone wishes to remind us about attending her salon tomorrow. She writes 'Please don't disappoint me, my dear duchess. I so very much wish for you and Lady Selena to meet my company. The poet Henry Travers will attend and he is a fascinating man.' "

"I should very much like to meet him," said Selena. "Oh, we must go."

"I really don't think it at all wise to do so."

Selena regarded her sister-in-law with a puzzled expression. "But why not, Hetty? I thought you liked Lady Blackstone."

"Oh, I do. But, I fear the guests at her salon are not exactly . . . well, the sort of people your brother would wish us to see. They are artists, of course."

"I don't understand how James can be such a great art lover and so disapprove of artists."

"But, my dear, many artists are not at all respectable." Henrietta paused and appeared to be considering her words. "Indeed, I fear many of them are quite shocking."

Selena raised her eyebrows in mock surprise. "Are they?" A mischievous look in her green eyes. "Then I shall certainly want to attend Lady Blackstone's salon." Selena burst into laughter at her sister-in-law's alarmed expression.

Henrietta managed to smile. "So you were gammoning me, Selena."

"But I do wish to meet Mr. Travers. I so admire his work. Do say we might go."

"If James approves."

"Well, he might if you tell him the alternative is spending an evening at the opera."

The duchess brightened. "That is a good idea. James detests the opera. I shall give him the choice. Of course, he is still very angry about the painting. I scarcely saw him this morning. He went out riding and hasn't returned. I am a bit worried. He never misses breakfast."

"You mustn't worry," said Selena. "My brother will get over it."

"I do hope you're right, my dear," said Henrietta. Then looking toward the door, the duchess saw Sophie come dashing into the room with Fluff at her heels. "Mama, Aunt Selena."

"Good morning, my darling," said the duchess, opening her arms to receive her daughter's embrace.

After hugging her mother, the little girl went to Selena to receive a kiss. "How are you this morning, Sophie?" said Selena, smiling at her niece.

"I am very well. But Fluff and I would like to go to the park."

"That is a good idea," said Selena.

"We must wait until your father returns from his ride," said the duchess. "I must speak with him. But do sit down, my dear."

Sophie took a seat beside her aunt. "I wish you had called me to see Lord Heathfield when he was here," she said.

"We have had this discussion before, I believe," said Henrietta. "I cannot call you away from your studies every time we have callers or you will be an ignorant young woman."

"But to see Lord Heathfield," said Sophie. "And a prince. How I should like to see a prince."

"A prince looks like any other gentleman," said the duchess. Then seeing her daughter's disappointed look, she added, "Well, I promise I shall call you if he comes again."

Sophie brightened. "Oh, good. I do hope he calls again. You must invite him to tea, Mama."

"We will see," said Henrietta vaguely. She was glad to see her husband come into the room. "My dear, you were gone a very long time. I was beginning to worry."

"Worry?" said the duke. "Whatever for?"

"Well, you might have fallen off your horse or something dreadful."

James smiled and Selena was glad to see that her brother appeared in a better mood. "I only took a rather long ride."

"You must be very hungry. You will want breakfast." The duchess rose to her feet and rang for a servant. "The duke will want breakfast now," she told the butler who answered her summons.

"And what mischief are you about, my girl?" said James, addressing Sophie.

"I'm being very good, Papa," she replied. "And so is Fluff. We'd like to go to the park. After your breakfast, we can all go. Do say you will. Please, Papa."

"Oh, very well," replied the duke, sitting down in a chair. "I imagine a walk to the park would be a good idea."

"Good," said Sophie, very excited at the idea of her father's accompanying them. The duke seldom went on walks to the park.

"James," said Selena, "we have had a letter from Lady Blackstone. She invites us to her salon this evening."

"Yes, I thought it might be rather amusing to go," said Henrietta. "Of course, there is the opera. You said we might go. And there are no other engagements tonight."

"The opera?" said the duke, frowning.

"Well, I shouldn't mind missing it if we could attend Lady Blackstone's salon."

"I don't know," said James. "Lady Blackstone has poets and painters and such about. I'm not sure they are fit company for you or Selena."

"But it does sound very interesting," said Selena. "Of course, I'd love to see the opera as well."

"Well, I suppose it wouldn't hurt to go," said the duke. "Perhaps von Gessler would be there."

"That is very likely."

"Then we shall go to Lady Blackstone's."

The matter now settled, the ladies accompanied the duke to the dining room where they kept him company while he ate his breakfast.

10

That evening the ducal carriage pulled up in front of the Blackstones' impressive townhouse. As a servant assisted her from the carriage, Selena was filled with anticipation. She was sure that Lady Blackstone's salon would be far more interesting than the other social affairs she had been attending in town.

The duke and the two ladies made their way to the front door, where a butler ushered them inside. Selena glanced about her as the servant led them up the stairs to the drawing room. She was very impressed with the house, which was decorated with exquisite taste and style.

Indeed, Lady Blackstone had made a good many changes to her husband's London house. She had transformed the rather gloomy, dismal interior, relegating the ancient stuffed deer head and her husband's fox-hunting paintings to the attic. Now the house was quite magnificent with its elegant French furniture and Italian paintings.

The butler led them into the drawing room. There was a great crowd of people squeezed into the large room and it was quite noisy. A number of men were arguing loudly at one end of the room and there were several other groups of ladies and gentlemen scattered about, talking and laughing. Despite the somewhat noisy atmosphere, Selena noticed one gentleman sprawled out on a sofa, sleeping.

Theresa, noting her guests' arrival, hurried over to them. Dressed in a rose-colored gown, a jewel-bedecked turban atop her blond hair, their hostess looked quite lovely as she smiled graciously at them. She made a deep curtsy. "Your grace and my dear duchess," she said in her charming accent, "and Lady Selena. I'm so honored that you could attend my little party."

Selena smiled. She would have scarcely called the large, boisterous group a "little party."

"It was good of you to invite us," said Henrietta, managing to smile despite her misgivings at seeing the somewhat unruly company gathered before her.

Before Theresa could reply, her brother appeared at her side. "Why, this is wonderful," said Count von Gessler, bowing gracefully to the duke and duchess. "How good to see you again." He then smiled his charming smile at Selena. "And Lady Selena. How marvelous that you could come." Taking her hand, he bent down to bestow a gallant kiss upon it.

The count had given a good deal of thought to Selena since meeting her at the duke's dinner party. Impressed with her beauty and rank and mindful of the dowry she would bring, von Gessler had decided that she was the perfect choice for his future bride. Of course, he wasn't certain how the duke would react to such a match. He knew that the English had a distinct prejudice against foreigners. Still, he got on very well with the duke and he knew that English ladies had a good deal to say about whom they would marry.

His first course of action, therefore, must be to win the lady's affections. The count didn't think that a particularly difficult task, for he was confident of his ability to charm members of the fair sex.

"Von Gessler," said the duke, taking him by the arm. "I wanted to speak with you about that Tintoretto."

"By all means, your grace," said the count.

"Privately," said James, leading him away.

"What a great crush of people," said Selena.

"Oh, yes," replied Theresa. "I must introduce you to everyone." She scanned the crowd. "Where shall I start? Why not with Mr. Travers? I know you are eager to meet him."

"Yes, I should like that very much," said Selena.

Theresa led Selena and Henrietta through the room to a group of people who were clustered around one of the guests. Selena, who had seen a lithograph of Henry Travers in a literary magazine, recognized him at once.

The poet was a romantic figure. He was a handsome, middle-aged man of average height, who wore his unruly black hair a bit longer than was fashionable. Travers disdained conventional style, preferring velvet coats that were more suitable to the last century. Rejecting the white linen neckcloths worn by other gentlemen, the poet wore a flamboyant silk scarf tied in a loose bow about his neck.

Selena studied Travers with interest, noting his lean face with its regular features. His complexion was dark and a bit weather-beaten. The poet's most striking feature were his eyes, which were very dark and framed by dark, bushy eyebrows.

Selena thought that he looked like a hero in a Gothic novel. As she approached him, he turned his intense dark eyes upon her with rather unsettling effect.

"I do not wish to interrupt you, Mr. Travers," said Theresa, coming forward through the other people who had gathered around him, "but these ladies would like to meet you. And I know that you will be very glad to make their acquaintance. I have the honor to present the Duchess of Melford and her sister-in-law, Lady Selena."

The other guests turned to view the duchess and Selena with keen interest. While there were other titled and distinguished personages in attendance, none could compare in rank and position to the ladies who were now coming forward to be introduced.

Travers, who had fastened his piercing brown eyes upon Selena, continued to stare at her. "Your grace," said Lady Blackstone, making the introduction, "Mr. Henry Travers. Lady Selena, this is the esteemed poet."

"This is a great honor indeed," said Travers, nodding to them in a way that suggested he felt the honor was theirs in meeting him.

"Lady Selena is a great admirer of your work, Mr. Travers," said Lady Blackstone.

"I am flattered," said the poet, fixing his dark gaze upon her green eyes.

Although Selena was feeling rather unsettled by Travers's scrutiny, she managed to smile.

"Tell me, Lady Selena, which of my poems do you think is my best?"

Surprised at the question, Selena hesitated a moment. "I don't know if I'm qualified to make such a judgment, but I will say your 'Tribute to Odysseus' is my favorite."

"Is it?" said Travers, apparently surprised at the answer. "Why, you are clearly a young lady with remarkable powers of discernment. It is my favorite as well. Do tell me why you like it."

This struck Selena as a very self-congratulatory sort of question, but she obliged him by speaking enthusiastically about the poem, noting its skillful use of metaphor and daring variation from standard meter. Travers accepted the praise with the air of a monarch receiving tribute. "How good of you to say so," he said. "And what an astute lady you are. None of those simpletons who purport to be critics understood what I was doing with the meter. It is quite wonderful to talk to a lady of such intelligence."

"Selena is very clever," said the duchess. "I must confess I don't read very much, and poetry quite confounds me. But I'm certain you must be a very good poet if Selena thinks so."

"Thank you, Duchess," said Travers.

The poet continued to regard Selena with keen interest. He was well accustomed to feminine attention. Ladies he had never met often sent him letters proclaiming their undying devotion.

While he usually thought his female admirers more of a nuisance than anything else, he was very pleased to think that Lady Selena appeared quite enamored of him. Although he proclaimed indifference to the aristocracy, he was, in truth, as impressed by titles as most Englishmen were. He knew that Lady Selena was the Duke of Melford's sister and, as such, was a person of consequence in Society. She was also very beautiful. Travers found himself wishing that there wasn't such a great crowd of people about so that he might become better acquainted with her.

"There you are!" cried a voice. Selena turned to see a well-dressed woman smiling brightly at them. She recognized her as Mrs. Sinclair. "My dear Duchess and Lady Selena, I heard that you were here and I came straight away to find you."

Travers frowned at Mrs. Sinclair. Why did this noisy woman have to appear when he was enjoying talking to Selena, he asked himself.

"Mrs. Sinclair," said the duchess, happy to see her friend.

Mrs. Sinclair took Henrietta by the elbow and pulled her away from the group around Travers. Selena followed them, not altogether unhappy to come away from the poet. "I was told that you received a call from Prince Maximilian," said Mrs. Sinclair.

Lady Blackstone, who had been standing beside the duchess, regarded Mrs. Sinclair with interest. "Prince Maximilian?"

"Prince Maximilian von Stauffenburg," said Mrs. Sinclair.

"However did you hear about that?" said Henrietta.

"Why, our cook heard it from the butcher's boy who had

stopped at Melford House this morning," said Mrs. Sinclair. "Do tell me about the prince."

"Well, he was very pleasant," said the duchess, "and his appearance had improved from our first meeting. Perhaps he isn't really handsome, but then I wouldn't call him unhandsome."

"And what did you think of him, Lady Selena?" said Mrs. Sinclair.

"He appeared to be an amiable, good-natured gentleman," said Selena.

"And how was your visit? What did you discuss?"

The duchess frowned a little. "Oh, dear, it is always rather hard to remember. I recollect he said that he likes dogs. And then he recited a poem."

"Recited a poem?" said Mrs. Sinclair. "How lovely."

"I imagine it was very nice," replied the duchess, "but it was in German so I had no idea what it was about." She looked over at Selena. "What else did we discuss with Prince Maximilian, my dear?"

"He did say how much he liked England."

"Did he?" said Mrs. Sinclair. "That is excellent. You know that Princess Charlotte has said she doesn't wish to leave England. Do you think Prince Maximilian would agree to make his home here?"

Lady Blackstone, who had been listening to this conversation with keen interest, frowned. "What do you mean, Mrs. Sinclair?"

"Perhaps you haven't heard, Lady Blackstone," said Mrs. Sinclair. "Prince Maximilian's name is being put about as a possible bridegroom for our dear Princess Charlotte. I was told that the Prince Regent asked about Brunconia yesterday. He was so favorably impressed with the young man when he met him." Mrs. Sinclair looked as though she had suddenly remembered something. "Why, you are Brunconian, aren't you, Lady Blackstone?"

Lady Blackstone nodded.

"Then you must be very excited by the idea."

"It has taken me by surprise," said Lady Blackstone, who thought it best to hide her dismay. She could imagine what her brother would think of it.

"I expect you know Prince Maximilian as he is one of your countrymen," said Mrs. Sinclair, smiling at the baroness.

She shook her head. "No, I haven't had the pleasure of meeting him. But you must excuse me. I believe it's time for Mr. Travers to read some of his poems. He promised to do so. Do find a seat over there and I shall have Mr. Travers make ready."

Lady Blackstone went off, announcing the impending reading to the guests, who eventually followed her instructions to take seats where they could. Selena, who along with the duchess and Mrs. Sinclair had seated herself, waited expectantly for Travers to begin his reading.

It seemed a very long time before the company was settled and ready to hear the poet. "I am so very pleased that Mr. Travers has agreed to read one of his poems. And after that Mrs. Stanley will sing for us," Lady Blackstone announced.

Everyone applauded as Travers stepped up before them. He looked rather solemn as he opened a book and then began reading in a very dramatic fashion. Selena noted that he had selected the poem she had told him was her favorite.

Travers had a melodious, deep voice and he read very well. But after a time, Selena found herself thinking of what Heathfield had told her in the bookshop. What was it, the earl had called Travers's poetry? Overblown, she remembered.

The poet's voice grew louder and more theatrical as he read on. "Perhaps it is rather overblown," thought Selena. When he had finished, the guests applauded enthusiastically and Travers looked very pleased with himself.

The rest of the evening passed quickly. After Mrs. Stanley, a talented soprano, sang several songs, the guests rose from their chairs to once again congregate into small groups for conversation. Selena was introduced to a number of interesting people. They included a French opera singer who, according to rumor, had once been Napoleon Bonaparte's mistress, a landscape painter whose work Selena admired, and a writer who had once been arrested for writing an uncomplimentary pamphlet about the Prince Regent.

The most interesting person she met was Miss Foxworth, an outspoken lady who believed in universal suffrage and equal rights for women. A tall, imposing-looking middle-aged woman, Miss Foxworth was a scholar and a writer. Having had the good luck to have inherited a considerable fortune, she published a literary magazine in which she often expressed her strong opinions.

They stayed until rather late. The duke, who had spent most of his time with von Gessler discussing his alleged Tintoretto, had been the one who insisted they leave. As they made their way home, the duchess declared that she had certainly enjoyed herself and was very glad that they had come. Selena had readily agreed, although, as the carriage made its way through the dark streets of town, she found herself thinking of Heathfield and wondering what he would have thought of Lady Blackstone's salon.

When all her guests had left, Lady Blackstone sat wearily down upon the sofa to sip one final glass of wine before retiring to bed.

"Another triumph, Theresa. I congratulate you."

The countess looked up in surprise to find her brother standing there. "I thought you'd gone, Rudolf," she said.

"No, I was assisting your man in removing a certain fellow who had fallen asleep in your sitting room."

"Oh, you should leave that to the servants."

"It was nothing. I rather enjoyed tossing the boy out the door."

"I do hope it wasn't anyone I like."

"His name is Winfield."

"Oh, then that is all right," said Theresa, taking another drink of wine. "I'm very bored with him. Would you like a glass before you go, Rudolf?"

The count nodded and took a seat beside her on the sofa while she filled a glass for him. "Thank you," he said, taking it from her.

"Did you enjoy yourself?"

"I must confess I've had more amusing evenings. The Duke of Melford was very tiresome about that Tintoretto of his."

"The sale you arranged?"

He nodded. "By the damndest bad luck, the Earl of Heathfield saw it and told him it was a forgery."

"Why, the effrontery of the man," cried Theresa indignantly.

Von Gessler shrugged and then took a drink of his wine. "Well, it is a forgery after all."

"What!"

"Whoever would have thought Melford would have discovered it? I was told on the best authority that it would never be detected."

"Oh, Rudolf, what a fool you are. How could you do such a thing?"

"Well, I shall be more careful in the future."

"But what did you say to the duke?"

"I told him that I was certain that Heathfield was mistaken. And then I told him that if he had any suspicion at all, I would take the painting back to its previous owner and his money would be refunded in full."

"And what did he say?"

The count smiled. "He said he wanted me to take the painting at once. He knows Heathfield is infallible in such matters. No one knows Venetian painting the way he does. Well, to soothe the duke, I promised to show him the Carpaccio. I imagine I shall have to sell it to him. Not that I mind. He'll pay a good price for it.

"Still, the matter irritates me. It is the fault of this Earl of Heathfield. Who would have thought he would go to Melford's house and see the accursed picture? I believe I detest the fellow even though I've never met him. Of course, he is connected to the von Stauffenburgs and that is reason to despise him."

"Yes," said Lady Blackstone thoughtfully. Although she had never been introduced to the earl, she found him terribly dashing. "Did the duke tell you that Prince Maximilian called upon him?"

"Yes, of course. That was when Heathfield saw the painting."

"Mrs. Sinclair was saying that there is talk that Princess Charlotte might choose Maximilian for a husband."

A scornful laugh escaped the count's lips. "What an absurdity! I do not believe that the Prince Regent of England will wish to ally himself with a bankrupt family of such a pathetic state as Brunconia."

"But what if he is very handsome? What if she falls in love with him?"

"*Gott in Himmel!*" exclaimed the count. "That is ridiculous."

"The duchess described him as not unhandsome. And she thought him personable. They say the Prince wishes Charlotte to marry as soon as possible. And Mrs. Sinclair said he has expressed interest in Brunconia. His Royal Highness has met Maximilian and was impressed with him."

"What? He met Maximilian?"

"Why yes. That is what Mrs. Sinclair said. She is a tattlemonger to be sure, but her information is always reliable."

Von Gessler frowned, unhappy at the news. It was bad enough to hear that Prince Maximilian had come to town. Now there was talk that he might have a chance to win the hand of Princess Charlotte. While the count thought that unlikely, one could never be sure. Well, there was no point in worrying about it now.

He rose from the sofa. "But I am very tired and in need of sleep. Good night, my dear." Leaning down, he kissed his sister on the cheek and retired from the room.

11

The next few days passed quickly for Selena, who had been kept busy with callers and social engagements. She did not see Heathfield, but when she and Henrietta called on Mrs. Sinclair, they heard more about him and Maximilian.

Mrs. Sinclair, who kept well informed about what was happening with the Prince Regent through her connection to the Prince's aide, Colonel Lyon, had been eager to tell them that His Royal Highness had called at the earl's residence.

According to Colonel Lyon, who had been present, the Prince Regent had talked a long while with Heathfield and Prince Maximilian. Royal George and the Brunconian prince had gotten on very well indeed, and Maximilian had been invited to call on Princess Charlotte.

Mrs. Sinclair had been very excited by the story. She had told the duchess and Selena that everyone was dying to meet Prince Maximilian. It was rumored, Mrs. Sinclair had informed them, that Maximilian would be at Almack's assembly rooms, and, therefore, the sought-after vouchers for admission were even more widely desired.

This information had made Henrietta determined to attend Almack's the evening in question. And besides, Selena hadn't yet been there. While it could be dull, conceded the duchess, Almack's was still a very good place to meet suitable gentlemen. There was always a chance that her sister-in-law would find a gentleman there to her liking.

Of course, Henrietta was beginning to think that her sister-in-law was far too particular where men were concerned. It distressed Henrietta that Selena had shown so little interest in any of the eligible suitors who continued to flock to their door. Several of them were attractive and charming and a few were, in the duchess's eyes, very good prospects. Yet, Selena remained indifferent to all of them.

When the duke was informed that they must attend Almack's, he adamantly refused to go. It took a good deal of persuasion for Henrietta to convince him otherwise.

Of course, the duchess knew that her husband was unhappy at the prospect of seeing Heathfield. But then, that couldn't be helped, she told him. After all, the earl was a member of the same elite circle of society and it was a fact of life that they would attend the same functions.

It would be easy enough for the duke to ignore him, said the duchess. And, she argued, if her husband avoided Heathfield all the time, how could he ever have the opportunity to snub him? The duke found a good deal of logic to this, and, therefore, agreed to escort the ladies to Almack's.

The Earl of Heathfield never went to Almack's. It wasn't that he found it so terribly tedious, for, in truth, he found it no duller than many other social affairs he attended. No, it was that there were always so many earnest-looking matrons in attendance with their marriageable daughters in tow, looking over the unmarried gentlemen as if they were so many bulls at a country fair.

Almack's, thought the earl as he dressed for the evening, was a place any sensible bachelor should avoid unless he were intent upon becoming a married man. Still, when Percy had insisted that there was no better place to introduce Maximilian into Society, Heathfield had allowed himself to be persuaded to attend the assembly rooms that Thursday.

On the positive side, there was always the possibility that Selena would attend. Knowing that his cousin had more than a passing interest in the lady, Percy had brought up the idea that she might be there. Of late, his lordship had been giving a good deal of thought to Selena and to the prospect of abandoning his bachelor status.

Heathfield was well aware that Selena's brother was a major obstacle. The duke would be adamantly opposed to his sister marrying a man he detested.

The earl frowned at the thought, wishing that he hadn't had to tell Melford his painting was counterfeit. But then, what else could he have done? Surely it was better for the duke to find out the truth now rather than later.

Heathfield's valet helped him into his close-fitting evening coat. He then critically surveyed his master.

"And do I pass muster, Barnes?" said Heathfield, noting the valet's scrutiny.

"Indeed, my lord," said Barnes, brushing a bit of lint from the earl's shoulder.

At that moment Maximilian entered the room. He was dressed in a new coat that fit him splendidly and made him look broad-shouldered and not in the least stout. His snowy white neckcloth was tied into a fashionable knot and his blond hair was combed into a modish style.

"Well, doesn't his highness look dashing, Barnes?" said the earl, smiling at his cousin.

"Yes, very dashing, m'lord," said Barnes.

"There, you have Barnes's approval," said Heathfield, "and he is the most critical judge in all of England. You do look dashed splendid, Max. Why, all the ladies will be dazzled."

"You are jesting, I think," said Maximilian, smiling.

"I am perfectly serious," replied his lordship. "But I must warn you. Almack's is well known for the predatory females who frequent it. No unmarried man is safe. You will be surrounded by single ladies vying for your attention."

"That does not seem like such a bad fate," said Maximilian.

"What a brave fellow you are, Max," said the earl. "It seems you approve of our English ladies."

Maximilian smiled. "I have seen many pretty ones to be sure. That is not to say that the Brunconian girls aren't very pretty as well."

"I'm sure they are, Max," returned his lordship.

"I do wish you could visit Bruncofia," said Maximilian. "How I should love for you to see it. My country is very wonderful. There are mountains and grand forests. And my father and mother would so enjoy meeting you."

While Bruncofia had never been on the earl's list of places he wished to visit, he politely assured his cousin that he would like nothing better than to journey to Maximilian's native land. He then suggested that they go to the drawing room to await Percy's arrival.

The earl and his cousin had scarcely arrived in the room when Percy entered. He was dressed with his usual care and attention to fashion. Percy was very pleased to see Maximilian looking so splendid in his new evening clothes. After commenting that the prince would doubtlessly cause a sensation at Almack's, the three cousins set off for the assembly rooms.

Selena entered the exclusive assembly rooms with a sense of eager expectation. It wasn't that she was excited to find herself at Almack's. Indeed, she wouldn't have wished to come if it hadn't been for the knowledge that Heathfield would be there.

That gentleman was occupying her thoughts with aggravating regularity. She often looked at the book of poetry he had given her, wondering about his feelings for her.

While Selena couldn't deny she felt a strong attraction to the handsome earl, she was rather wary of him. She had seen first-hand what sort of man he was where women were concerned. Her practical side told her that falling in love with Heathfield would cause only heartbreak and that she should put him from her mind.

Her brother had also declared that he didn't wish the earl's name to be mentioned in his presence. The duke had been furious at the earl's labeling his painting a forgery. While Melford respected Heathfield's judgment enough to know that the earl was telling the truth, he was sure that Heathfield was very pleased at his misfortune.

So Selena knew very well that she would be very foolish to fall in love with the earl. Yet, she was learning that one couldn't always be sensible about such things.

"There are a good many people here, aren't there?" said the duchess, surveying the crowd.

"Too damned many," said the duke, who wasn't too pleased to be there.

Selena looked around, wondering whether Heathfield was in attendance, but she didn't see him. They were soon joined by several ladies and gentlemen of their acquaintance.

After engaging in small talk for some time, the duke went off to join some of his friends, while Henrietta and Selena began to circulate about the room. Since there were many people eager to speak with the Duchess of Melford and her attractive sister-in-law, the ladies received a good deal of attention.

"Oh, look, Selena," said Henrietta as they moved on from one group of people, "there is Lady Blackstone."

Selena caught sight of the baroness, who was attired in a stunning gown of ivory silk with a large plume in her elegantly coiffed blond hair. She was standing beside a dandified young man who wore a skin-tight coat and knee breeches.

Catching sight of them, Lady Blackstone smiled brightly. She curtsied gracefully as Henrietta and Selena joined her.

"Your grace, Lady Selena, how wonderful to see you."

"Good evening, Lady Blackstone," said Henrietta.

The young gentleman standing beside Lady Blackstone regarded them eagerly. "May I present Mr. Winfield?" said the baroness. "I have the honor to introduce the Duchess of Melford and Lady Selena."

"This is a very great honor indeed," said the young man, making a deep bow.

Selena nodded courteously. She thought Winfield rather handsome in a boyish way. He didn't appear much over twenty and he had pleasing features and a bright smile. However, Selena did not approve of young men who took to extremes in fashion. Winfield's collar was ridiculously high and his neckcloth fluffed out absurdly. His coat appeared so tight that Selena found herself wondering how he could possibly have got into it.

They talked about the weather and then Lady Blackstone asked the duchess about her children. This caused Henrietta to beam with maternal pride and launch into several amusing anecdotes about Lady Sophie and dear little Harold.

Winfield, who found this conversation exceedingly dull, glanced about the room. "Why, look," he said, when the ladies paused in their discussion enough to give him the opportunity to speak, "there is Percy Hastings and the Earl of Heathfield. That must be Prince Maximilian."

The ladies looked over to see Heathfield, Percy, and Maximilian enter the room. Their arrival caused a good many heads to turn in their direction.

While most all attention was directed toward the prince, Selena found herself watching the earl. He looked very handsome in his elegant black evening clothes.

"They say Prinny may be considering him as a suitor for the princess," said Winfield.

"What nonsense," said Lady Blackstone.

"Well, I should like to meet him in any case," said Winfield. "Do excuse me, ladies. I shall be off to see if Hastings will introduce me."

Lady Blackstone eyed the young man with disapproval, but he

didn't seem to notice. Bowing, Winfield took his leave and headed in Maximilian's direction.

"I expect you are most unhappy to see Prince Maximilian, Lady Blackstone," said Henrietta.

"I fear I cannot help disliking him," said the baroness, watching the prince with keen interest. "You know how my family was cruelly used and sent into exile."

"That was horrible," said the duchess. "Of course, Prince Maximilian is very young and he had nothing to do with that. Indeed, perhaps one day when he is the ruler of Brunconia, you might appeal to him."

"I want nothing to do with him," said Lady Blackstone, casting a disdainful glance in Maximilian's direction. "Do excuse me, I must find my brother." With these words, Lady Blackstone took her leave.

"Isn't it dreadful to think that Prince Maximilian's father was so unjust to Lady Blackstone's family?" said Henrietta.

Selena shook her head. "We have only heard one side of that story, Hetty. I don't doubt there is another."

At that moment they were joined by two gentleman, one of whom asked Selena to dance. Since she couldn't think of a civil way to refuse, Selena assented, allowing the gentleman to escort her to the room where the orchestra was playing.

Heathfield had spotted Selena shortly after entering the assembly rooms. While he would have liked to make his way over to her, he was prevented by the great swarm of people who soon surrounded them.

It seemed that virtually everyone in attendance was most eager to be presented to Maximilian. Nearly every lady and gentleman who had the least acquaintance with either Percy or the earl seemed to come forward.

Heathfield was, therefore, tied up for a good long time making introductions. Percy was utterly delighted by the interest his cousin inspired. Maximilian smiled at everyone. Gregarious and amiable, he spoke with each person and appeared to make a very favorable impression.

When the earl was finally able to leave his cousin's side, he went in search of Selena. He found her dancing with a stout middle-aged gentleman.

Standing there watching the dancers, he reflected that Selena looked radiantly lovely that evening in the golden candlelight that illuminated the room. She was wearing a gown of pale green satin that perfectly complemented her deep red curls.

When the music ended, Heathfield stepped forward quickly to claim a dance. "Lady Selena," he said, "I should be very grateful if you would allow me the next dance."

Selena, who hadn't realized he was nearby, regarded him in surprise for a moment. "Lord Heathfield."

"Will you dance with me?"

Selena hesitated. What would her brother say to see her dance with the earl? Yet, she wanted very much to do so.

"You needn't fear that I'm a poor dancer," he said.

"That's not what I fear," returned Selena.

"Then you fear me, I suppose?"

"I fear my brother's wrath. You know he dislikes you."

"And I dislike him, so we are even."

Selena frowned. "He will be exceedingly vexed if I dance with you."

"And I shall be exceedingly vexed if you do not," said Heathfield smiling his charming smile at her. "Come, what harm is there in a dance? You may say to Melford that you couldn't refuse me. After all, my cousin is Prince Maximilian." He smiled again and she could only smile in return.

"Very well, but I daresay I shall regret it."

"I know I won't regret it," said the earl in a soft tone that had an unsettling effect on Selena.

She tried hard to appear nonchalant as the earl escorted her to a place beside the other couples who were getting into position. The dance was a round dance with a slow tempo and a number of complicated steps and formations.

"Are you enjoying Almack's, Lady Selena?" asked his lordship, taking Selena's hands in his own and leading her in a sedate circle.

"Yes, it's very nice," said Selena. "Although I must admit that the refreshments are hardly exceptional."

"Indeed, all you'll find here most times is bread and butter. But then there are other things more important. Why, to be seen here is essential to success in Society. You realize there are persons who would sell their own grandmother to obtain entry to this august establishment?"

Selena laughed. "Isn't it utterly silly? I cannot understand why success in Society is so sought after."

He smiled again. "That is because you are a success. It is human nature to want what one does not have."

"Perhaps," she said, looking into his blue eyes.

The earl, looking down at her, had an almost overpowering urge to kiss her full, inviting lips. Fortunately for his lordship it was time to hand Selena off to another gentleman while he became the temporary partner of a stout gray-haired lady.

When he returned to Selena, his lordship had recovered himself sufficiently to smile languidly as he stepped forward and then back. "I hope Lady Sophie is well."

"She is very well. And Sophie will ask about Duncan so I hope he is in good health."

"Excellent health," returned the earl, turning Selena in a circle. "I know he'd love to see your niece. Why don't you bring her to the park? Perhaps Wednesday at two o'clock would suit?"

"Really, I don't believe that would be a good idea," said Selena.

"The duke wouldn't approve, I suppose."

"He certainly would not. Don't forget that my brother detests you, my lord."

"Detests? Before you said dislikes," said his lordship, raising one eyebrow.

"I was only being polite," replied Selena with a mischievous smile. "Detests is the more precise term." The dancers turned around and began to walk in a circle. "Could you not be more agreeable to my brother? Why must you be his enemy?"

"It's dashed hard to change one's habits," said the earl, "and I have locked horns with Melford for years. Oh, very well, I suppose I could attempt being pleasant to him."

"Good," said Selena, directing her dazzling smile toward his lordship, who once again found himself wishing he could take her into his arms and crush his mouth against hers.

At that point the music came to its conclusion. There was applause and the gentlemen bowed to the ladies, who curtsied in return. Heathfield was very disappointed to see the dance at an end. He was about to ask for another when the duke appeared beside them.

After directing a withering look at the earl, he took Selena by the arm and led her off. "I am very disappointed in you, Selena. You know I didn't want you to dance with that man."

"James, it is very hard to refuse a gentleman without giving offense."

"I've seen you refuse others," he said. "And what does it signify if you offend Heathfield? By God, I wish you would." He shook his head. "What could you be thinking to dance with him? And besides being a man who hates me and wishes me ill, he is a notorious libertine."

Selena tried to restrain her temper. "You are treating me like a child, James," she said.

"And if you act like a child, how else am I to treat you?" said the duke.

Selena regarded her brother with an indignant look, but before she could reply, she noted that two gentlemen were approaching. Percy Hastings and Prince Maximilian came forward. "Your grace, Lady Selena," said Percy. "I hope you will forgive the intrusion, but my cousin has a request to make of Lady Selena." He turned expectantly to Maximilian.

"Would you do the very greatest honor to dance with me, Lady Selena?"

For a moment, Selena was afraid that her brother would make an uncivil remark, but the duke only stood regarding her with a frown. She could tell by his expression that he expected her to refuse the prince. "I should be very happy to do so, your highness," said Selena, smiling at Maximilian.

"Thank you with all my heart," said the prince, offering her his arm.

Selena allowed Maximilian to lead her away. Although she hadn't looked at her brother, she didn't doubt that the duke was very upset with her. "Are you having an enjoyable evening, sir?"

"Indeed so," said Maximilian. "Everyone is so charming to me. The English are a most agreeable people." He smiled at her. "Especially the ladies."

"You are very kind," said Selena smiling up at him.

Maximilian, who was again reminded of his beloved Frederica, smiled again. As they joined the other couples who were waiting for the music to start, the prince glanced around, noting with some satisfaction that a good number of the assembly were watching them with keen interest.

Scanning the crowd, he smiled benevolently at the curious onlookers. Then his eye fell upon a tall, good-looking gentleman who was frowning grimly at him. The man's expression startled

Maximilian. Was the fellow frowning at him? he wondered. The man continued to regard him with a malevolent look.

"Lady Selena," said Maximilian, "do you know the man standing there? He is looking at me in a most unfriendly way. The tall man there by the lady with the blue dress."

Looking in the direction of the prince's gaze, she caught sight of von Gessler. The count continued to stare at them, a sour look on his face. "Oh, that is the Count von Gessler," said Selena.

"Von Gessler?" said Maximilian, his eyes widening in surprise. The music was starting and the ladies and gentlemen were bowing to each other in anticipation of the start of the dance. However, the prince only stared at von Gessler. "Do you know this man, Lady Selena?"

"I have met him, sir," replied Selena, growing a bit anxious at Maximilian's expression.

The prince, who had seemed so amiable, now was frowning grimly. "There is a von Gessler from my country," he said. "If it is he . . ." His voice trailed off.

"The dance is beginning, sir," said Selena.

"Is he from Brunconia?" said Maximilian.

"Why, yes, he is," said Selena.

The dancers started to move and Maximilian took Selena's arm and began to lead her in the steps of a quadrille. However, he seemed very preoccupied.

"Do you know more about von Gessler, madam?" said Maximilian.

"He is a friend of my brother's," replied Selena, unsure what to say about von Gessler. "He is an art collector."

"That is not surprising," said the prince, frowning again. He went through the motions of the dance, but said little else. Selena tried to distract him with other conversation, but it was obvious that Maximilian was thinking about von Gessler.

At the conclusion of the dance, Maximilian muttered an apology. "I beg your pardon, Lady Selena, but my mind was so much on that man. Perhaps you would do me the favor of introducing me to him."

"Yes, if you wish," said Selena, who really didn't want to bring the two men together. "But there are many other people here you would like much better, your highness. Yes, there is Admiral Witherington and his wife. They are very interesting. I'd be very pleased to introduce you to them."

"No, it is von Gessler I will see."

"Very well, sir," said Selena as the prince offered her his arm. They walked the short distance to where von Gessler stood. Noting that the two men were regarding each other like a pair of angry bulls, she had considerable misgivings. Yet she hoped that her presence would prevent any unpleasantness. "Prince Maximilian, this gentleman is Count von Gessler. Count, I have the honor to present his highness, Prince Maximilian von Stauffenburg."

Frowning, the count made a rigid bow. Maximilian fixed an icy gaze upon von Gessler. "Your family is known to me," he said stiffly.

"As yours is known to me," said the count.

The two men stared at each other in a moment of ominous silence. Finally Maximilian spoke. "You are related to Count Karl Joseph von Gessler, I think?"

"I am his son."

This admission made Maximilian view his fellow countryman with a look of disgust. He spoke one word in German, and von Gessler responded by growing very red in the face. Maximilian then let loose a stream of furious words, also in German.

Selena watched the two men in dismay. The prince was beginning to shout, and everyone within range was watching with a mixture of horror and excitement.

Suddenly, to Selena's amazement, Maximilian pulled off his white glove and struck von Gessler hard across the face. There were gasps from the ladies and gentlemen who had been witnessing the scene.

Von Gessler blinked in astonishment as Maximilian uttered one more indignant German phrase. While Selena had no idea what he had said, she suspected it was a most grievous insult, for the count lost all self-control, pouncing on Maximilian and shoving him to the floor. Cries of horror came from the ladies and gentlemen. Maximilian jumped up quickly and rushed toward his opponent and the two men became locked in a violent struggle.

"Maximilian!" The Earl of Heathfield was suddenly there beside his cousin. "Stop it! Stop it, I say!" His lordship grabbed the prince, pulling him from his adversary. Fortunately, two other gentlemen had come forward to restrain von Gessler. "Remember where you are, gentlemen!" shouted Heathfield as von Gessler and Maximilian struggled to break free and resume their battle.

Then, seeming to calm themselves, they ceased struggling and glared at each other.

"Release me," said von Gessler. "I shall do nothing more." When the gentlemen let him go, he muttered a few more words in German before turning and abruptly stalking off.

Maximilian glared after him, trembling with fury. "I shall kill him," he said in English.

"Good God, Max, you must control yourself," said the earl, still holding him tightly by the arms.

"I am better," said the prince, watching von Gessler vanish through the throng of people who had gathered to witness the scene. The earl released him.

"You are hurt, sir," said Selena, noting that there was blood on Maximilian's cheek where von Gessler's signet ring had cut him. "May I have your handkerchief, Lord Heathfield?"

The earl produced the handkerchief, which he handed to Selena, who dabbed at Maximilian's face.

"Selena!" The Duke of Melford's voice made her turn to see her brother standing there with a disapproving look. "Come away. You are wanted elsewhere!"

Maximilian reached up to take the handkerchief and as he did so his fingers brushed against hers. His pale blue eyes met her green ones. "Thank you, Lady Selena. You are very good. I am very sorry."

Selena smiled. She then turned to exchange a glance with Heathfield. Frowning, the duke took his sister firmly by the elbow and pulled her away.

Heathfield shook his head at his cousin. "Good God, Max, what can you be thinking to make such a spectacle of yourself?"

"I know I should not lose my temper," said the prince, "but it was von Gessler!"

By this time Percy, who had been at the far side of the room when the altercation took place, arrived. "What in heaven's name was that about?"

"It was von Gessler," said Maximilian.

"Von Gessler?" returned Percy, quite distraught at the commotion his cousin had caused. "I don't care if it was the devil himself. One doesn't make a scene at Almack's."

"I think we'd best take Maximilian home," said Heathfield, placing his hand on the prince's shoulder.

Percy nodded and the three cousins left Almack's. When they

had settled themselves into Heathfield's carriage for the ride home, Percy folded his arms across his chest. He was very put out with his Brunconian cousin. Maximilian had spoiled what had been his triumphant entry into Society.

"Perhaps you should explain who this von Gessler is and why you wished to murder him," said Percy, frowning at Maximilian, who was seated across from him next to Heathfield.

"Von Gessler is a traitor! His father ruined my family and impoverished my country."

"What do you mean, Max?" said the earl.

"It was many years ago. My father had come to the throne of Brunconia when young. His most trusted minister was Count Karl Joseph von Gessler, and my father was very fond of him. He looked to von Gessler almost as a son looks to his father.

"Years passed and my father allowed von Gessler great authority. He trusted him completely. But the country grew poorer each year. My father could not understand why this was so, but always von Gessler would say there is no money for this and no money for that.

"When I was a boy, we lived very well. We seldom left the palace so we did not know what it was like for our people. But they were very poor, so poor they often had little to eat.

"One very cold winter there was unrest. Many people came to the palace seeking food. Von Gessler ordered the soldiers to drive them away. It was the first time my father quarreled with him, and he began to distrust von Gessler from that day.

"Slowly he learned the truth. Von Gessler had been taking money from the treasury for years. He had stolen a vast amount of wealth from Brunconia, sending it to Switzerland and Prussia.

"When my father had enough evidence against him, he sent his guard to arrest von Gessler. But von Gessler had spies everywhere. He and his family had fled the country. They had taken all they could, including jewels and paintings from the royal household. And many others of the nobility who were friends of von Gessler left as well, also taking much of the country's wealth with them.

"There was very little left. My father blamed himself, and he tried to do what he could to aid those who had suffered most. But now Brunconia is a poor country and so many suffer because of von Gessler. So you see why I lose my temper when I meet this man who is the son of the greatest enemy of the Brunconian people."

"I do understand," said Percy, "and I daresay this von Gessler is a villain, but upon my honor, Max, I wish you'd held your temper. I don't know what the Prince Regent will say when he finds out that you've been brawling at Almack's. And he'll hear of it, you can be sure."

"I'm sure Max feels bad enough about this evening, Percy," said Heathfield.

Maximilian nodded glumly and they continued on in silence.

12

Later that evening Selena, Henrietta and the duke departed from Almack's. Melford wasn't in the best of moods, for he had been very upset to find his sister in the thick of the excitement involving Prince Maximilian and von Gessler.

Since he had been deep in conversation with some of his friends, Melford hadn't seen Selena dancing with Maximilian. When he had gone to investigate the commotion, he had been quite shocked to have found his sister wiping blood from the prince's face with Heathfield standing beside them.

Melford leaned back against the leather seat and tried to see his sister's face in the darkened carriage. Henrietta was sitting beside him and, knowing that her husband was vexed with Selena, the duchess was trying to distract him with light-hearted chatter.

However, when Henrietta paused a moment, the duke took the opportunity to speak. "Selena," he said, adopting a censorious tone, "I was very displeased with your behavior this evening. It was bad enough that you danced with Heathfield, but then to find you in the middle of a brawl with that foreign prince. God in heaven, have you no sense?"

"I do wish you would stop being so insufferable, James," said Selena irritably.

"You forget that your behavior reflects upon me and Henrietta. You know my feelings about Heathfield. And then you dance with his boorish cousin, who disgraced himself with that display of public drunkenness."

"He wasn't drunk," said Selena.

"Then that is all the worse," said the duke, "for if he were sober there is no excuse at all for his behavior. Poor von Gessler might have been killed."

"I don't know what von Gessler said to him," said Selena, "but I believe the prince was sorely provoked."

"Nonsense," said the duke. "I'm told he acted like a madman. Von Gessler said there is madness in the family. I'm glad it showed itself so that there will be no more talk of this prince and Princess Charlotte. The fellow may as well pack himself back to Brunconia."

"I spoke with Lady Blackstone after the incident," said Henrietta, "and she told me that Prince Maximilian's father was often unaccountably violent. And Lady Blackstone said that her family was so mistreated by this prince's father. She was very upset at her brother being attacked."

"I'm not sure how much we can believe Lady Blackstone," said Selena. "She is hardly objective. Indeed, I would like to hear Prince Maximilian's explanation of what happened."

"You are to keep away from him," said the duke. "He is very likely mad."

"What nonsense," said Selena.

"That is enough," said the duke sharply.

Selena made no reply. Staring resentfully out the window, she said nothing more during the rest of the ride home.

In the morning Heathfield joined Maximilian for breakfast. "Good morning, Max."

"Good morning, dear cousin," said the prince.

Heathfield thought that Maximilian seemed a bit less cheerful than usual. "How is that cut on your face?"

"It is nothing," said the prince, dismissing it with a wave of his hand.

The earl went to the sideboard and perused the selection of food. "I hope you're hungry, Max. It appears that Cook was prepared to feed an army."

Maximilian, who usually appeared thrilled at the breakfast fare, stared gloomily at the silver chafing dishes. After selecting a single sausage and a small helping of eggs, he sat down at the table.

When Heathfield took his seat, he noted that his cousin was eating his meager breakfast with far less enthusiasm than was his custom. "Is something wrong, Max?"

The prince shrugged. "It is only that I am sorry to cause embarrassment. Percy was vexed with me."

"Oh, don't worry about Percy," said the earl. "I believe no one will blame you very much for losing your temper when they learn the cause. I only wish there was something that could be done to recover some of what was stolen from your country."

"Yes, I wish that could be so," said Maximilian. "But, in any case, I shall see my family's honor vindicated."

"What do you mean?"

Maximilian, who had taken a bite of sausage, chewed for a moment and then swallowed. "When I kill von Gessler in the duel."

The earl was glad that he hadn't been eating anything for he might have choked at this surprising remark. "What the devil do you mean, Max?"

"I challenged him to a duel, and he accepted."

"What?" cried Heathfield, eyeing his cousin in astonishment. "Is that how you arrange a duel in Brunconia? By brawling first?"

Maximilian reddened, but made no reply.

"This is ridiculous. Why didn't you mention this duel before?"

"I didn't wish to upset Percy," said Maximilian. "You will be my second, won't you?"

"I'll be no such thing," said Heathfield. "Of all the crackbrained notions I've ever heard, this is by far the worst. I'll have no part of it."

Maximilian appeared hurt. "You will not be my second?"

"I most assuredly will not. Come, Max, you can't be serious."

"I am," said Maximilian. "And if you are my friend, you will assist me."

"I won't assist you to get killed," said the earl.

"I will not be killed," said Maximilian. "I am a very good shot."

"That may be, but it doesn't mean you won't get killed. For all we know, von Gessler may be a better shot. No, Max, this won't do at all."

"I have challenged him and I will fight," said Maximilian stubbornly. "My honor and the honor of Brunconia demand it."

Heathfield regarded his cousin in some frustration. "So you are determined?"

"Yes," said Maximilian resolutely.

Heathfield shrugged and then turned his attention to his breakfast. What was he to do about this? he asked himself.

"Mr. Hastings is here, my lord," said the butler, entering the dining room.

"Do show him in, Preston."

When Percy entered, he greeted his cousins before going to the sideboard and helping himself to breakfast.

"You're up early, Percy," said the earl.

"Well, I couldn't sleep," said Percy, taking a seat at the table. "I was too worried."

"Worried?"

"Well, you know my father will be coming from the country and what will I tell him about Max after last night? I can hardly be sanguine about his chances with Princess Charlotte."

"I fear there is more to worry about than that," said the earl. "Our cousin neglected to inform us that he had challenged von Gessler to a duel."

"What!" exclaimed Percy.

"Yes, Max informs me he is quite determined to meet von Gessler on the field of honor."

"But it just isn't done, Max," said Percy. "Oh, there are a few hotheads dueling, I admit that, but I assure you it has quite gone out of fashion."

"It is not about fashion," said Maximilian. "It is about honor."

"Honor is all very well," said Percy, "but one can get hurt in duels, you know. You must forget about this dueling business. You would serve Brunconia far better by marrying Princess Charlotte than getting killed in a duel."

"He doesn't intend to get killed," said the earl.

"Heathfield will not be my second," said Maximilian with a mournful expression. "Would you, Percy?"

"Would I be your second?" replied Percy. "My dear Max, I will not."

"Then I must do without a second," said Maximilian.

"Indeed, that wouldn't do at all," said Heathfield. "One must have a second. Perhaps you could send a letter to Brunconia and ask one of your friends to come."

"That would take weeks."

"Well, I see no alternative," said Heathfield. "You can hardly go to a duel without a second. What does it signify if the duel waits a while? Better to go into these things with a cool head."

"I don't think . . ." began Maximilian, but he was interrupted by the appearance of the butler, who regarded the earl apologetically.

"I beg your lordship's pardon," he said, "but Mr. Reynolds is here. He says that it is a matter of some urgency."

Mr. Reynolds was Heathfield's solicitor and, while the earl was never very eager to see him, he nodded. "Very well, Preston. Show him to the library." Rising from the table, Heathfield told his cousins that he wouldn't be long.

When he had gone, Percy started to eat his breakfast again. "Now let's not talk of this dueling business any longer, Max. It will give me indigestion. Indeed, I find the thought of pistol balls whizzing about quite upsetting.

"Let us speak of something more pleasant. For example, Princess Charlotte. I'm sure she is eager to meet you."

Maximilian frowned. "Perhaps it is foolish of me to think I can wed Princess Charlotte. And perhaps I do not wish to do so."

Percy appeared stunned. "Not wish to do so? Whatever can you mean?"

Maximilian shook his head. "What if I find I do not like this princess?"

"Oh, I daresay you will like her, Max. She is a pleasant enough girl."

Maximilian frowned. "I did not tell you this, Percy, but I was very devoted to a young lady in Brunconia." He sighed. "But I know a prince cannot marry as his heart wishes, but I love my dearest Frederica."

"Oh, dear," said Percy, disturbed at this information.

"I thought that we would wed, but Frederica is very poor. My father said that I must marry a wealthy woman, that it was my duty to do so. I agreed to come to England and try to win Princess Charlotte's hand."

"I am very sorry, old lad," said Percy sympathetically. "Being a prince has its disadvantages. But think of being married to the heiress to the English throne! It would be so splendid for Brunconia."

"Perhaps," said Maximilian, "but sometimes I think it would not be very good to be married to the English princess."

"What!" cried Percy, regarding his cousin in alarm. "Whyever not?"

"It is that a man wants to be master of his house and how can one be master if he is married to an English princess who is to be Queen? If I must marry for money, could I not marry some other wealthy lady? For example, Lady Selena. I like her very much and she is very rich, is she not? She would bring a very large dowry. I know she is not of royal blood, but she is the sister of a duke, and an English duke is very important, is he not?"

"Yes, but Lady Selena is not a princess."

"But Lady Selena is very beautiful and kind. She is like Frederica," he added wistfully.

"I do hope you aren't going to say you are in love with Lady Selena," said Percy, viewing his cousin with a look of dismay.

"No, I am in love with Frederica," said Maximilian. "But I do like her very much. And I may not like Princess Charlotte."

"My dear Max, you haven't even met her. I'm sure you'll like her."

Maximilian frowned. "But I may not, and she may not like me. Lady Selena likes me, I think."

Percy regarded his cousin in frustration. "You must forget all about Lady Selena. You must think only of Princess Charlotte." When Maximilian looked as though he didn't wish to take this advice, he continued hastily. "It is pointless to fancy yourself marrying Lady Selena. She is to marry someone else."

"Marry someone else?"

Percy nodded. "Yes, of course."

"Who?"

"Who?" repeated Percy. "I fear I'm not at liberty to say."

"Not at liberty to say?" said the prince, eyeing his cousin skeptically.

"The engagement hasn't been announced as yet." Percy hesitated, unsure what to say. He certainly couldn't have Maximilian pining after Selena Paget. Indeed, he must nip the idea in the bud before his cousin abandoned his goal of wedding Princess Charlotte. He hesitated before plunging ahead. "Well, if you really must know, Lady Selena is to marry your cousin Heathfield."

Maximilian's blue eyes widened in surprise. "Marry my cousin?"

"I must swear you to secrecy, Max. Heathfield would have my head if he knew I told you. They are secretly engaged to be married."

"Engaged?" cried Maximilian.

"Shhh . . ." warned Percy. "It is a secret. You know that Heathfield and Lady Selena's brother are on very bad terms. The duke would not countenance the match. That is why no one knows of it. Heathfield hopes that one day he will make amends with Melford. Then the engagement can be announced."

"But why did not Heathfield tell me this?"

"Oh, I'm sure he'll tell you, but it is difficult for him to discuss the subject. He is so in love, you see."

"Poor cousin Heathfield," said Maximilian. "How miserable for him."

Percy nodded. "You mustn't worry. It will work out in the end, I'm sure. But you mustn't give up your idea to marry Princess Charlotte. Don't forget what it would mean to Brunconia."

His cousin nodded sadly. "*Ja, ja,* you are right," he said.

The sound of approaching footsteps caused Percy to speak once again in hushed tones. "That is probably Heathfield. Remember, you mustn't say a word about Lady Selena to him." The prince nodded again and they both waited for the earl's return.

13

When he rejoined his two cousins after meeting with his solicitor, Heathfield could not fail to note that his Brunconian cousin seemed rather depressed and preoccupied. Suspecting that Maximilian was reflecting on the unfortunate business with von Gessler, he tried to distract the young man by suggesting they go see a man about a horse the earl was thinking of buying.

Later when they were at the stables of a prominent horse breeder, Maximilian seemed indifferent to the horse the earl was considering. He hung back, leaning glumly against a gate, lost in his own thoughts.

At first opportunity, Percy informed Heathfield about Frederica, causing the earl to regard his cousin sympathetically. Hoping to take Maximilian's mind off his lost love, the earl called to him, asking his opinion about the horse.

The prince only shrugged and stayed where he was. While his cousins talked of horses, Maximilian found his mind wandering. He thought of Lady Selena, and how she reminded him of his dear Frederica. Not that Frederica had red hair or green eyes. No, she had blond hair and hazel eyes and she was short and rather plump. In actuality, Maximilian reflected that Lady Selena and Frederica didn't look very much alike at all. No, the likeness was more in their personalities.

A sad smile appeared on Maximilian's face. Since coming to England, he had tried not to think of Frederica. For a time the excitement of the great city of London had pushed her from his thoughts. But now he found himself missing Frederica dreadfully.

That evening Maximilian was feeling so despondent that he refused to accompany Heathfield to the theater after dinner. Saying he had a headache, the young prince begged the earl to go without him. Maximilian wouldn't hear of Heathfield's staying home on his account. Thinking it might be just as well for his cousin to have a quiet evening, the earl had left Maximilian sitting in the drawing room with Duncan at his feet.

Yet after a time of quiet reflection, Maximilian grew agitated. Retreating to his room, he put on his old Brunconian military coat and hat. Although he knew that Percy wouldn't approve of his appearance, the prince drew comfort from his old familiar clothes. He then left the house, walking briskly down the darkened street.

Maximilian walked for a long time, thinking of Frederica and then of Count von Gessler and the duel. His thoughts grew increasingly gloomy as he traveled farther and farther from the earl's fashionable residence.

After a time, he found himself on a street lined with shops. His eye alighted on a large hanging sign with a painting of a fierce looking wolf. Above the picture were the words Wolf's Head Tavern. Feeling himself in need of some liquid refreshment, Maximilian made his way inside the establishment.

Most of the patrons of the Wolf's Head took little note of the prince's entrance. However, one young gentleman, a dandy who was sitting at a corner table, regarded him with considerable interest. "Why, look at that fellow, Fairchild. Have you ever seen a more hideous coat? And that hat!"

Fairchild, another young dandy in a tight-fitting plum colored coat, directed his attention toward Maximilian. Languidly lifting up his gold quizzing glass, he eyed the prince with interest. "By heaven, do you know who that is, Boswith?"

His friend regarded him in surprise. "You do not mean to tell me that the fellow is somebody?"

"Indeed, yes. Why, he's that Brunconian prince! Remember I told you of that frightful scene at Almack's."

Boswith viewed Maximilian in surprise. "Good God! I hardly think he'd be taken seriously as a suitor for Princess Charlotte."

"Well, he was a good deal better dressed at Almack's. But I assure you, that is Prince Maximilian!"

Boswith kept his gaze on the prince. He then turned back to his friend. "Gad, I wish I'd been there. Come, Fairchild, you must introduce me to him. I should like to meet this prince."

"I don't know," said the other gentleman, noting that Maximilian was gazing gloomily at the glass that had been set before him. "I met him only briefly. He probably won't remember me."

"What does that signify? He was doubtlessly introduced to so many people that he could scarcely know whom he has met."

"But by the look on his face, I doubt he wants company."

"A man needs company most when he is blue-deviled," said Boswith.

"Oh, very well," said Fairchild, rising from his chair. The two young gentlemen approached Maximilian. Fairchild stepped forward and made a bow. "Your highness," he said.

Surprised at being recognized, Maximilian nodded to the two gentlemen standing before him.

"I was fortunate enough to be introduced to your highness at Almack's last evening, Your Highness. I am Roger Fairchild and this is my friend, the honorable Mr. Cecil Boswith."

"An honor to meet your highness," said Boswith, bowing again.

The prince nodded. "And very good to meet you, Mr. . . . ."

"Boswith," said that gentleman quickly. "I do hope your highness is enjoying your stay in town."

Maximilian nodded again. "Yes, yes, it is a very interesting place, this London." When the gentlemen continued standing there before him, Maximilian gestured for them to join him. "Do sit, gentlemen. You must have a drink with me." The two men seemed overjoyed at this suggestion and quickly took places at the prince's table.

Although Maximilian was not at first pleased at being disturbed, he soon began to warm to his new companions. Fairchild and Boswith were pleasant, talkative young gentlemen. After partaking of the prince's generosity in buying them a drink, they reciprocated by buying him one and then another. Maximilian bought the next round, and then Fairchild and Boswith called for still more ale. After a while, Maximilian began to think Fairchild and Boswith were the most congenial of men.

The prince took a long gulp from his glass and set it down with a loud thump. "This English ale of yours," he said, "it is not so good as our Brunconian beer. But, it is not so very bad," he added with a grin.

"I'm gratified to hear it," said Boswith, noting that the royal gentleman was rapidly approaching a state of inebriation.

Maximilian took another long swig of the ale. Putting the glass back down, he suddenly frowned. "No, it is not like Brunconian beer," he said glumly.

"I daresay you miss Brunconia," said Fairchild, exchanging an amused look with Boswith.

Maximilian nodded. "Brunconia," he said sadly. "It is very beautiful." He turned to Boswith. "Like my Frederica. *Ja,* she is *sehr schön.* And Lady Selena. She is a beautiful English lady. Do you not think her very beau-ti-ful, my dear sirs?"

Boswith and Fairchild exchanged a glance, before regarding the prince with interest. "Lady Selena Paget?" asked Fairchild.

"Lady Selena Pag-et," said Maximilian. "She is so very beautiful. So very beau-tiful." He looked down at his now empty glass with a melancholy expression.

"Oh, I do think Lady Selena very lovely," said Boswith, sensing that some especially choice bit of gossip was soon to be his. Was Prince Maximilian in love with the Duke of Melford's sister? It would be a new piece of news to spread about. "She has won many hearts to be sure."

The prince nodded. "This I do not doubt, but she is to marry my cousin." He suddenly looked guilty. "Shhh . . .," he said, holding an unsteady finger to his lips. "It is a secret."

Fairchild couldn't hide his surprise. "Lady Selena Paget is to marry your cousin? You mean Percy Hastings?"

"*Nein,* I mean Heathfield." Maximilian looked suddenly disturbed. He added in a loud whisper. "Shhh . . . it is a secret. You must not tell anyone. Do you understand?"

Boswith smiled. "Of course, of course, your highness. I wouldn't tell a soul." But even as he spoke these words, the dandy was deciding whom he would honor first with this delectable piece of news.

14

The morning sun streamed into Selena's sitting room as she sat writing a letter at the small, ornate cherry desk. Fluff lay beside the desk, sleeping soundly. After penning a few words, Selena paused to stare out of the window. She was finding it hard to concentrate on her letter.

She found herself thinking about what had happened at Almack's two nights ago. It had been a most unfortunate incident, one that would keep Society talking for a good long time. Selena wished she knew what had caused Prince Maximilian to lose his temper. She had thought him an amiable mild-mannered sort of man. Selena couldn't believe that Maximilian was the monster that Count von Gessler had painted him to be.

A thoughtful expression appeared on Selena's face. Perhaps she was merely giving Prince Maximilian the benefit of the doubt because he was Heathfield's cousin. After all, she couldn't deny that she was very much attracted to the earl.

Restlessly getting up from the desk, Selena walked over to the window and looked down at the view. The small garden behind the house was quite lovely with its colorful array of primroses and tulips. As she continued to gaze down from the window, there was an excited bark from behind her. Glancing around, she found that Fluff was gazing up at her with an expectant look. Selena smiled. "So you're done with your nap, are you? Why don't we go out to the garden? It is too nice a day to stay indoors."

The little red and white dog ran to the door, wagging her tail furiously. Selena laughed. Fetching her bonnet and placing a shawl around her shoulders, she left the room, accompanied by the eager dog.

As she walked down the hallway, she heard a sudden commotion coming from the nursery. Selena recognized the indignant voice of her niece and then the loud wailing of her three-year-old nephew. Selena hurried to the nursery where she found the children's nanny speaking in comforting tones to Harold, who was sitting sobbing on the floor. Sophie stood to one side of them with her head hung down.

The children and their nanny looked up as Fluff bounded into the room, making a beeline for the distraught boy. Jumping up into Harold's lap, Fluff began to lick his face. Little Lord Hillsborough was so surprised by the dog's fervent attention that he abruptly quit crying and then he began to giggle as the dog continued to lick him.

"I'm sorry that the children disturbed you, my lady," said the servant.

"Oh, no, that is quite all right," said Selena, "but whatever is the matter with my nephew?"

"I fear Lady Sophie stepped on her brother's toy horse and broke it. His lordship was quite upset."

"I didn't mean to, Aunt Selena!" cried Sophie, looking as if she was also about to burst into tears. "I was just telling Nanny how I wanted to be a ballet dancer. I was showing her how I could dance and I didn't see Harold's silly old horse."

"It's not silly!" cried the boy and, remembering his grievance, he once again began wailing. Fluff, upset by this, jumped off his lap and hurried over to Selena as if for protection.

Crouching down next to the boy, Selena picked up the toy. The wooden horse's tail was broken and it dangled at an odd angle. "Come, Harold, don't cry," said Selena gently putting her arm around the little boy, "your horse's tail can be mended. We will have William see to it. I promise your horse will be as good as new." The boy's sobbing eased a little and he looked over at her.

"Jupiter will be all better?" he sniffed. Selena nodded and the little boy quit crying. "That is a good boy, Harold. Now, we'll have Nanny take your horse to William and I shall take you both out to the garden for a time. It is such lovely weather. You don't object to that, do you, Nanny?"

"Indeed not, my lady," said the servant, happy at the prospect of a break from her duties. "I shall fetch their coats and hats."

A short time later, Selena and the children went out into the garden with Fluff running merrily alongside them. Sophie had brought along a ball and she was gaily throwing it for the little dog to chase. Harold, who had by now forgotten the tragic episode of his toy horse, was laughing as Fluff dashed madly after the ball.

They had been outside for nearly half an hour when their play was interrupted by the appearance of the butler. "I beg your pardon, my lady," said Walker. "Lord Heathfield is here. He asked if you would see him."

Selena tried hard not to show her surprise at this communication. She hadn't thought that Heathfield would call at the house. Indeed, her brother would be very displeased to hear of it. She knew the duke didn't want him received.

"Lord Heathfield!" cried Sophie happily hurrying over to her aunt. "Oh good! I should like to see him. Perhaps Duncan is with him." She looked at the butler. "Did he bring his dog, Walker?"

"No, my lady," said the servant.

"Oh, that is too bad," said Sophie, very much disappointed.

Selena shook her head. "It is a very odd time for anyone to pay a call. Do tell Lord Heathfield we are not at home, Walker."

"Oh, Aunt Selena," cried Sophie. "I should so like to see Lord Heathfield again. Couldn't you have Walker show him to the garden?"

Selena hesitated. While she knew very well that she shouldn't admit the earl, she did wish to see him again. Her brother and sister-in-law had gone out and there was nothing to prevent Heathfield's paying a visit.

"Oh, very well," said Selena. "I must say I am curious why he would call at such an hour. Walker, do show Lord Heathfield out here to the garden."

"Very good, my lady."

In a short time, Heathfield was ushered into their presence. Fluff, overjoyed to see him, rushed forward with a happy bark.

"Good morning, Fluff," said the earl, reaching down to pat the dog. He then bowed to Selena. "Lady Selena, how good of you to receive me. I apologize for calling at such an hour." While he had hoped to find Selena alone, Heathfield smiled good-naturedly at the children. "How charming you look this morning, Lady Sophie."

Smiling delightedly, the little girl smiled and made a polite curtsy. "Thank you, Lord Heathfield. And you look very handsome. Just like the prince in the story Aunt Selena read to me last night." Sophie turned to Selena. "Doesn't he look like the handsome prince, Aunt Selena?"

The earl grinned at this remark, and then looked expectantly at

Selena. "Do not think I shall puff up your vanity, my lord," she said, meeting his gaze with a smile.

Harold provided a diversion by hurrying over to look up at the tall earl. "And good morning to you, young man," said the earl.

Sophie felt an introduction was in order. "Lord Heathfield, this is my little brother, Harold, Lord Hillsborough."

The earl put out his hand to the boy. "Lord Hillsborough, I'm very pleased to meet you."

Harold put his little hand into Heathfield's and smiled shyly.

"How is Duncan, Lord Heathfield?" said Sophie.

"He is very well indeed. You must come to the park with us one day very soon."

"I'd like that," said Sophie eagerly. She then looked from the earl to Selena. "I believe I should take Harold in to Nanny."

Selena eyed her niece in surprise. "I want to stay in the garden," said Harold firmly.

Sophie took his hand. "I believe William has mended your toy horse. Shall we go see?" Harold seemed more willing, and his sister led him away after saying farewell to the earl.

"Your niece is very perceptive for one so young," said Heathfield, watching the children head toward the house. "She knew I wanted to speak with you alone."

"I don't know that you should. My brother will be furious when he hears that I've received you," said Selena.

"It is so very inconvenient having your brother despise me," said his lordship with a smile.

"You have always done your best to vex him. And then telling him that his Tintoretto was a forgery! He still hasn't got over that."

"I didn't want it to be a forgery," said Heathfield. "I shall be more than happy to assist him in the future by examining any paintings he may wish to buy. You must tell him that I'm more than happy to advise him."

Selena couldn't help but smile at the mischievous expression on his handsome face. "I truly doubt he'll want your advice," she said. Although Selena knew that she should send the earl on his way, she didn't really wish to do so. "Would you sit down, Lord Heathfield?" she said gesturing toward some wrought-iron benches.

The earl nodded, eager to do so. After waiting for Selena to take a seat under a rose arbor, he sat down beside her. The bench was not very large and Selena found the earl's close proximity to be rather unsettling. She looked sideways at him and noted that he didn't look in the least discomfited.

"How is Prince Maximilian?" said Selena thinking it best to make conversation. "I have been thinking of him and that unpleasant incident at Almack's."

"I'm very sorry you had to witness that. My cousin lost his head and behaved rather badly. But, I assure you, he had very good reason to forget himself."

Selena eyed the earl with great curiosity. "I did suspect that Prince Maximilian had been sorely provoked. I know that Count von Gessler considers the prince's father his enemy. He told us a dreadful story."

"What did he say?"

"That his father was once Prince Maximilian's father's most trusted minister. And that he was badly treated and forced into exile. Indeed, according to the count, his family would have been executed has they not fled the country."

"That is his version of it. I shall tell you Max's." Heathfield then began to recount the treacherous story of the count's father and how he had stolen the treasury of the tiny principality of Brunconia, plunging Maximilian's family and the country into poverty.

Selena listened raptly to the tale and when the earl was through telling it, she shook her head. "That is abominable! I suspected he was lying. There is something about the man I do not like. Indeed, Fluff took an instant dislike to him."

Heathfield smiled. "I'm sure that Fluff is an excellent judge of character."

"I'm not so sure of that, my lord," said Selena with a smile. "She seems very fond of you."

Heathfield grinned and then they both laughed. The earl then returned to the more serious matter of Maximilian. "It was very ill luck that von Gessler was at Almack's. You see, my cousin has challenged him to a duel."

"A duel!" cried Selena. "He can't be serious!"

"Maximilian is very determined to go through with it. He claims he must avenge the honor of his family and Brunconia."

"But you must stop him from acting so foolishly."

"It isn't so easy stopping others from behaving foolishly," said his lordship. "And Maximilian is very stubborn in this matter."

"Surely, there must be something one can do," said Selena. "The idea of dueling is quite ridiculous. If I have the opportunity I shall certainly tell von Gessler that."

"That would be much appreciated," said the earl, who despite his serene appearance, was very much aware of Selena's being there beside him. It was hard to refrain from putting his arm around her shoulders and pulling her to him.

"I fear that the incident at Almack's may jeopardize Prince Maximilian's prospects of marrying Princess Charlotte," said Selena, hurrying to fill the awkward silence that had ensued.

"Well, I've never thought there was much chance of that in any case," said Heathfield. "Poor Max. I've recently learned that he's left his true love behind in Brunconia."

"Oh, dear," said Selena.

Heathfield smiled and leaned closer toward her. "I wish Max could marry the woman he loves. While it isn't really the fashion, marrying for love now seems a logical thing to me." This remark combined with an intent gaze into Selena's eyes, very much disconcerted her. She looked questioningly at him as he began to move his face toward hers. Just when their lips were about to touch, there was a loud shout from behind them.

"Selena! Where are you?"

Both Heathfield and Selena sprang back in surprise. Coming toward them was the grim figure of the Duke of Melford. Selena regarded her brother in some confusion while the earl got up from the bench and walked out to meet the duke.

"Melford," he said in a friendly voice. "Good morning. I must compliment you on your delightful children. I had the great good fortune to meet them."

Ignoring him, the duke turned his stern gaze on his sister. "I think you had best return to the house, Selena. I must speak to Heathfield."

Selena began to protest, but the earl's slight shake of the head stopped her. Rising from the bench, she nodded to the earl before walking back to the house.

Once his sister had gone, Melford glared at Heathfield. "How dare you come here to see my sister, knowing full well that I do not wish you in my house."

"I am sorry, Melford," said his lordship, adopting a conciliatory tone. While he had always disliked the duke, he now had no wish to upset him.

"I know what you're about, Heathfield."

"What I am about?" said the earl, raising his eyebrows in surprise. "What can you mean, sir?"

"You wish to injure me by these attentions to my sister. You believe that you can ingratiate yourself into Selena's affections and turn her against me. If you think that I will sit idly by while you seek to compromise my sister, you are very much mistaken!" The duke was growing very agitated as he said this.

"I assure you I have no nefarious scheme where Lady Selena is concerned. My intentions are completely honorable."

"Honorable? When have you ever acted honorably where women are concerned?"

Heathfield bristled at this remark, but he replied calmly. "I wish to marry your sister, Melford."

"Marry her?" cried the duke. "You cannot imagine that I should ever allow you to marry her."

"I believe it is Lady Selena's decision whom to marry," said his lordship.

"Then she will have to choose between her family and you. Upon my honor I'll never speak to her or allow her to see my family if she marries you."

"Do be reasonable, Melford," said the earl, remaining cool in the face of the duke's anger. "I know we've disliked each other in the past, but I should like to make amends."

"I suggest you leave here, sir," said Melford. "I have no wish to continue this conversation."

Heathfield stared at the duke in some frustration. Then, feeling there was no point in saying anything else, he bowed stiffly and took his leave.

15

When Melford returned from the garden he was in an exceedingly bad temper. The duchess, who had gone to see the children upon her return to the house, now came down from the nursery to find her husband pacing the drawing room in some agitation.

"Whatever is the matter, my dear?" said Henrietta.

"Heathfield was here. I found him in the garden with Selena."

"Oh, dear," said the duchess. "Sophie told me he had come. She has the silliest notion that Heathfield and Selena will marry. You can't think that Selena wants to marry him?"

"I don't care what she wants. I won't have my sister marry him. I won't even consider it."

"But perhaps he is fond of her," said Henrietta.

"Rubbish," muttered the duke. "I am quite certain that he only wants to hurt me. What better way than through my sister?"

At that moment Selena entered the room. "I imagine you're discussing me," she said, frowning at her brother.

"And why not, when I find you with that man?" said the duke. "I had thought you far too sensible a girl to be taken in by Heathfield. He is an unscrupulous rakehell. I suppose you will tell me you fancy yourself in love with him."

"I shan't tell you anything," said Selena irritably. "And I suggest you cease treating me as if I were just out of the nursery. I am three and twenty."

Henrietta, who wished to prevent further unpleasantness, stepped in. "Perhaps it is best not to speak of this any further. It would be best to discuss the subject later when both of you have cooled a bit. And I so want to tell you about the exciting time we had on our ride through the park this morning. Do sit down, Selena. It was very exciting.

"We had ridden to the park. James had wished to take some exercise so we alighted from the carriage. Just at that moment who should come along but the Prince Regent himself. His phaeton pulled up beside us and we had a very pleasant chat."

"And you will be interested to hear that His Royal Highness asked me what I knew about that unfortunate incident at Almack's," said Melford, frowning at Selena. "He said he was most distressed to hear that Prince Maximilian had acted so badly. The Prince Regent had formed a good opinion of him. Now he believed he was mistaken. I told him what I knew. I thought he should know what Count von Gessler had told us."

"But it is very likely that what the count has said is utter nonsense," said Selena. "I have had heard a very different account and I think it far more credible."

"And where did you hear this other account?" said the duke, eyeing his sister with disapproval.

"From Lord Heathfield."

"Just as I thought. He and Percy Hastings would do anything to advance the cause of their kinsman. One cannot believe a word they say about him."

"And you can believe von Gessler?" said Selena. "He certainly would say whatever put him and his family in a good light."

"Count von Gessler is an honorable man," said the duke. "I don't know if that can be said of Heathfield."

After regarding him in some frustration, she rose from her chair. "Do excuse me. I think it best that I go to my room." She left the room, going quickly to her bedchamber. There she sat down in an armchair and appeared thoughtful.

Things had certainly got into a muddle, she reflected, thinking of Heathfield. It was very clear that she had strong feelings for him. And if he proposed marriage . . . She frowned. He hadn't proposed, and it wasn't clear that he would do so. After all, she hardly knew him. And if he did ask for her hand, how could she accept him, knowing that Melford would have nothing to do with her if she married against his wishes?

Selena's frown grew deeper. "What shall I do, Fluff?" she said, scooping the little dog up into her arms. Then, sitting down on the chaise longue, she deposited the spaniel beside her. "James is being odious," she said with a sigh, causing Fluff to peer up at her with a questioning gaze. "Sometimes I think that it might have been better to have stayed at Melford Castle. Then we wouldn't have met Heathfield and had such bother." Even as she said it,

Selena knew that she didn't mean it. "Yes, I confess I am speaking nonsense," she said, smiling at the dog. "I'm glad we came to London, aren't you?"

Fluff cocked her head in reply, causing Selena to smile again. Then, thinking that a book might distract her, she took up a volume from the table beside her and started to read.

After a while, she put down her book. She found herself thinking of what Heathfield had said about Prince Maximilian. She wished that she had proof that what he had said was true. She would take great pleasure in making her brother realize that von Gessler was a scoundrel. If only there was someone else she might consult, an impartial person who knew the truth about what had happened in Brunconia.

Selena stroked Fluff's silky ears thoughtfully. There must be someone in London who would know about Brunconia and Prince Maximilian's family. Suddenly, she had an idea. Of course! Miss Foxworth. She remembered meeting that redoubtable lady at Lady Blackstone's salon. Surely a person of Miss Foxworth's renown and scholarly accomplishments would know about Brunconia.

Selena decided to consult Miss Foxworth as soon as possible. "I shall go to Lady Blackstone's salon with Henrietta," she said aloud. Her sister-in-law had mentioned that they might go again tomorrow evening. Miss Foxworth attended regularly and would doubtless be there. It would be the very opportunity to find out more about the Brunconian situation. Thus resolved on this plan, Selena settled down once again to her book.

16

Henrietta had been very much relieved when Selena had joined them at luncheon, for Selena's usual good temper appeared completely restored. She was very civil to Melford, who prudently made no mention of Heathfield during the meal.

When Selena expressed her wish to attend Lady Blackstone's salon, the duchess was very pleased. While she had been skeptical at first of going there, Henrietta had had such an interesting time, that she was eager to return.

The duke, however, had no wish to attend the salon again. He hadn't enjoyed himself when they had gone there before. There were too many people he didn't know talking of things he didn't understand. Still, he had no objection to his wife and sister going if they wished.

The following evening Selena and Henrietta set off for Lady Blackstone's. They had started rather late, because the duchess had had a good deal of difficulty deciding what to wear. When they finally arrived at the Blackstone residence, it was crowded with people.

Selena looked around, trying to spot Miss Foxworth. She was quite pleased when her eye alighted on that lady. Miss Foxworth wasn't hard to find. Her tall figure was attired in a saffron yellow dress and she wore a turban of multicolored silk. When Selena caught sight of her, she was having an animated discussion with a red-haired man, who was gesticulating wildly as he spoke.

"How delightful that you have come!" said Lady Blackstone, greeting them warmly. As always, the baroness was dressed at the height of fashion. She wore a lovely white gown, exquisite in its classical simplicity. Around her neck was an extraordinary necklace.

Selena couldn't help staring at it. The necklace had the look of great antiquity. It was a large swan-shaped pendant fashioned from gold and decorated with some of the largest diamonds Selena had ever seen.

"Good evening, Lady Blackstone," said Henrietta, smiling brightly at the baroness.

"Your grace," said the baroness, making a graceful curtsy. "And Lady Selena."

Selena nodded in reply. "I have looked forward to coming again. I enjoyed our last visit to your salon."

"I am so glad," said Lady Blackstone. "And Mr. Travers will be so pleased. He has been asking about you, Lady Selena. I daresay he was very much taken with you."

Selena wasn't sure how to reply to this remark so she changed the subject. "What a lovely necklace, Lady Blackstone."

The baroness smiled. "Thank you. I must say it is a great favorite of mine."

"It quite takes my breath away," said Henrietta, eyeing the glittering stones with admiration.

"It is a von Gessler family heirloom," she said. "My brother has loaned it to me for this evening. I had to beg him to allow me to wear it. He worries about it so when it isn't locked up so I promised I would return it to him as soon as possible. But I think it a pity to never allow anyone to see it."

"Yes, indeed," said Henrietta. "What is the use of jewels if they aren't to be worn? That is what I'm always telling my husband."

"Lady Selena!" A masculine voice interrupted the conversation, and Selena turned to see Henry Travers approaching. He was wearing a blue velvet coat, and around his neck was a red silk scarf tied in an extravagant bow. Selena noted that his unruly hair seemed even wilder than the last time they had met.

"Lady Selena!" he repeated, bowing low before her and then fixing his dark eyes on her face. "The gods are extraordinarily kind in bringing you here."

Although Selena had an urge to laugh at this remark, she nodded graciously. "Mr. Travers."

The poet then bowed to Henrietta. "Duchess."

"How do you do, Mr. Travers?" said Henrietta, eyeing the poet with an expression akin to alarm. She was sure that her husband wouldn't be very pleased hearing him spout flummery to Selena.

"Very well, madam," he said. "Indeed, I am exceedingly well. And now that you lovely ladies are here, my happiness is complete. I am nearly finished with a new poem. It is my greatest achievement."

"How lovely," said Henrietta uncertainly.

Although Selena's admiration of Henry Travers had been somewhat dimmed by meeting him, she couldn't help but be interested in his new work. "A new poem? That is exciting."

"It is called 'The Summer of Aphrodite.' "

"That is very nice, I'm sure," said Henrietta.

"Lady Selena has been my muse," said the poet.

"Has she?" said the duchess, unsure what Travers meant by that.

"Yes, she has truly inspired me," said the poet.

"Will we hear some of your new poem this evening?" said Lady Blackstone.

He shook his head. "It isn't quite finished. A poem must be polished carefully like a precious stone before revealing it to the public."

"Yes, I'm sure that is a good idea," said Henrietta.

"But when will it be ready?" said Lady Blackstone, who was rather disappointed. Having the debut of the famous poet's new work would have been a considerable coup for her salon.

"One cannot say," said Travers gravely. "It could be days or weeks or months."

"Well, you must promise me that you will read it first at my salon," said the baroness.

"Very well," said Travers, "but only when Lady Selena is present."

Selena felt rather embarrassed by the intent gaze now being directed at her by the poet. "Oh, there is Miss Foxworth. I must speak with her."

"Miss Foxworth," said Travers with a frown. "My dear lady, I must protest. Why would you wish to speak with that gorgon? She is my deadliest enemy."

Selena laughed. "Surely you exaggerate, Mr. Travers."

"Indeed, I do not," he said emphatically. "She'll try to poison you against me."

"Don't worry, sir," said Selena, smiling brightly, "I promise Miss Foxworth won't change my opinion of your genius in the least. But do excuse me." She hurried off, happy to leave Henry Travers.

Miss Foxworth had evidently concluded her conversation and

was now standing alone, regarding the company with the look a mother might have watching toddlers at play. When she saw Selena, she smiled. "Lady Selena."

"Miss Foxworth, I'm so glad to find you here. I wanted to speak with you."

"I must say I am in want of intelligent conversation," said Miss Foxworth. "I saw that you were speaking with Henry Travers. I daresay you are in want of intelligent counterstating as well."

Selena smiled. "I do wish I'd never met him. I liked his poetry so much better before I did so."

"His work is unmitigated balderdash," said Miss Foxworth. "I admit he does produce a good phrase here and there, but all in all, I feel his worth is far exceeded by his reputation. But, pray let us not speak of him."

"I shall be happy to talk of another subject," said Selena. "Indeed, I wished to ask you about Brunconia."

"Brunconia?" said Miss Foxworth, raising her eyebrows in surprise.

"I was wondering about it. I have met Prince Maximilian von Stauffenburg, Count von Gessler, and Lady Blackstone. I'd never even heard of Brunconia before coming to town and now I've met three Brunconians. I thought you'd know about it."

"My dear young lady, what is there to know about Brunconia? It is, by all accounts, a dreary place with little to commend it but a few mountains. And those are of unexceptional height I'm told."

"Have you been there?"

"Indeed not. No one visits Brunconia, not if one can help it. Surely you aren't thinking of going there."

Selena smiled. "Certainly not. I'm only curious."

"I confess I know very little about the subject," said Miss Foxworth, "although I can find Brunconia on a map of Europe, which is more than most can do. But I do know someone whom you might speak with, Professor MacNeil. He is a very well respected historian and scholar. Perhaps you are familiar with his history of the Holy Roman Empire?"

"No, I fear not."

"Well you must read it. It is splendid. Yes, MacNeil is a very sound man. He lived in Brunconia for some months a few years ago, which is where he met Mrs. MacNeil. She was employed as a governess by some minor princeling or other.

"If you wish to learn about Brunconia, you should call on Professor MacNeil. He lives in London. I have his address and I shall send it to you."

"If it wouldn't be too much trouble," said Selena.

Miss Foxworth assured her it was no trouble in the least and that she'd send the address to Melford House by the morning post. The redoubtable lady then began to tell Selena about a new pamphlet she had just written advocating her revolutionary position that women should have all the rights accorded to the male sex.

"I shall send you my pamphlet as well, my dear," said Miss Foxworth after expounding on her topic for some time. She seemed pleased that Selena had been so attentive and sympathetic. They were joined by two gentlemen. One, a stout young man of florid countenance, was eager to speak with Miss Foxworth about an essay he hoped she might publish.

Selena took her leave, walking through the crowded room toward Henrietta. "Lady Selena!" A masculine voice caused her to stop and turn around. Coming toward her was Count von Gessler. He was dressed with his usual understated elegance, and Selena had to admit that he looked very handsome.

"Count von Gessler," she said, smiling politely.

"What a great pleasure it is to see you once again," he said as he maneuvered himself through the guests to her side. "It is very crowded here. May I escort you to the anteroom? There are fewer people there. And I shall get you a glass of punch. You are doubtless thirsty, for it is rather warm."

"That would be very kind," said Selena, allowing the count to take her elbow and lead her out from the great crush of people. The room did seem very hot with so many guests in such a relatively small space. Selena was escorted to a smaller room that opened onto the main one. There were only a couple of other people there, two gentlemen who were holding an animated conversation about the state of Ireland.

Von Gessler left Selena for a short time, returning with a glass of punch. "I do not know why my sister invites so many. It is always very noisy."

"Oh, I don't mind," said Selena, accepting the glass of punch and taking a sip. Although she didn't really like von Gessler, she was glad at having this opportunity to talk to him. Perhaps she could help stop the ridiculous duel between him and Prince Maximilian.

"I was speaking with the duchess," said von Gessler, smiling at her. "What a charming woman."

"Yes, she is that."

"What a pity the duke did not come. I have great admiration for your brother, Lady Selena."

"And I know he has great respect for you," said Selena.

"His grace is very kind," said the count, nodding. "It is unusual for a gentleman of your brother's rank to take such an interest in the arts." Fixing his gaze on Selena, he changed the subject. "You look very beautiful this evening, my lady."

"Thank you," said Selena in a perfunctory tone. "Count von Gessler, I heard the most alarming story concerning you and I wished to find out if it were true."

"Alarming?" said the count, his eyes widening in surprise. "Do tell me what you have heard."

"It is that you intend to fight a duel with Prince Maximilian von Stauffenburg."

"Oh, that," said the count.

"Then it is true."

Von Gessler shrugged. "Yes, I fear so."

"You can't possibly mean to carry through with it."

"I do indeed," said the count. "As a gentleman, I have no choice but to do so. Prince Maximilian insulted me in the most infamous manner. You were there, madam. He had no provocation whatsoever. Indeed, we had never before met. Upon learning my name he heaped upon me the most opprobrious slurs upon my character. I have no alternative but to meet him on the field of honor."

"I am so sorry," said Selena, adopting a sorrowful expression. An idea had occurred to her that might help prevent the duel. "I beg you to reconsider. You will very likely be killed! Think of how devastated your family and friends will be to lose you."

"I am touched that you are afraid for me" said von Gessler, "but as I have said, I have no choice."

"I do wish it could be otherwise," said Selena, hoping she looked appropriately concerned. "I will say that you are a brave man, sir," said Selena. "Considering Prince Maximilian's reputation, I think you are the bravest man I know."

This remark startled the count. "His reputation?"

"His reputation for dueling." When he regarded her in surprise, she continued. "You mean you haven't heard about him? Oh, dear."

"My dear Lady Selena, I don't know what you mean."

Her mind racing to come up with a plausible story, Selena suddenly thought of Sir Edward Phipps, a diplomat she had met at one of Henrietta's parties. She regarded von Gessler gravely.

"When you told us about Prince Maximilian and his family, I was very much surprised. He seemed like such a nice young man. And then later when I was speaking with Sir Edward Phipps— you do know Sir Edward Phipps, don't you, Count?"

Von Gessler nodded. "I have met him."

"He is a very distinguished gentleman. He travels a good deal in his diplomatic duties. It seems he was in Brunconia not long ago. We began talking about Prince Maximilian, and I remarked that the prince seemed to be a very amiable gentleman. Sir Edward Phipps told me that I had been very much deceived. It seems Prince Maximilian has a violent temper, and despite his young age he has fought in many duels. He is a deadly marksman. He has already killed three men in Brunconia."

The count frowned at her. Was she joking, he thought. She appeared to be deadly serious. "It was Sir Edward Phipps who told you this?" said von Gessler.

Selena nodded. "Do call on him, Count von Gessler. He will tell you all about Prince Maximilian. I daresay what he said was most upsetting. You must find a way out of this dreadful duel. Surely there is something you can do."

"I don't know," said the count uncertainly.

At that moment Henrietta appeared. "There you are, Selena," she said. "You must forgive me, dear count, but I promised Mrs. Withycombe I'd fetch Selena. She's been asking to see her."

"Do think about what I've said, Count von Gessler," said Selena. After giving him an earnest look, she walked off with her sister-in-law.

"Whatever were you talking about?" said Henrietta. "The count looked rather perturbed."

"Oh, it was only small talk, Henrietta," replied Selena with a faint smile. She wondered if her strategy would work. Of course, Sir Edward Phipps hadn't said a word about Maximilian. For all Selena knew the prince couldn't hit a barn at ten paces. Yet Sir

Edward was a man of unimpeachable reputation and she knew that he had left for France that very morning.

Perhaps von Gessler wouldn't believe her. She wasn't sure what he would do even if he did, but at the very least he would find the news quite unsettling.

17

While Selena conversed with Lady Blackstone's guests, the Earl of Heathfield attended the theater with Percy and Maximilian. Although his lordship usually liked nothing better than to see a play, he didn't enjoy himself very much that night. He was in a strange reflective mood, and he found that he was too preoccupied with thinking about Selena to concentrate on the performance.

When he returned home to his bed, he had a hard time falling asleep. Then in the middle of the night he awakened. Again he thought of Selena, imagining her there beside him.

When the early morning light peeked in through the narrow opening between the drapes, he realized that he had slept very little. Exhausted, but in a state of agitation, he arose, dressed, and went riding.

Mounted on his fine black gelding, the earl rode a good distance across the city, all the time reflecting about Selena. Heathfield knew that he wanted to marry her. However, the problem of accomplishing the marriage loomed large before him. For even if she would accept him, the earl knew that without Melford's blessing, matters would be very difficult.

The earl stayed away a long time, stopping at an inn to have some luncheon. He didn't return home until later in the afternoon. When he entered his residence, his butler informed him that Maximilian had gone out. Percy had called and, after waiting for some time for him to return, his two cousins had left the house.

Heathfield's solicitor arrived with a number of matters requiring his lordship's attention. Heathfield was glad of the mundane distractions that allowed him to forget about Selena for a time. When the lawyer had gone, the earl went to his drawing room where he began to go through a pile of letters that had accumulated over the past few days.

It was nearly five o'clock when Maximilian and Percy entered the drawing room. Looking up from a letter, Heathfield noted that both of his cousins looked rather somber.

"Good afternoon, cousins," said the earl. "By God, you both look grim."

"We should look grim," said Percy, plopping into an elegant French chair across from Heathfield. "We have just been to see Princess Charlotte."

"What?" said Heathfield, quite surprised. "I didn't know you were going to call today."

"I hadn't planned on it," said Percy with a frown. "But I had a note from my father saying we must call on her at once. He felt we'd been cooling our heels too long. And as my father will arrive in town tomorrow, I thought it best to go to Warwick House at once. We waited for you as long as we could."

"Well, how did it go?" said Heathfield, turning to Maximilian, who was standing with his arms folded across his chest. "What did you think of Princess Charlotte?"

"I did not meet her," said Maximilian.

"You didn't meet her?"

"She did not receive us," said Percy. "I must say, I was dashed disappointed. We were told Her Royal Highness was indisposed."

"Well, there will be another day, after all," said Heathfield. "You'll meet her soon enough, Max."

"I'm not so sure of that," said Percy gloomily. "I'll wager that the Prince Regent heard about that business at Almack's."

"You don't know that for certain, Percy."

"But I do suspect it."

"Don't look so blue-deviled, Percy," said Heathfield. He smiled at Maximilian. "Do sit down, Max. I'll ring for tea."

"I do thank you, Cousin," said Maximilian, "but I am not feeling so well. I shall go to my room if you will permit." He made an oddly formal bow, and then he left them.

"What the devil is wrong with Max?" said the earl. "I can't believe he was that disappointed at not meeting Princess Charlotte."

"It's not that at all," said Percy with a frown. "He keeps pining for his Frederica. Indeed, the heart has gone out of him where this business of Princess Charlotte is concerned."

"Well, you mustn't take it so hard, Percy. You must have known it was a long shot, after all. One doesn't just arrive from

Brunconia, declare he wishes to marry the heir to the British throne, and that's that."

"But he was willing to give it a try when he came here. Indeed, I thought he liked the idea. All the way to Warwick House he talked about Frederica and how he didn't know if he could live without her."

"Poor old Max," said Heathfield. "I don't know what we'll do about him. But will you stay for tea?"

Even in his disheartened state, Percy could not refuse refreshments. He nodded, and his cousin rang the bell.

Miss Foxworth had been prompt in sending Selena a note containing the address of Professor MacNeil. She also had written that she would write the professor, explaining that Selena might call.

Selena wasn't sure how best to accomplish the visit. After all, she didn't have her own carriage and most of the time when she went out, Henrietta accompanied her. Since the duchess expected Selena to go with her when she paid her usual social calls, there was little opportunity for Selena to go anywhere alone.

The problem appeared to be a difficult one. Yet, being a resourceful young woman, Selena was sure that she could solve it. After all, it was London and it was easy to hire transportation.

The day after receiving the letter from Miss Foxworth, Selena sent her trusted lady's maid out to hire a chaise. Then she excused herself from accompanying Henrietta on her calls that afternoon by saying she had a dreadful headache.

After the duchess had gone, Selena set off, telling the duke's butler that she was going for a short walk in hopes that the exercise would help her headache. A few blocks away, she met the hired chaise and soon was on her way to Professor MacNeil's.

As she rode along, Selena felt rather proud of herself. Of course, it bothered her to have to be so deceitful. Yet, as the vehicle made its way through the streets of town, she reflected on how restricted her life was in town. Indeed, decided Selena, Miss Foxworth was right in thinking that women should be able to do as they pleased.

The professor lived in a respectable middle-class neighborhood of handsome but unpretentious brick row houses. After pulling the horses up at the destination, the driver hopped down to assist Selena from the vehicle.

Going to the door, Selena rapped at it with the brass door knocker. "I do hope he is at home," she thought as she stood waiting for the door to open. In a few moments a maid appeared. The servant, a girl of no more than sixteen, stared wide-eyed at Selena. "Yes, madam?"

"I should like to see Professor MacNeil. I am Lady Selena Paget."

"Do come in, m'lady," said the girl, bobbing a curtsy. She led Selena to a parlor. "I'll tell the master you're here, m'lady."

"Thank you," said Selena, pleased at hearing MacNeil was at home.

In a few minutes the maid returned to escort Selena up the stairs to the drawing room. "Mr. MacNeil will be but a few moments, m'lady."

Selena glanced around the room. It was pleasant and comfortable looking. There were some excellent watercolor paintings on the wall. Selena went over to study one, a landscape of mountains.

"Lady Selena."

Selena turned around to see a short, smiling man approach her. "Miss Foxworth said to expect you." He spoke with a Scottish accent, gently rolling the *r* in Foxworth. MacNeil was a pleasant looking man of middle years whose chestnut-brown hair was graying about the temples.

"Good afternoon, Professor MacNeil. You are very good to receive me."

MacNeil invited her to be seated. Then, sitting down himself, he regarded her expectantly. "Miss Foxworth wrote that you were interested in Brunconia."

"Yes, I am."

"Well, I must admit I was a wee bit surprised to hear that. There is little interest in that part of Europe. Of course, I know that Prince Maximilian is in town. I've heard that he is one of the princes here to court Princess Charlotte."

Selena nodded. "Have you met Prince Maximilian?"

"Aye, that I have. He's a good lad. I've met many of the von Stauffenburgs. They're a charming family. When I was in Brunconia they were very hospitable."

"Did you stay in Brunconia long, Professor MacNeil?"

"Five months it was." He gestured toward the watercolor painting that Selena had been looking at. "That is Brunconia. One of the views of the mountains."

"Why, it is quite beautiful" said Selena, studying the painting once again.

"Aye, it is not unlike the highlands of Scotland," said MacNeil. "Perhaps that is why I liked it so well. And also because I met my dear wife, Elizabeth, there. I'm happy to answer any questions you might have about Brunconia. What is it you wish to know, Lady Selena?"

"I'd like to know about Prince Maximilian's family. I was told that they are very poor."

"Very poor indeed," said the professor. "They live simply and have little money. Indeed, members of the Brunconian royal family live little better than their subjects. Of course, in earlier years, they were more prosperous. You see, Maximilian's father, the grand duke, had a dishonest minister who robbed the royal treasury over many years. Most of the wealth of the country was lost. Even the crown jewels were stolen."

"You're speaking of von Gessler."

"Aye," said MacNeil, nodding. "You've heard of him?"

"I know his son, Count von Gessler. He has said that it was his family who was mistreated by Maximilian's father. According to the count, the grand duke is mad."

"What nonsense," muttered MacNeil. "Von Gessler's father was a villain to be sure." The professor rose from his chair. "I have some books that might be of interest to you. Would you come to the library?"

"Yes, of course," said Selena, getting up and following Mac-Neil from the room.

While the library wasn't a large room, it was crammed with an astonishing number of books. The walls were lined with shelves overflowing with volumes. MacNeil pulled one from the shelves. "This includes a history of Brunconia. It's written by Heinrich Muntz of the University of Heidelberg. I don't suppose you read German, Lady Selena."

"Not a word."

"But you may be interested in the illustrations in any case. I believe there is a very good engraving of the royal palace." He thumbed through the book, opening it to a picture of an impressive residence. "It doesn't look so impressive now. A fire destroyed the west wing and there was no money to rebuild it."

Selena stared at the picture for a time before turning the page. There were additional illustrations, drawings of a crown and scepter and some ornate necklaces. "The crown jewels of Brunconia," said MacNeil. "They are all lost now, doubtlessly scattered around Europe."

Selena turned another page to find more pictures of jewelry. Her eye alighted on one necklace, a pendant in the shape of a swan. "Good heavens," she said, looking over at MacNeil with a surprised look. "I have seen this! Lady Blackstone was wearing it at her salon."

MacNeil appeared very much interested. "Von Gessler's sister?"

Selena nodded. "She said it was an old family heirloom."

"Aye, that it is, but not her family's," said the professor disgustedly.

At that moment two ladies appeared in the library. "I do hope we aren't disturbing you, my dear," said one of them, a handsome woman in her thirties who smiled brightly at Selena. "We just arrived home and Tilly told us that you had a guest."

"Elizabeth," said MacNeil, ushering them inside. "You must come and meet Lady Selena. Lady Selena, may I present my wife, Elizabeth? And this young lady is our guest, Princess Frederica von Hohenthurn of Brunconia, who has just recently arrived in London."

Princess? Selena tried to mask her surprise as she curtsied to the young lady who was standing there regarding her with her remarkable hazel eyes. She certainly hadn't expected to meet a princess at the home of Professor MacNeil. The princess looked very young, perhaps only seventeen or eighteen. Petite and plump, she had a pretty doll-like countenance that was framed with blond curls. Princess Frederica was attired in a plain blue dress with high collar and long sleeves.

"And now we have two titled ladies in our home, Elizabeth," said MacNeil, smiling at his wife. "How many professors of history can say that?" He turned to Selena. "My wife was the princess's governess in Brunconia. Her highness will be staying with us for a time."

While Selena thought it extraordinary that a princess would come to London and reside with her former governess, she was far too well bred to reveal her surprise. Selena smiled at the young woman. "It is an honor to meet your highness."

"It is very good to meet you, Lady Selena," said the girl in excellent English.

"I do hope you will stay to tea, Lady Selena," said Mrs. MacNeil. "It will be ready in a moment."

"I should like that very much," said Selena, very eager to do so.

Mrs. MacNeil was delighted. While she was on intimate terms with members of Brunconian royalty, she had no such connection with the British aristocracy. The idea of having a duke's sister for tea was quite exciting. "Then do let us go to the drawing room."

MacNeil scooped up the book he had been showing Selena and they all made their way to the drawing room. They had scarcely sat down when two maids entered with the tea things.

"I do hope you weren't boring her ladyship with those old books of yours, John," said Mrs. MacNeil, smiling indulgently at her husband.

"Indeed not," said the professor. "Lady Selena wasn't in the least bored."

"No, indeed," said Selena. "I called on Professor MacNeil in order to learn about Brunconia. I didn't know I'd be fortunate enough to find Princess Frederica here."

"You wished to learn about my country?" said Frederica.

"Why, yes," said Selena. "I'm sure many people will want to know about Brunconia now that Prince Maximilian has come to England."

"Lady Selena has met Prince Maximilian," said MacNeil.

"You have?" said Frederica with more than a little interest. "How is he?"

"Very well," said Selena.

"Did you see him recently?"

"Yes, at Almack's," said Selena. "And I met him another time in a book shop."

"A book shop?" said Frederica. "That does not sound like Maximilian."

"He was there with his cousin Lord Heathfield," said Selena, suppressing a smile. "I imagine you know Prince Maximilian well."

Frederica nodded gravely. "Yes, very well." She put down her teacup. "Since I was very young."

"I daresay Prince Maximilian will be very pleased to see you, your highness," said Selena. "One always enjoys seeing a familiar face from home."

At this seemingly innocuous remark, Frederica looked at Selena with a strange expression, and then she burst into tears. "My poor dear," said Mrs. MacNeil, handing the young lady a handkerchief. "There, there, don't cry, my pet."

"Oh, I am sorry," said Selena, as Frederica sobbed into Mrs. MacNeil's handkerchief.

"It is only that Princess Frederica cannot see Maximilian. Indeed, she promised she wouldn't see him," explained Mrs. MacNeil, placing a sympathetic arm around the girl's shoulders.

"How can I bear it?" cried Frederica between sobs. "Not to see him!"

The professor stared at his wife and her young guest for a moment. Then, being extremely hungry, he took up a lemon tart and began to eat it. "You must try one of these, Lady Selena," he said. "Our cook's recipe is quite delicious."

"Thank you, Mr. MacNeil," said Selena, feeling very awkward as Frederica continued to weep in a plaintive fashion, "but perhaps I should leave."

"Oh, no," said Frederica, wiping tears from her face. "I am very sorry. I do not mean for you to go. I do apologize for such an outburst."

"But you are very upset," said Selena soothingly. "I'm sure it would be better if I left."

"No, I wish you to stay," said Frederica, pulling herself together. "I am very ashamed for acting so. I must explain, Lady Selena."

"There is no need to explain anything to me, I assure you."

"No, I wish you to understand." Frederica dabbed at her eyes with the sodden handkerchief. "You see, my father did not want me to leave Bruronia. But I was so miserable and so missed my dear Miss Thompson. Oh, I should say Mrs. MacNeil, of course. I so missed her that I begged Papa to allow me to go to London. Finally, he agreed, but I promised him that I would not see Maximilian. I gave him my solemn oath. And Maximilian is not to know I am here. Please do not tell him, Lady Selena."

"I shan't tell him," said Selena. "But why don't you wish him to know you are in town?"

The princess sighed. "Because we love each other so much. We had hoped to marry. But then it was suggested for Maximilian to marry Princess Charlotte. All agreed that such an alliance would be good for Brunconia. Princess Charlotte is so very rich and England is so powerful.

"Although Maximilian had no wish to marry anyone but me, he agreed to come to England to attempt to win Princess Charlotte's hand. He said that duty was more important than personal happiness." She sniffed. "He is right, of course. He must do what is good for Brunconia. That is why I mustn't see Maximilian. He mustn't think of me at all. Indeed, he has probably forgotten all about me."

"Oh, I'm sure he hasn't, your highness," said Selena. "No, how could he?"

"No, of course, he couldn't," said MacNeil. "Come, come, Princess Frederica, take heart. You must be brave. Indeed, you must take your mind off the prince. I'll tell you something you'll be interested in hearing." Wiping his fingers carefully on his linen napkin, he took up the book he had brought in from the library. After turning it to the page of illustrations of the Brunconian crown jewels, he handed it to Princess Frederica.

"Lady Selena has seen the swan necklace. Karl Joseph von Gessler's daughter has been wearing it."

"What!" cried Frederica, turning to Selena in astonishment. "You have seen this necklace?"

"Yes, not two days ago. Lady Blackstone said that her brother, Count von Gessler, was allowing her to wear it, but then she would return it to him for safekeeping."

The princess muttered a few words in German. "My dear!" cried Mrs. MacNeil, who appeared shocked at hearing such words coming from her former charge.

"I am sorry," said Frederica, "but it is hard to remain a lady when learning such a thing as this! One of the von Gesslers wearing the Swan of Brunconia! It must not be tolerated! We must get it back at once. It belongs to the royal family and our people."

"That may not be so easy," said the professor. "But perhaps there is something that could be done. I shall consult my good friend Richardson. He will know how the law would regard the matter."

"What Count von Gessler's father did is certainly dreadful," said Selena, "but do you believe he and his sister know the truth? They were very young when they left Brunconia."

"I don't doubt that this von Gessler knows all about it," said MacNeil. "I've heard about him from a friend of mine in Berlin.

He is a deceitful rogue who cares for nothing but increasing his fortune. It's said he even sells art forgeries."

"He does?" said Selena, thinking of her brother's ill-fated Tintoretto.

"Aye, he's a mercenary sort of man. It's said he has been involved in all manner of deceitful intrigues throughout Europe."

"Yes," said Frederica, frowning darkly, "it is horrible that a member of that family has the necklace. It is said that when the Swan of Brunconia was stolen, our luck left with it. I must find a way to get it back."

"My dear girl," said Mrs. MacNeil, "really there is nothing you can do. You must know that."

"But there must be, Tommie," said the princess, addressing Mrs. MacNeil by the nickname she had used for years. Noting the steely-eyed resolution in the girl's face, Selena found herself liking Princess Frederica. She knew that if she were in her position, she would feel the very same way.

"Well, if there are legal means, Richardson will know of them," said MacNeil.

"I must say I have learned a good deal about Brunconia today," said Selena. "And I have confirmed my feelings about Count von Gessler. I do wish there was something I could do about the necklace." Glancing over at the mantel clock, Selena realized that it was time for her to go. "I didn't know it was so late. I fear I must go. It was so good meeting you. Do call on me at Melford House. Perhaps you might come tomorrow afternoon."

"Why, how kind," said Mrs. MacNeil. "That would be lovely."

"I should like that," said Frederica, smiling at Selena.

"Good, then we will expect you." Selena rose from her chair, took her leave, and was soon on her way back to Melford House in the hired chaise.

18

Selena sat at her dressing table while her maid arranged her hair, tying the long red tresses up into a knot at the back of her head and carefully fixing the curls that fell around her face. As she stared into the mirror, Selena reflected on her visit to the MacNeils. It had been a great surprise meeting Princess Frederica. She wondered what Prince Maximilian would do if he discovered that she was in town.

"There, m'lady," said the maid, eying her handiwork with satisfaction. "I'm finished."

"Thank you, Betty," said Selena, rising from the dressing table.

At that moment Sophie peeked into Selena's dressing room. "Aunt Selena?"

"Good morning, Sophie."

The little girl smiled brightly as she entered the room. Fluff, who had been curled up on the floor while her mistress was having her hair done, jumped to her feet and raced over to greet Sophie. "Dear Fluffkins," said Sophie, kneeling down to receive the little spaniel's exuberant greeting. Then, once Fluff had calmed down a bit, she looked up at her aunt. "Could you take me to the park this morning? It is a lovely day."

"That is a good idea," said Selena. "But don't you have your lessons?"

"Oh, Miss Dobbs is in bed with a cold," she said, smiling happily. "What great good fortune!"

"Not for Miss Dobbs," said Selena, smiling in return.

"Oh, it is a pity for her," said Sophie, trying to sound appropriately sympathetic. "Yes, poor Miss Dobbs."

Selena laughed. "Yes, poor Miss Dobbs. I don't envy her at the best of times having to teach a minx like you."

Sophie grinned delightedly. "It would be great fun to go to the park. Fluff would like it, wouldn't you?" The dog wagged her tail enthusiastically.

"Well, I have no objection, Sophie, as long as your mother says you may go."

"Yes, she has said we may go after breakfast." She frowned suddenly. "But she wanted Nanny and Harold to go as well."

"What a very good idea," said Selena.

"But he is such a baby," said Sophie. "It is much better for just us to go."

"Don't be silly. It will do Harold good to have an outing. Now, let us go to breakfast. I'm quite hungry this morning."

Sophie expressed the opinion that she was utterly ravenous and the two of them left the room with Fluff running ahead.

They found Henrietta in the dining room. The duchess seemed in a cheerful mood although she was a trifle worried about other family members coming down with Miss Dobbs's cold. The duke was not there as he had had his breakfast early and was now holed up in the library with an architect who was supervising restoration work on one of the ducal residences.

Although Sophie suggested that her mother accompany them to the park after breakfast, Henrietta had a previous engagement with her dressmaker, who was coming to the house later that morning. The duchess was also adamant that Harold and Nanny go to the park, saying that Selena would be glad of having Nanny along to make Sophie behave herself.

Since the carriage was having a wheel replaced, it was decided that they would walk to the park. And so after breakfast the little group started out from the house with Selena and Sophie walking in front followed by Nanny and Harold. Selena was dressed in a stylish pelisse of gray-blue silk and matching bonnet. Sophie wore her favorite pelisse, a wine-colored creation with military style epaulets and gold braid trim on the front and a new bonnet adorned with satin ribbons. Holding Fluff's leash, Sophie walked proudly. She knew that she and her aunt looked very fashionable.

They hadn't walked very far when a carriage pulled up alongside them. Glancing over, Selena was surprised to recognize the two ladies seated in the phaeton as Mrs. MacNeil and Princess Frederica.

"Lady Selena," cried Mrs. MacNeil, waving to them.

"Why, it is Mrs. MacNeil and Princess Frederica," said Selena.

"Princess?" Sophie's eyes grew wide.

Smiling, Selena walked over to the carriage. "How good to see you."

"You must think we are quite dreadful appearing at such an hour," said Mrs. MacNeil. "I was taking Princess Frederica out this morning to see some of town. My uncle loaned us his carriage, dear man that he is. We both wanted to see where you live so I had the driver go by Melford House."

"I must introduce you to my niece and nephew," said Selena. "This is Lady Sophie and this is Harold, Lord Hillsborough. And Nanny Walters and this is Fluff. Children, these ladies are Mrs. MacNeil and Princess Frederica of Brunconia."

Sophie made a well-practiced curtsy and Harold bowed politely.

"What lovely children," said Frederica, smiling warmly at them. "And such an adorable little dog."

Sophie regarded the ladies with keen interest. She was thrilled at meeting a princess. She thought Frederica very pretty even though she didn't seem as grandly dressed as one would expect for a princess. Indeed, Frederica was wearing a very plain dove-gray pelisse and a wide-brimmed hat adorned with silk roses. Observing that the hat looked rather old and faded, Sophie wondered why the princess didn't stop by one of the fashionable milliners and buy something more modish.

"And what do you think of London, your highness?" said Selena.

"It is very grand," said Frederica. "And so much of everything! I do like it exceedingly well."

"You have a fine day for a walk," said Mrs. MacNeil.

"Yes," said Selena. "I am taking the children to the park."

"Perhaps you might come with us," said Sophie. "There is a pond and there are ducks."

"Ducks?" said Frederica with a smile. "I love ducks very much. I wonder if English ducks are like Brunconian ducks."

"You might come and see," said Sophie eagerly.

"How very kind, Lady Sophie," said Mrs. MacNeil, "but we shouldn't intrude."

"You aren't intruding at all," said Selena. "The park isn't very far. We could meet you there."

"Could we not walk, Tommie?" said Frederica, looking at her former governess. "We have been riding such a long time."

"Why not?" said Mrs. MacNeil. She addressed the driver. "Rogers, we will walk to the park. Do meet us there."

The driver nodded, and then he jumped down to assist the women down from the phaeton. They all set off down the street.

Frederica, who dearly loved children, made a great fuss over them, telling Sophie that she looked very beautiful, that Harold was as handsome a boy as she had ever seen, and Fluff was an exceedingly fine dog. Such remarks as well as her bright smile quickly endeared her to Selena's niece and nephew.

Harold took her hand. "Are you a real princess?" he said, looking up at her.

"Yes, a Brunconian princess," she said. Then she added a trace wistfully, "But that is not so grand as an English princess, I will admit."

Selena, who had heard this remark, was certain that Frederica was thinking of Princess Charlotte. Poor girl, thought Selena. How dreadful it must be to be in love and know that the man she wishes to marry must wed someone else.

Selena walked alongside Mrs. MacNeil. That lady glanced back at Frederica, who was now laughing with the children. "I must say I am relieved to see the princess appearing so cheerful. I fear she has been quite melancholy."

"One can easily understand it," said Selena.

"Yes," replied Mrs. MacNeil. "But I hope that I can keep her busy meeting new people and seeing new things."

"That is a good idea," said Selena. "I know that my sister-in-law can arrange a good many invitations for you. I shall be happy to speak to her."

"I do appreciate that, Lady Selena," said Mrs. MacNeil, "but Frederica doesn't wish to go about in Society. She fears meeting Maximilian, you see. And besides that, she hasn't proper clothes for appearing in the first circles. Her family is very poor. But you mustn't worry. London has many distractions. And soon we'll be going back to our home at Cambridge. We have many friends there, and I believe Princess Frederica will enjoy it."

"Yes, I'm sure she will," said Selena.

When they arrived at the park, Frederica proclaimed it very lovely. There were large flowerbeds ablaze with color and the grass was brilliantly green in the bright sunshine.

The children soon were pulling Princess Frederica toward the pond where she was to inform them how English ducks compared to Brunconian ones. Nanny Walters followed behind, cautioning his young lordship to stay far away from the edge of the water.

Frederica, who was thoroughly enjoying herself, waved toward Mrs. MacNeil and Selena. "Tommie! Lady Selena! Do come!"

They started across the grass. Selena caught sight of a tall figure walking briskly down the path with a large dog at his side. Recognizing Heathfield, Selena was filled with the sense of excitement the sight of him always engendered. Seeing her, he raised his tall hat. She hesitated.

"What a handsome man," said Mrs. MacNeil. A shrewd woman, she could tell by Selena's expression that the younger woman was more than moderately interested in the newcomer. "Oh, I must join Frederica and the children. But do wait for the gentleman. I can see he'd like to speak with you."

Selena hoped that the color wasn't rising to her cheeks. Mrs. MacNeil walked away, leaving Selena to stand there watching the earl approach.

His long strides crossed the ground quickly and soon he was standing before her. "Lord Heathfield," she said, fixing her green eyes on his blue ones.

"Lady Selena," he said, tipping his hat and bowing slightly.

"Good morning, Duncan," said Selena, looking down at the huge hound.

Duncan wagged his tail sedately and Selena reached over to stroke his neck. "But where is Fluff?" said his lordship.

"With the children," said Selena nodding toward the pond.

"I didn't recognize the lady who was with you."

"That is Mrs. MacNeil."

"I don't believe I know her," said the earl.

"Her husband is Professor MacNeil," said Selena. "He is an historian."

"MacNeil?" said his lordship. "Not John MacNeil, the author of *The Holy Roman Empire*?"

"Why, yes," said Selena, regarding him in surprise. "I believe Miss Foxworth said he had written a book on that subject."

"Miss Foxworth? The lady publisher?"

"Yes."

"I must say, you've met some interesting people. I didn't know Miss Foxworth appeared at Society functions."

"I met her at Lady Blackstone's," said Selena.

"Lady Blackstone's? Oh, yes, the famous salon."

"You've never been there?"

"I've heard Henry Travers recites his poetry there." He made a face. "I felt it best to stay away. Oh, I am sorry. I know you're fond of his work."

"I daresay I'm not nearly as fond of it as I once was," said Selena. "Meeting the poet has rather disillusioned me."

Heathfield smiled again. "But if one can meet Miss Foxworth and John MacNeil there, perhaps I should visit Lady Blackstone's."

"Oh, I didn't meet Mr. MacNeil there. I consulted Miss Foxworth about who might know about the Brudonian situation and she suggested I see Professor MacNeil. You see, I had heard Count von Gessler's account of his family's ill treatment at the hands of Prince Maximilian's father. You told me a very different story so I wished to hear about it from an unimpeachable source."

"Then I'm not an unimpeachable source?"

Selena smiled. "You are Prince Maximilian's cousin."

"And prejudiced in his favor. So you called on MacNeil?"

She nodded. "And he knew all about the count's father. It is true that he behaved in an infamous manner, betraying his trust and stealing from the royal treasury. Why, he even stole the crown jewels of Bruconia!

"This is certainly true for I saw Lady Blackstone wearing a swan necklace that appeared in a book on Bruconia that Professor MacNeil showed me. Poor Princess Frederica was very upset to hear of it."

"Princess Frederica?" said Heathfield. "Princess Frederica of Bruconia?"

Selena put her hand to her mouth, realizing that she had been terribly indiscreet. She had promised Princess Frederica that she wouldn't inform Maximilian that she was in town, and now she'd told his cousin. "Oh, dear."

"You can't mean that Princess Frederica is in London?"

"Yes, she is in town. Indeed, there she is by the pond with the children. But I promised her that I wouldn't tell Prince Maximilian."

"It appears she came a very long way to win him back," said Heathfield, staring over at Frederica. "Why else would she have come here?"

"She was miserable and missed Mrs. MacNeil, who was her governess. And I believe she sincerely wishes to avoid Prince Maximilian. She knows it is his duty to marry Princess Charlotte. I implore you not to say a word to him."

"Well, I must say this business of Maximilian's marrying Princess Charlotte never seemed very likely to me. I can't see the harm in telling Max. He's been very homesick lately. Indeed, today he stayed in bed, complaining of a stomach upset. It would do him good to see her."

"Oh, no, he mustn't. He must make a wealthy marriage, and Princess Frederica is very poor."

"Well, I thank Providence that I may marry for love," said his lordship, directing a meaningful look at her.

"That is something few princes may do," said Selena, blushing in what his lordship thought was a charming manner.

"Did you tell Princess Frederica about the duel?"

"No, I didn't wish to upset her. I cannot imagine what she'd do if she heard of it." Selena frowned. "You must dissuade your cousin from meeting von Gessler."

"He is very set upon dueling. I've told him what I think of it. But Maximilian isn't reasonable where von Gessler is concerned."

Selena nodded gravely. "I tried my best to convince the count that dueling with your cousin was a very bad idea. When I saw him at Lady Blackstone's, I told him that Prince Maximilian was a crack shot and that he had killed three men already in duels."

"The devil you say!" exclaimed the earl.

She smiled. "I don't know that he believed me. And even if he did, I daresay it probably won't matter."

"Well, it may unnerve him a bit," said his lordship. "But I have no intention of allowing my royal cousin to get killed in a duel." He grinned. "After all, how could I ever visit Brunconia after taking such bad care of the heir to the throne?" They smiled at each other. "I haven't said that I think you look dashed beautiful."

Selena looked into his eyes and she had a most unladylike urge to throw herself into his arms. "You are too kind, my lord," she said softly.

At that moment a childish shout made Selena turn away from the earl. "Duncan!" Sophie was running toward them, chasing the deerhound with Fluff racing beside her. Harold was hurrying after them as fast as he could until Nanny Walters snatched him up into her arms. Frederica and Mrs. MacNeil followed behind at a more sedate pace.

Duncan was soon before them, wagging his tail happily. Coming up to him, Sophie threw her arms around the dog's neck. "Dear, dear Duncan!" she said.

The big hound endured her childish exuberance with good spirits, while Fluff started barking wildly, apparently disturbed by Sophie's display of affection for a canine rival.

"Fluff, it's Duncan!" said Sophie. "Really, you must behave yourself."

Fluff continued to bark, causing Selena to scoop her up. "Calm yourself, you silly girl." Fluff stopped barking, but looked down at the enormous dog rather indignantly.

Heathfield laughed. "Poor Fluff." He smiled down at Sophie. "Good morning, Lady Sophie."

"Good morning, Lord Heathfield," said the girl.

By this time Nanny Walters, Mrs. MacNeil, and Frederica had joined them. Mrs. MacNeil had told her former charge that Lady Selena had seemed very interested in the gentleman who appeared in the park. Having a very romantic nature, Frederica was very pleased to hear it.

Selena hesitated, unsure if she should introduce Heathfield. Sophie stepped in. "Lord Heathfield, you must meet Princess Frederica and Mrs. MacNeil." She turned to grin at the ladies. "May I present Lord Heathfield?"

At the name Heathfield, Frederica had turned a bit pale.

"Your servant, your highness," said his lordship, bowing politely, first to Frederica and then Mrs. MacNeil. "Mrs. MacNeil."

"Lord Heathfield," said the princess, regarding him in confusion.

"Don't be alarmed, Princess," said Heathfield. "Lady Selena has told me I mustn't tell Maximilian you're here. I give you my solemn promise that I won't say a word to him."

"Oh, I do thank you, my lord," said Frederica. "I do hope Maximilian is well."

"Very well, although he had a slight stomach upset today. I'm sure he'll be fine very soon."

Frederica seemed so alarmed at this news that the earl wished he hadn't said anything about his cousin's indisposition. "He is ill?" she cried.

"Oh, no, not really ill," insisted his lordship.

"You mustn't worry, my dear," said Mrs. MacNeil.

"No, you shouldn't worry at all," said Heathfield. "No, Prince Maximilian is doing very well. Of course, he misses Brunconia."

"Does he?" said Frederica, rather heartened by this remark.

"Oh, yes."

"And you won't say I am here?"

"No, I shan't say a word," said his lordship.

"It is best that way," said Frederica with a sigh.

Noting that Sophie was listening with an intent expression, Selena thought it best to change the subject. "The princess has only recently arrived in England. Mrs. MacNeil was showing her London this morning. It was very lucky that they came by."

"Yes," said Frederica. "How fortunate to meet Lady Selena again and the children. And this is a lovely park."

"And Princess Frederica said that our ducks are far more handsome than Brunconian ducks," said Sophie.

They all laughed. "I'm sure her highness is only being polite," said Selena. "I daresay there are fine ducks in Brunconia."

Frederica smiled and admitted that, yes, there certainly were handsome ducks in her homeland as well.

19

When Henrietta was informed by a very excited Sophie that they had met an actual princess, the duchess had been astonished to hear that the lady in question was a princess of Brunconia. Selena was very glad that Sophie tactfully kept quiet about meeting Heathfield.

Once Sophie and Harold had been taken to the nursery, the duchess asked Selena how she had met Princess Frederica. Selena tried to be as vague as possible, leaving Henrietta rather confused.

Yet because the duchess had a good deal on her mind that day, she didn't pursue the subject. In the evening there was to be a party at Melford House. A good many people had been invited and the servants had been rushing about all day preparing for the event.

Selena and Henrietta spent the afternoon going over some final preparations for the party. When it was time to dress, Henrietta hurried away, eager to make ready.

In the evening when the guests began to arrive, Selena did her best to appear charming and pleasant to everyone. She was glad that Count von Gessler didn't appear for she wasn't sure how she could be civil to him. Lady Blackstone arrived with her husband, and Selena was polite but rather distant to her.

As the night progressed, the ducal residence was filled with the chatter of guests and the sound of the orchestra. Many eager gentlemen flocked around Selena, begging her to reserve them a dance.

Knowing how important the occasion was for her sister-in-law, Selena tried to be gracious to everyone, agreeing to dance with any who asked her. After a while she grew rather tired of dancing and she was glad when it was time for supper. The guests just as eagerly abandoned the dancing in order to take advantage of the sumptuous repast set upon long tables adorned with flowers, fruit and blazing candles set in candelabras.

While she was sitting eating her food, Selena had the distinct impression that people were staring at her. Of course, she had become accustomed to exciting the interest of members of Society.

Yet, as Selena sat at the table, chatting with the lady on her right, it seemed that the guests were exhibiting more than the usual amount of interest in her. While she told herself that she was imagining things, she had the impression that people were talking about her. In particular there was a man named Boswith, a gentleman she knew only very slightly, who kept looking in her direction and then leaning over to say something to his companion.

As the evening went on, Selena felt increasingly uncomfortable. After the supper, there was entertainment, first an excellent tenor and then a talented pianist. Selena tried to concentrate on the music, but she was unsettled by the number of ladies who kept talking behind their fans and then looking over at her with knowing smiles.

When the affair was finally over, Selena was relieved. "I must say it went splendidly," said Henrietta, tired but elated at the obvious success of her party.

Eager to go to bed, Selena said good night to her sister-in-law and then started to leave. "One moment, Selena," said Melford, who had come up behind her.

"Yes, James?" said Selena, turning to see that the duke had a grim expression on his face. "Is something the matter?"

"Yes, is something wrong, my dear?" said Henrietta.

Melford looked around, noting the army of servants tidying up after the guests. "Come to the library. We can talk there."

Selena was quite perplexed. "I'm so very tired, James. Whatever it is, can't we discuss it in the morning?"

"No, it is best discussed now."

Henrietta seemed very alarmed at her husband's tone. "What is wrong, my dear?"

"Let us go to the library," said Melford, taking his wife's arm and escorting her out. Selena followed them wearily. Walking into the library, she sank down into the closest chair. "What is it, James?"

"Yes, do tell us," said Henrietta.

"Before he took his leave this evening, Sir Richard Oglesby

told me something I found utterly astonishing." He frowned at Selena. "There is a rumor going about that you and Heathfield are secretly engaged."

"What!" cried Henrietta, regarding her sister-in-law with amazement. "It can't be true!"

"It isn't true," exclaimed Selena.

"It isn't?" said Melford, very relieved at his sister's denial.

"No, it isn't," said Selena. "Why would Sir Richard tell you such a thing?"

"He said that no one scarcely talked of anything else all evening. It seems young Cecil Boswith was putting it about," replied the duke. "Oglesby felt obliged to tell me as a friend of the family."

Selena frowned. So she hadn't been mistaken in thinking that people were watching her. The guests had been discussing her alleged engagement.

"And he heard it from Cecil Boswith?" said Henrietta.

Melford nodded. "And Boswith told Oglesby that he was told the news from Prince Maximilian von Stauffenburg."

"Well, this is very peculiar to be sure," said Henrietta. "I can't imagine why Prince Maximilian would have told him such a thing."

"I can imagine it," said the duke. "I am sure that Heathfield is behind it. He started the rumor, knowing how furious I'd be."

"That is ridiculous," said Selena.

"Is it? I don't think so. Heathfield has been the bane of my existence for years. I don't think there is anything he wouldn't do to vex me. Yes, he is the sort of man to do something like this. Now everyone in Society will be linking your name with his. It's monstrous!"

"Well, I think you are making too much of it," said Selena hotly. "I will not hear any more about it. I am very tired and it is late. I'm going to bed." Rising from her chair, she walked out of the room, leaving Melford to complain to his wife about Heathfield's treachery.

In the morning Selena awakened to a dreary wet day with rain falling steadily. She had slept surprisingly well and the morning was already well advanced by the time she dressed.

Looking out onto the rain-soaked street below, Selena appeared thoughtful. So everyone in Society now thought she was engaged to marry Heathfield?

It was a peculiar and vexatious situation. How had the rumor gotten started, she wondered. Surely Heathfield had nothing to do with it. Or had he?

Frowning, Selena turned away from the window. She must see Heathfield. Yes, she should call on him at once. But how was that possible? She could hardly go to his home unaccompanied. And Henrietta would never agree to go with her knowing how Melford felt.

Selena pondered the problem. Perhaps she would see him in the park. Yes, he very likely would appear there again. But it was raining too hard for a walk this morning and one couldn't depend on good weather tomorrow. Perhaps she might send him a note, telling him about the rumor.

Thinking that this was the best solution, Selena sat down at her desk and took out a piece of paper. Yet when she had dipped her pen into the ink, she found she couldn't think what to say to him. It would be far better to speak with him. Indeed, it seemed very indiscreet to discuss such matters in a letter.

After considering the matter for a time, Selena had an idea. She began to write. "My Lord, Will you meet me at Rutledge and Jones, Booksellers, at 2 o'clock tomorrow afternoon? I have a matter I must discuss with you. Selena P." She blotted the brief message and then folded it, sealed it with candle wax and addressed it. When she was done, she called for her lady's maid and requested that Betty post the letter at once.

The Earl of Heathfield sat at the breakfast table, eating a piece of buttered toast and thinking about his cousin Maximilian. He hadn't seen Maximilian that morning for the prince had risen early and gone out. Heathfield had been surprised to hear this for his royal cousin had spent most of the previous day in his room, feeling rather unwell.

When the earl had arrived home after seeing Selena and Princess Frederica in the park, he had wished he could have told Maximilian that his lady love was nearby. Yet, he had promised the princess that he wouldn't tell Maximilian and so he had kept silent despite a strong urge to do otherwise.

Rising from his chair, the earl went to the sideboard and took some kippers from a silver chafing dish. He thought of Selena and how splendid she looked when he last saw her.

As he brought his plate to the table, the door opened and in came Maximilian and Percy. They both appeared to be in exceedingly good spirits.

"Good morning, Charles," said Percy, smiling broadly. "It is a fine day, isn't it?"

"A fine day?" said the earl. "The last time I looked out the window it was gloomy and raining."

"Yes, that is true," said Percy, "but it is a fine day, nevertheless. And I feel ravenous. You don't mind if I have a bit of breakfast, do you?"

"Of course not," said his lordship, sitting down at the table. "But how are you feeling, Max?"

"Ah, much better, my dear Heathfield," said Maximilian, piling food onto his plate. "Yes, I feel very good. *Ja, sehr gut.*"

"We have what seems very good news," said Percy. "Can you guess where we've been?"

"I shouldn't even try," said his lordship.

"We have been to von Gessler's house."

"Whatever for?"

"To make the arrangements for the duel."

"Good God!" exclaimed the earl.

"You see, I agreed to be Max's second. I knew you'd be angry."

"Indeed I am!"

"Well, he had no one else to ask. There was only you and I, and you were so adamant about refusing."

"I begged Percy to help me," said Maximilian. "He did not wish to do so."

"Now before you take me to task, cousin," said Percy, "allow me to tell you the good news. Von Gessler has flown off. He's left town for the country. And his servant said he's not expected back for several weeks."

"What can it mean but that he is a coward who will not meet me on the field of honor?" said Maximilian.

"Well, I'm damned," said the earl. "It must have been what Selena said to him."

"What do you mean?" said Percy.

"When I saw her yesterday in the park, she told me that she'd informed von Gessler that Max was a crack shot and that he'd killed three men. She was hoping that the count would be more concerned about saving his skin than his honor."

"What a splendid girl," said Percy. "This is famous news, isn't it, Max? It appears we don't need to worry about the duel."

"But if there is no duel I shall not be able to obtain satisfaction from that villain."

"We'll think of some other way so that von Gessler will get his comeuppance," said Percy. "Indeed, I think the best thing would be for Max to succeed with Princess Charlotte. Von Gessler won't like it in the least to see our Max married to the future Queen." He grinned broadly. "And that is the other wonderful news. We are expected at Warwick House tomorrow afternoon for tea with Princess Charlotte!"

The earl noted that Maximilian didn't seem to share Percy's enthusiasm for this news. "That is very good," said Heathfield. "Indeed, Max, you'll finally be meeting the princess."

Maximilian nodded glumly.

"You will come with us, Charles?" said Percy.

"I daresay you won't need me," said Heathfield, but Percy was insistent. However, later that day when the evening post arrived, the earl received Selena's note. After reading it, he decided that his cousins must see Princess Charlotte by themselves. He had a more important engagement.

20

In the morning Selena suggested to Henrietta that they go shopping in the afternoon. Since the duchess enjoyed nothing better, she was more than happy to agree. After all, declared Henrietta, she was in great need of a new hat and she was always eager to visit her favorite milliner's shop.

Later that day when the two ladies set off in the ducal carriage, Henrietta could talk of nothing but hats. Selena, while she didn't share her sister-in-law's passion for the milliner's art, chatted amiably about the new styles of hats and bonnets as portrayed in the lady's magazines.

By the time they arrived at the milliner's shop, Henrietta was very eager to see what was new there. After a servant assisted the ladies down from the carriage, Selena turned to the duchess. "Could we go to the bookshop first, Hetty?" said Selena, motioning toward the bookseller's establishment, which was located a short distance away.

"Books?" said Henrietta. "I thought we had come to see hats."

"Yes, of course, but I also wanted to buy a new book. It won't take long."

"Why, you always take so long poking about in there," said the duchess.

Selena tried not to smile. She'd been counting on her sister-in-law's being far more eager to look at hats than books. "I have an idea, Henrietta. You go into Madame Claire's and I shall go have a look at the new books. Then I'll join you."

"Yes, I suppose that would be all right, my dear," said Henrietta, "but you must promise not to take too long. I shall need your opinion on the hats."

Taking her leave of the duchess, Selena walked to the bookstore. There she stood looking at books and awaiting the earl's arrival. It was a quarter of an hour before two o'clock and Selena hoped that Heathfield would be prompt.

A few minutes later, she saw his tall, handsome figure enter the shop. Catching sight of her, he smiled and hurried to her side. "I was very surprised to receive your note. Is something the matter?"

Selena looked down at the book she had been examining and then back up at him. "There was a party at Melford House last night."

"I wish I could have been there," he said, fixing his blue eyes on her face. "I would have liked to dance with you again."

This remark rather disconcerted her, but she regained her composure quickly. "There was a rumor being spread about that you and I are secretly engaged to be married. My brother was very upset. He thought that you had started the rumor, knowing how angry he would be to hear it."

The earl's dark eyebrows registered surprise. "You don't believe that?"

"No," said Selena, shaking her head. "But the man who told my brother of the rumor said that he'd heard it from someone who heard it from your cousin, Prince Maximilian."

"Why, that is utterly ridiculous," said his lordship. "Max wouldn't say such a thing."

"It is all very odd."

"Yes, I should say it is," said Heathfield. He grinned. "But it is a pity to waste what seems to me a splendid rumor. Why don't we become engaged? Will you marry me?"

"I do think you could be serious."

"But I am completely serious."

Selena looked up at him, noting that his eyes had a mischievous gleam. "It would serve you right if I said yes."

"Then you *will* marry me?"

Selena blushed, aware that a man and woman near them were listening to their conversation. "Really, my lord," she whispered.

Heathfield lowered his voice. "Why shouldn't we marry?"

"For one thing, we hardly know each other," said Selena, frowning at him. "And another, my brother would disown me."

"Lady Selena!" A feminine voice startled Selena. Turning around, she was rather dismayed to recognize Lady Blackstone. The fashionable baroness was splendidly attired in an elegant dress and primrose-colored spencer. Her blond curls peeked out from beneath an attractive French bonnet.

Lady Blackstone was regarding Heathfield with keen interest.

"Lady Blackstone," said Selena, feeling very awkward.

"I do not believe I have met this gentleman," said the baroness, adopting the seductive smile she reserved for dashing gentlemen.

While Selena had no wish to introduce them, she seemed to have no alternative. "Lady Blackstone, may I present Lord Heathfield?"

"Lord Heathfield?" said the baroness. "Yes, of course. How good it is to finally meet you."

"Your servant, Lady Blackstone," said the earl, bowing politely.

"I have heard so much about you, my lord," said Lady Blackstone. "I know that you are a connoisseur of fine art like my brother."

"Your brother, madam?" said the earl, feigning ignorance.

"Count von Gessler."

"Oh, yes, Count von Gessler," said Heathfield, exchanging a glance with Selena. "I haven't had the pleasure of meeting the count. I heard he has gone to the country."

"He has gone to the country?" said Selena, very much surprised.

"Yes, business called him there. He has a house in Sussex, you know."

"I'm sure your brother hated to leave London at such a time," said the earl, smiling at Selena. "One misses so many interesting events."

"Yes, that is true," said Lady Blackstone. "I know my brother hated to miss the lovely party at Melford House, Lady Selena. It was quite wonderful." She smiled meaningfully at Selena. "The conversation was so very interesting."

"Yes, it was a nice party," said Selena, silently cursing her ill luck to be seen by Lady Blackstone. It was a very awkward situation and she was certain that Lady Blackstone would waste no time in spreading it about that she had seen the two of them together. Of course, it had been interesting to learn that von Gessler had left London. Did that mean that he had abandoned the duel?

"So you are a book lover, Lord Heathfield?" said the baroness, batting her long eyelashes at him.

"I am very fond of books," he replied.

"Then I must tell you of a wonderful new work by a protégé of mine." Lady Blackstone started talking about a novelist she had taken under her wing.

Selena stood there trying to look interested, but she wished that Lady Blackstone would take her leave. She thought suddenly of Henrietta. The duchess would soon begin to wonder what had become of her. It would never do for Henrietta to come to the book shop to find her and discover her there with Heathfield. At the first opportunity, Selena announced that she must be going, and then hurried off, leaving a much delighted Lady Blackstone alone with the earl.

21

After arriving home from the bookshop, Heathfield retired to his library to write some letters. Sitting down at his desk with Duncan stretched out nearby, he found himself thinking of his meeting with Selena. When it was nearly five o'clock, Maximilian and Percy came in.

Percy looked particularly pleased. "Well, Charles, it went exceedingly well. Princess Charlotte seemed to like our cousin."

"Did she?" said the earl.

"Oh, yes," said Percy. "The visit went splendidly."

"Do tell me all about it," said Heathfield as his cousins seated themselves across from his desk.

"Well, Princess Charlotte looked very well," said Percy. "And she was very pleasant to us. Miss Knight and the Duchess of Leeds were there as chaperones. The duchess is a good friend of Aunt Margaret's, you know, so we had a long discussion of Uncle Roger's gout. And then the Princess asked Max about Brunconia and we had tea."

"The teacakes were very good," said Maximilian.

"I do believe Princess Charlotte was quite taken with Maximilian," said Percy. "Yes, the visit went very well indeed." Percy glanced at the ornate clock that stood in the corner of the library. Realizing that he had another engagement, he said farewell and left the library, whistling a sprightly tune.

When he had gone, Maximilian cradled his head on his hands and sighed. "I fear she liked me, Cousin Heathfield."

"You should be pleased."

"But perhaps she will wish to marry me."

"My dear Max, isn't that the idea?"

"Of course, but I don't want to marry her. It isn't that I didn't like her. But I want to marry Frederica. I am in love with her. I think about her so far away in Brunconia. Now that I am gone there will be many suitors. And how can I bear it if someone else marries Frederica?

"But I must not think of that. I must do my duty for my country. If Princess Charlotte will have me, I must marry her."

Heathfield eyed his cousin sympathetically. "Don't lose heart, Max. After all, you don't know for sure that the Princess wants to marry you. And one never knows what the Prince Regent thinks. He blows hot and cold often enough."

Maximilian made no reply, but sat glumly in his chair.

"There is something I must ask you, Max," said the earl. "I heard the oddest story—that you told someone that I was secretly engaged to Lady Selena."

A sheepish expression appeared on the prince's beefy countenance. "I am sorry."

"You mean you did say that?"

Maximilian nodded. "Yes, I did. I should not have told, but I was rather drunk, you see. I know you didn't wish anyone to know of it."

"You mean you believe that I am secretly engaged to Lady Selena?"

"Then it is not true?"

The earl shook his head. "Why on earth did you think so?"

Maximilian looked down and said nothing.

"Was it Percy? Did he tell you that?" When Maximilian remained silent, Heathfield nodded. "So it was Percy. I shall have to find out why he would have told you this."

"But I thought you were in love with Lady Selena."

"I am in love with her," he said matter-of-factly. "Yes, I am. And I should like to marry her, but I am not nor have I ever been engaged. Well, I shall take this matter up with Percy when I see him. You look tired, Max. Why don't you rest before dinner?"

"You are very kind," said Maximilian, rising from his chair and exiting from the room.

Shortly after his cousin had left, Heathfield's butler appeared in the library. "Excuse me, my lord," said the servant, speaking without the slightest trace of emotion despite the fact that he knew his master would be quite amazed with the information he was about to impart, "but the Duke of Melford is here to see your lordship."

The earl's dark eyebrows arched in surprise. "The Duke of Melford?"

"Yes, my lord. I showed his grace to the drawing room."

"Very good, Preston," said Heathfield, and the servant nodded and retreated from the room.

The earl sat for a moment longer at his desk, pondering what his unexpected caller could want. "It must have something to do with this rumor being put about town that I am engaged to Selena," he said, addressing Duncan, who was lying near his feet. The deerhound regarded his master questioningly, causing the earl to smile as he rose from his chair. Well, he would find out what Melford wanted.

As he left the library, Heathfield resolved to be on his best behavior. It was important that he mend his unfortunate relationship with the duke. After all, the fellow was Selena's brother and he would be his brother-in-law.

Making his way to the drawing room, the earl opened the door to find his guest standing before one of his paintings. "Melford," he said in a genial voice, smiling over at the duke.

That gentleman abruptly turned around and regarded the earl with a sour expression. "Heathfield," he said coldly.

Undeterred by this unpromising greeting, the earl walked over toward the duke. "I just bought that Rubens. What do you think of it?"

Melford, who had been eyeing the painting enviously a moment before, gave an indifferent shrug. "An adequate example of his lesser works," he sniffed.

Heathfield found himself thinking that the duke was an annoying individual, but he only smiled. "You didn't come here to talk about art, did you, Melford?"

"No, I did not," returned the duke.

"Sit down, Melford," said his lordship, gesturing to a chair.

"I prefer to remain standing," replied the duke, crossing his arms in front of him and regarding Heathfield with a disdainful gaze. "What I have to say to you shall not take very long. I have only come to tell you to stay away from my sister."

"Come, Melford, I know we have had our differences in the past, but isn't it time we put them aside?"

"Time to put them aside?" sputtered the duke. "As if that can be so easily done! Why, you have enjoyed making sport of me ever since we were boys together at Eton. You buy paintings out from under my nose just to spite me. The Titan . . ." Melford suddenly stopped as if this episode was too painful to recount. "And now, you try to cause me pain by paying attentions to my sister. I can't think of anything you have done that is more despicable than that! For you to harm Selena and her good name just because you dislike me is contemptible!"

"Good God, Melford, don't be an idiot," muttered the earl, abandoning his attempt at diplomacy. "I hold your sister in the highest esteem. My feelings for her have nothing to do with you. I would never do anything to hurt her."

"Oh, you wouldn't?" returned Melford. "Well, you have already harmed her with this accurst rumor you have spread about town that you are engaged to her. Yes, I see you know what I'm talking about. I suppose you thought it a great joke to have my sister's name bandied about with yours."

"You are very much mistaken" said the earl, frowning. "I just learned of the rumor today. I don't know why the story was put about, but I promise you that I will get to the bottom of it."

The duke eyed him disapprovingly. "Yes, well it is too late now in any case. Selena's reputation has already been sullied by having her name connected with yours."

"Don't be absurd. I do wish to marry your sister. That will put an end to talk soon enough."

"You cannot honestly believe that I would allow you to marry Selena?" Melford appeared incredulous at the idea. "By God, I would never allow it. Not only are you my greatest enemy, but you are a rake and a scoundrel. You'd make her miserable. She deserves better than you, and I intend to make sure she marries someone worthy of her."

While up to this point, the earl had retained his composure admirably, these words and the sneering way in which they were said made him lose his temper. "Dammit, Melford, I have endured enough of your insults! I'd have you tossed out of my house if you weren't Selena's brother."

"I warn you, Heathfield, not to mention my sister's name again," snapped Melford.

The earl suddenly laughed. "God, Melford, you are the same insufferable ass that you were as a boy. I remember you at Eton and how you treated the boys who you felt were beneath your touch. Yes, I enjoyed giving you your comeuppance then and I still do."

Melford purpled with rage. "I forbid you to speak to my sister again! I won't allow you to even be in the same room with her!"

"Don't be a fool, Melford. It should be Selena's choice whether she wants to see me." He paused. "Or whether she decides to marry me."

The duke looked as if he might have an attack of apoplexy. "My sister will never marry you, Heathfield! And I cannot express my contempt for a man who would ruin the life of a wonderful girl only to hurt her brother."

"By God, Melford," said Heathfield in an angry voice, "this has nothing to do with you. Indeed, it is the greatest misfortune that Selena is your sister. It is clear that you know as little about my feelings for Selena as you do about art!"

"What?" cried the duke, momentarily taken aback by this remark. His face then grew livid with rage as the earl's insult took full effect on him. He shook his fist in the air. "You . . . you . . . blackguard! I should have you horsewhipped!"

"I suggest you get out of my house, Melford," said the earl in an icy tone, "or I will personally throw you out!" The duke hesitated for only an instant, and then he stormed out of the room.

After Melford had departed, Heathfield paced about angrily, swearing under his breath. It was intolerable, taking such abuse from that prig Melford, he thought. He had had every right to become furious with the duke. A man could only stand so much. Surely Selena would understand that.

With the thought of Selena, the earl stopped pacing and his angry look was replaced with a serious expression. Well, he had made a mess of it. He had hoped to mend fences with Melford. Now the duke hated him more than ever. Heathfield frowned. What would Selena think of him after hearing about this meeting?

Heathfield suddenly plopped down in a chair and stretched out his long legs before him. Yes, he had been a fool to lose his temper and insult the duke. How could he ever make amends with him now? Whatever Selena's feelings for him might be, how could she ever agree to marry a man her brother so despised? The earl glumly shook his head, reflecting that he had no idea how to set matters right.

22

Selena and Henrietta were seated in the drawing room discussing Henrietta's plans for a new garden walk when the duke stormed into the room. Still seething from his visit with Heathfield, he leaned against the mantelpiece and stood regarding the two women with an irate expression.

Henrietta noted her husband's countenance with alarm. "Good heavens, James," she said, "whatever is the matter?"

Selena, who was ensconced on the sofa next to her sister-in-law, also eyed the duke curiously. Her brother certainly appeared to be in a foul temper over something.

"I have just come from seeing Heathfield," said Melford, frowning grimly.

Selena could hardly have been more astonished. "Heathfield?" she repeated.

Henrietta's round face took on an even more concerned look. "You do not mean to say you called upon him, my dear?"

The duke nodded grimly. "I did. I felt it was my duty to do so for Selena's sake."

"For my sake?" said Selena, raising her eyebrows. A sudden flush appeared on her face. "Oh, James, what did you say to him?" she asked in a dismayed tone.

"I told him to stay away from you."

"What?" cried Selena.

"Oh, dear," said Henrietta, glancing from her sister-in-law to her husband and fearing for the worst.

The duke nodded. "I thought the fellow needed a talking to, spreading that rumor about that you and he were secretly engaged."

"But he didn't do any such thing," protested Selena.

"And how do you know that?" asked her brother coolly.

Selena hesitated for a second and then said defiantly, "Because I asked him about it when I saw him today."

"You saw Heathfield today?" said the duke. He fixed a severe look on his wife. "And why was I not told about this, Henrietta?"

Henrietta shook her head. "But I have been with Selena all day and I never saw the earl."

"We met in the bookstore," said Selena, casting a somewhat guilty look at her sister-in-law.

"The bookstore," said Henrietta, momentarily puzzled. A look of enlightenment seemed to strike her. "Oh, Selena, you didn't plan to meet him there?" When Selena didn't reply, her brother gazed at her in disbelief.

"Good God," he muttered, "so now you're arranging assignations with the man?"

"Don't be ridiculous," said Selena in a scornful voice. "It wasn't an assignation. I just wanted to find out if he knew anything about the rumor." She paused. "And he didn't."

Melford regarded her incredulously for a moment and then burst out angrily, "And you think you can believe a word he says? My dear sister, how can you be so beetle-brained? Meeting a notorious libertine like Heathfield in public! The gabblemongers will really have a field day now!"

"You are making too much of this, James," said Selena. "And I think you are very wrong in your estimation of Lord Heathfield's character."

After eyeing his sister as if she were a complete simpleton, he turned to his wife. "I fear he has won her affections with his deceit and trickery," he said sadly. He looked back at Selena. "I will tell you of Heathfield's sterling character. He is a rakehell, totally unscrupulous where women are concerned. He has had a score of mistresses and he is so indiscreet that any woman unfortunate enough to be his wife would soon be an object of pity. And if you believe he has affection for you, I must remind you that he has devoted himself to making my life miserable. He would think nothing of ruining your reputation just to get at me."

"That is ridiculous," began Selena, but he cut her off.

"Is it!" cried the duke. "He admitted that he has hated me since we were at Eton and that he has enjoyed vexing me. Yes, he thinks it is a great joke to do so, whether it is by taking a painting that I have wanted or by having a dalliance with my sister."

Selena's face had grown pale at these words. "I can't believe that he would behave in such an infamous manner," she said.

"My dear sister, I assure you that Heathfield is capable of

doing anything that he thinks would harm me," said Melford, pleased to see that he was finally making an impression on her. "The fellow formed a dislike of me during our school days, all because I didn't approve of some of his ill-bred friends. Why, you should have heard how he insulted me!"

Selena got up from the sofa. "If Lord Heathfield insulted you, James, I do not doubt that he was sorely provoked into doing so. Indeed, I feel quite provoked with you myself at this moment."

The duke's face reddened. "Don't be a fool, Selena. You are acting like a silly moonling over the man. You must stay away from him. In fact, I will see that you do!"

Selena regarded her brother with a furious look. "And what will you do, brother? Lock me in my room?"

"If need be," he said. "By God, Selena, I'm sorry you ever came to town. You should have stayed in the country. Yes, and perhaps you had better go back there before you disgrace yourself any further!"

Selena gave him one last angry look and then she hurried from the room.

"Oh, dear," said Henrietta, looking quite upset. The duke merely frowned again and decided that his sister had completely taken leave of her senses.

That evening Selena refused to come down to dinner, staying in her room with her dog Fluff as her sole companion. When she failed to appear at breakfast the following morning, Henrietta was quite concerned.

"James, shouldn't you speak to Selena?" she asked, watching him as he took up a piece of ham from his plate.

He stopped his fork in midair and looked at her. "I have nothing more to say to her," he said coldly. "I only hope that, on reflection, she will realize her folly."

Henrietta hesitated a moment. "But, my dear, what if Selena is in love with Heathfield? I very much fear that she is."

The duke scowled. "And what would you have me do? Let her marry the man?" He took a bite of the ham and eyed his wife somewhat resentfully.

Henrietta looked surprised. "You don't mean that Heathfield told you he wanted to marry Selena?"

James was chewing his food and took an infuriatingly long

time to reply to his wife's question. "He said something to that effect," he said.

"But, James," said Henrietta, "perhaps he is serious about marrying her."

Melford gave his wife a disapproving look. "Don't be a gudgeon, Henrietta. If he says he wants to marry her, it's only to plague me."

"But surely he wouldn't enter into a marriage with Selena simply to . . ." She stopped when she noted her husband's censorious expression. Sighing, she took up her own fork and half-heartedly pushed at the food on her plate.

The duke shook his head as he took up a piece of toast. "No, it is best that Selena leave town for a time until this all blows over. We must pack her off to Northumberland at first opportunity."

"Northumberland?" repeated Henrietta in dismay. "But my dear, do you think that wise? What if Heathfield should follow her there? It is very near to Scotland, after all."

Melford looked thoughtful. "That is true. She can't go back there alone."

Henrietta looked alarmed. "You can't think of us all going there, James?" she cried. Henrietta had never been overly fond of the wild countryside and provincial society of Melford Castle, and she shuddered to think that they would be staying there during the height of the Season in town.

The duke shook his head. He was not very desirous of leaving London, either, and especially not to go to his isolated ducal seat. "No, I shouldn't want to journey there now. But perhaps one of our other houses closer to town. I've heard that von Gessler has gone to his country estate that is very near to Gateswood Lodge." He paused. "I shall have to give it some thought."

Henrietta nodded. She wasn't particularly pleased at the thought of Gateswood Lodge, which had little more than pastoral scenery to recommend it. Still, it was far better than Melford Castle, which was remote, gloomy, and uncomfortable. Taking up her teacup, Henrietta wished that her sister-in-law had fallen in love with a more acceptable gentleman than the Earl of Heathfield.

23

Later that morning, Selena sat on a chair in her bedroom staring down at a book in her lap. After absently flipping a page, she closed the volume and placed it on a small table next to her. Glancing at the small dog at her feet, she sighed. "Oh, Fluff, what am I to do?"

Looking up at her mistress, Fluff cocked her head as if puzzling over the question. Selena smiled and reached down to lift the dog into her lap. How could James have done such a thing, going to see Heathfield like that? she asked herself for the thousandth time as she stroked Fluff's silky fur.

Selena sighed again. She had been quite disturbed at hearing about her brother's calling upon the earl the previous day. To think that James had gone there to tell Heathfield to stay away from her was too humiliating.

Still angry with her brother, Selena had remained in her room, having no wish to see him. James had had no right to treat her as if she were a misbehaving child, she thought. And she could only imagine the offensive things he had said to Heathfield. Really, James had behaved quite abominably, she decided.

Getting up from her chair, she carried Fluff over to the window. Selena looked down at the fashionable street below and remembered how her brother had said she should have stayed in the country. Well, perhaps James was right about that. She feared that coming to London had been a terrible mistake. She should go back home to Melford Castle and never see the Earl of Heathfield again.

Turning away from the window, Selena frowned. The idea of never seeing the earl again was quite upsetting. She thought of Heathfield, remembering the look in his blue eyes as he had smiled at her.

"Oh, Fluff," she said again, "I'm in a terrible muddle." Petting the spaniel's long ears, she shook her head. She couldn't deny it any longer. She was in love with Heathfield. It was really too ridiculous.

Her unhappy reflections were suddenly interrupted by a slight tap on the door. "Selena?" said Henrietta in a tentative voice. "Please, may I come in?"

Selena walked over to the door and opened it a crack. When she realized that Henrietta was alone, she swung it open wide. "Have you come to visit the prisoner?" she asked with a sardonic smile.

"Oh, Selena," said Henrietta, hurrying into the room, "I'm so sorry about yesterday. I fear James was rather . . . intemperate in going to see Heathfield like he did."

"He had no right to do such a thing, Hetty! What must Heathfield think?"

Henrietta regarded her sister-in-law closely. "You do care for him, don't you, my dear?"

Selena looked down at Fluff and then met her sister-in-law's gaze. "Yes, I confess that I do. But I assure you, Hetty, I'm not about to do anything foolish. It was very bad of James to act as if I was ready to fly off with Heathfield."

"You mustn't be too angry with James," said Henrietta quickly. "He is only concerned about you. And . . ." She paused. "Well, Selena, Heathfield does have a reputation with women. . . ."

"I know that well enough," said Selena. Realizing that she had spoken somewhat sharply, she smiled. "I'm sorry, Hetty. I'm afraid the whole business has made me quite cross. I was thinking that James might be right. The best thing may be for me to go back to Melford Castle."

"Oh, no, my dear, there is no need for such drastic measures," said Henrietta quickly. "I'm certain things will sort themselves out."

Although Selena could scarcely share her sister-in-law's optimism, she nodded. "Perhaps," she said doubtfully.

"Now do come with me for a walk, Selena," said the duchess. "It will do you good to get outside." When Selena hesitated, she added, "James has gone to see his tailor and then he was going to his club. He won't be back until much later."

Selena smiled. "Very well." After donning a pelisse and fetching her bonnet, she accompanied Henrietta outside.

After their walk to the park, the two ladies had luncheon. Then the two sisters-in-law spent some time with the children. When Sophie and Harold returned to the nursery, Selena and Henrietta made their way to the drawing room.

Once there, the duchess eagerly took up a new fashion magazine that had just arrived. Scanning the pages, Henrietta made comments on several of the designs, pushing the magazine over to Selena to get her opinion.

"I do like that dress, don't you, Selena?" asked Henrietta, casting an admiring glance down at one of the pictures. "Why, it would be splendid in that blue silk that you just bought the other day."

Selena smiled. "It is lovely, but truly, Henrietta, I have no need for another dress, especially if I am to return to Melford Castle."

"Oh, you mustn't think of returning there . . ." began her sister-in-law. She was interrupted by the appearance of the butler, who announced that they had visitors, the Princess Frederica and Mrs. MacNeil. After instructing the servant to usher the ladies in, Henrietta turned to Selena.

"This is a surprise," said Henrietta.

"I did ask the princess and Mrs. MacNeil to call upon us," said Selena.

"I do wish I had known they were coming," said Henrietta, glancing down at her dress. "I should have worn something else."

"Nonsense, Henrietta," said Selena, "that dress is charming." In fact, Henrietta did look very pretty in the stylish peach-colored muslin dress with its high neck and tight-fitting sleeves.

"But I'm not sure it is the thing for receiving a princess," said Henrietta doubtfully.

Thinking of the plain, worn frock Frederica had been wearing, Selena smiled. "You may trust me when I say you look quite grand enough to receive Princess Frederica."

Any fears Henrietta had about her wardrobe quickly disappeared as the young princess and her former governess entered the room. Although Frederica was very good looking with her blond hair and striking hazel eyes, she was attired in what Henrietta considered a rather shabby green pelisse, which the duchess suspected was several seasons old. The duchess noted that Mrs. MacNeil, while dressed rather plainly in a blue pelisse and plain bonnet, was better attired than her royal companion.

Although disappointed by her guests' lack of grandeur, Henrietta smiled at them and rose to receive them.

Selena made the introductions. "Princess Frederica, Mrs. MacNeil, may I present my sister-in-law, the Duchess of Melford?"

Frederica fixed a charming smile on her hostess. "Your grace, I am so pleased to meet you. And what a lovely home you have." Frederica looked around the room with an appreciative eye. "I have never seen such a charming room."

Henrietta beamed at this compliment and urged the ladies to sit down. "You will have tea, won't you?" she asked and the ladies readily agreed.

"Selena had told me about meeting you," said Henrietta, who was still rather unclear as to how her sister-in-law had become acquainted with the ladies.

"Oh, yes," said Frederica. "Tommie and I have so enjoyed meeting with Lady Selena and also your two dear children." She went on to comment on how pretty little Sophie was and how handsome Harold was and how intelligent and well-behaved both of them appeared to be.

There was nothing that Henrietta liked better than hearing her children praised. She found herself liking the princess very much. The girl was really quite fetching with her lovely eyes and charming accent. It was a pity that she apparently didn't have any decent clothes to wear, thought Henrietta sympathetically.

The four ladies had a very congenial time discussing Frederica's impressions of London and Mrs. MacNeil's adventures when she was in Brunconia. Henrietta was rather disappointed when Mrs. MacNeil finally announced that they must be going.

After the princess and Mrs. MacNeil had taken their leave, Henrietta continued to talk about the visit. "I did like Princess Frederica," she said to Selena. "She is such a delightful girl and so very pretty. It is a shame that she was wearing those old clothes."

"I fear the princess and her family are very poor," said Selena. "She cannot afford anything new."

"Then she must find a wealthy husband," said the duchess. "Perhaps Count von Gessler."

"Count von Gessler!" cried Selena. "Why, Princess Frederica believes his father responsible for the ruination of Brunconia."

"That wouldn't endear him to her, I suppose," said the duchess.

Selena laughed. "Indeed not." She thought of the financial woes of Brunconia and how the von Gesslers had stolen so much from the country. And now the count and his sister were living in great wealth, enjoying the fruits of their father's treachery. Selena looked thoughtful, wishing there was some way for Brunconia to reclaim the money that had been stolen from it.

An idea occurred to her. If only Brunconia could get back some of its wealth, perhaps Prince Maximilian and Frederica could get married after all. Now that Selena had fallen in love herself, she felt great sympathy for the Brunconian couple.

Selena suddenly decided that she could at least do a small thing by giving Frederica the fabric she had just bought for a new dress. She looked at her sister-in-law. "I was just thinking, Hetty, wouldn't the princess look lovely in that new blue silk I just bought?"

The duchess was quick to seize upon the suggestion. "Oh, my dear, that color would suit her exactly!"

"Well, I shall give it to her," said Selena. "I shall take it over to her tomorrow."

"What a very good idea," said Henrietta. "And she must go to my dressmaker." Eagerly picking up the fashion magazine, Henrietta quickly thumbed to the design she had looked at earlier. "This would be quite charming on her. Oh, Selena, if she had a new dress, she would make quite a sensation at Lady Newberry's ball! I will have to see that she is sent an invitation. Why, with her title and looks and some new clothes, I daresay the princess could make a good match."

"I don't think the princess is interested in finding a husband," said Selena, thinking of Prince Maximilian.

"Nonsense!" cried Henrietta. "The poor girl must marry a wealthy English gentleman. It would solve all of her problems."

Selena smiled slightly at the irony of her sister-in-law's remark. First, Maximilian was to marry a rich English princess and now Frederica was to marry a rich English gentleman. And, wishing once again that there was something she could do so the two of them could marry each other, Selena listened as Henrietta chatted on about what a success the princess would be in her gown.

24

Heathfield sat at the desk in his library, thoughtfully staring down at a sheet of paper before him. After dipping a quill pen into ink, he began to write. However, after a few minutes, he paused to reread what he had written. Uttering a curse, he grabbed up the paper and crumpled it into a ball.

Duncan, lying at the foot of the desk, seemed perturbed by his master's loud epithet. The canine's head shot up and he gazed at the earl with doleful brown eyes.

Heathfield reached down and gave the dog a pat on the head. "Sorry, old boy," he said apologetically, "I'm just having a devil of a time trying to write this letter." Duncan appeared to accept this explanation and quickly rested his head back on the floor to resume his nap.

Since his unfortunate meeting with Melford the previous day, the earl had given much thought as to how he could repair the dangerous breach between himself and Selena's brother. He had finally decided that he would make the duke a peace offering by writing him a note of apology.

However, as Heathfield tried to compose such a note, he found it galling that he should have to lower himself to Melford. After all, it was the duke who had begun the altercation by insulting him in such an infamous manner. Why should he have to apologize to that pompous idiot? he asked himself. Perhaps it would be better to try and make his case to Selena.

Taking up another piece of paper, he picked up his pen again. 'My dear Selena,' he quickly wrote, but then he became stymied as to what to say to her. Leaning back in his chair, the earl stared glumly out the window.

"Pardon me, my lord," said the butler, entering the library.

Heathfield was quite happy to have any interruption from his fruitless endeavor. "Yes, Preston?"

"There is a gentleman at the door, my lord. A Mr. MacNeil. He said he is acquainted with Prince Maximilian. When I told him his highness was out, he inquired whether he might see your lordship."

"MacNeil? Why, that must be Professor MacNeil. I shall be very glad to meet him. Do show him in, Preston."

"Very good, my lord." The butler retreated and returned a short time later with MacNeil at his heels. "Mr. John MacNeil," announced the servant in a sonorous tone. The earl got up from his chair and gave his visitor a welcoming smile. Duncan barked once and then he walked over to give MacNeil a friendly sniff.

"You're a fine fellow," said the Scotsman, patting the dog's neck, "and one of my own countrymen."

"That is Duncan, sir," said the earl.

MacNeil smiled broadly. "And he has a good Scots name as well." Turning from the animal, he looked over at the earl. "Lord Heathfield," he said, bowing, "you are very kind to receive me."

The earl stepped forward and extended his hand. "MacNeil. I'm pleased to meet you. I must say I very much admire your books. Your work on the Holy Roman Empire was quite brilliant."

"Och, thank you, my lord," said MacNeil, astonished that a member of the aristocracy had actually read one of his academic tomes. Heathfield motioned him to a chair and the Scotsman sat down.

MacNeil was gratified by the friendly reception he was getting from his lordship. He looked around at the tall bookshelves around him. "You have a very large collection, my lord. And far neater than mine. My books seem to end up in piles on the floor. Much to my wife's dismay, I might add."

Heathfield laughed. "So you are acquainted with my cousin Max?"

MacNeil nodded. "Aye, my lord. I met Prince Maximilian and his family when I spent several months in Brunconia doing research on a book."

"I see," said the earl. "Lady Selena told me she called on you seeking information about Brunconia."

"Aye, she did," said the Scotsman, nodding. "What a fine lady she is, charming, intelligent, and very beautiful."

Heathfield smiled. "I will agree with you on all those points, sir."

MacNeil smiled back at him. "My wife and our houseguest are calling on Lady Selena this afternoon. I'm told that you met our guest."

The earl nodded. "I had the pleasure of meeting Princess Frederica. I wish I could tell Maximilian that she's in town. He's very much in love with her."

"I wish you could, my lord," said MacNeil, "but Frederica agrees that they mustn't meet. 'Tis a pity, but, considering the state of the Brunconian treasury, Prince Maximilian must have a wealthy wife."

"Are matters in Brunconia so very grave?"

"Aye," said MacNeil. "Karl Joseph von Gessler was a crafty scoundrel who bled the country dry. There is little money in the country. And yet there is wealth in Brunconia if it could be reached."

"What do you mean, sir? What wealth are you speaking of?" said the earl.

"Why, mineral wealth. Coal, iron and copper are there in abundance. But it would take considerable capital to open mines. And, as you know, capital is in short supply in Brunconia. It would also require men with some expertise in mining and no one in the entire country has such knowledge."

"But surely there must be others wishing to invest in such enterprises," said Heathfield.

"Brunconia is remote and mountainous and even if foreign investors could be found, the grand duke is leery of outsiders. He doesn't want the country to be robbed again." He shook his head. " 'Tis a sad situation." Not wishing to overstay his welcome, the professor rose to his feet. "But I must be going, my lord. I should be grateful if you tell Prince Maximilian that I called. I'll call again another day."

"Of course," said the earl, smiling as he stood up. "I know Max will be sorry that he missed you. And do call again soon."

MacNeil nodded. "Thank you, my lord. I shall." He bowed to the earl and left the room.

Sitting down again, Heathfield considered what MacNeil had told him. So there was mineral wealth in Brunconia. If it could be mined, the Brunconian people would have the raw materials they would need for industry and commerce. Getting up from his desk, he walked over to his bookshelves and pulled out an atlas of Europe. Taking the large volume over to his desk, he opened it up to the page that featured the tiny principality of Brunconia.

He had scarcely begun to study the map before him when the door to the library opened and his cousin Perry strode into the room. "Charles," he said in a jovial voice, "Preston said you were squirreled away in here."

The earl looked up. "Percy," he said. "You appear disgustingly cheerful today."

After giving Duncan an ear rubbing, Percy sat down in the chair recently vacated by MacNeil. "I'm in a dashed jolly mood, Charles. It seems our fortunes are looking quite bright. I just called upon Aunt Margaret. She had a letter from the Duchess of Leeds saying that Princess Charlotte was quite favorably impressed with Cousin Max the other day.

"Everything is going exceedingly well. It seems the business at Almack's has been forgotten now that Count von Gessler has left town. Indeed, I don't think there are any other princes about to offer serious competition to Max. Oh, I did hear something about Prince Leopold of Belgium, but I doubt he will be taken seriously now that Her Royal Highness is smitten with Max."

"Smitten with Max? Don't you think you're doing it a bit brown, Percy?"

"Oh, very well. Perhaps she isn't precisely smitten with him, but it did seem she liked him. And he is much better looking than the Prince of Orange. But what is the matter, Charles? You look so serious. And who was that gentleman who just left your house as I arrived? A short middle-aged fellow. He got into this frightful carriage that was pulled by the sorriest horseflesh I'd ever seen."

"That was John MacNeil," said Heathfield, "the author of *The History of the Holy Roman Empire*. He just paid a call upon me."

"Good God," said Percy, making a ludicrous face. "I thank Providence I came so late. What a dull fellow he must be."

"What a great Philistine you are, Percy."

His cousin grinned. "Yes, that is true. But you are bookish enough for the both of us, Charles. So did you and this fellow MacNeil discuss the Punic Wars or some such thing?"

"Actually, he had come to visit Max."

Percy appeared surprised. "Max? I can't imagine our cousin knowing such a dry, dusty person as that."

The earl nodded. "MacNeil did scholarly research in Brunconia for a time and became acquainted with Max and his family."

"Then I doubt that they are bosom companions," he said, rather relieved. He paused. "Where is Cousin Max anyway?"

"He went out for a walk earlier. MacNeil was quite disappointed to miss him."

"Another one of his melancholy walks," said Percy, shaking his head.

"Yes, I'm afraid Max is unhappy. He's homesick for Brunconia."

"I know, I know," sighed Percy. "Poor old Max. But he must try and buck up. Soon he will wed Princess Charlotte and I daresay he will be able to visit Brunconia every now and then. Of course, I hope he doesn't mention such an idea to Princess Charlotte before they are married. The poor girl would undoubtedly be horrified at the idea."

"So you are still set on this marriage, are you?" asked Heathfield.

"What?" said Percy in a startled tone. "Of course, I am. And Father is counting on it. No, Max must pull himself together and do his duty. I do hope he doesn't get drunk again."

The earl regarded his cousin closely. "Speaking of Max, there is something I have to ask you about. It has to do with a rumor that is being spread about town about me and a certain lady."

Percy looked slightly uncomfortable, but he managed to smile. "Really, Charles, there are so many rumors spread about you and 'certain ladies' that I can't keep them straight."

"This one involves Lady Selena Paget," said Heathfield, fixing a severe eye on his cousin.

"Good Lord, not Lady Selena again," said Percy.

"Yes. Someone was saying that Lady Selena and I are secretly engaged."

"By Jupiter, you and Lady Selena!" said Percy with mock gaiety. "My felicitations, Cousin!"

"Thank you, Percy, but your felicitations are premature." The earl leaned back in his chair. "When Max was drunk, he told the tale about Lady Selena and me to Cecil Boswith."

"Tut," said Percy, shaking his head, "Boswith is one of the worst gossips in London."

"Yes, the rumor has apparently gone all over town," said Heathfield. "It has even reached Lady Selena and her brother."

Percy cringed a little. "Oh, no. Don't tell me Melford has heard the story?"

"He has. And he paid a most unpleasant visit on me yesterday, ordering me to stay away from Selena."

"Good God, Charles. But you must remember that I warned you about having anything to do with Melford's sister."

Heathfield scowled. "Dammit, Percy, I want to know why you told Max such a lie to begin with."

Percy sighed. "So Max told you?"

"He didn't want to, but it wasn't difficult for me to figure out. Why did you tell him such a thing?"

"It was really quite innocent, Charles. I only did it because I was afraid Max was expressing too much of an interest in Lady Selena."

"What?" Heathfield raised his dark eyebrows in astonishment.

"Oh, Max was moping around about having to marry Princess Charlotte. He had gotten it into his head that he didn't want to marry her. An affront to his manhood or some such thing being married to a future queen. Instead, he mentioned that Lady Selena might be a better choice being an heiress and the sister of a duke. And then he said she reminded him of his beloved Frederica."

"Selena reminded Max of Frederica?" Heathfield thought of his meeting with the princess and couldn't see any resemblance between the two young women at all. Indeed, such a comparison struck him as ludicrous.

"I hope you won't think Max has fallen in love with Lady Selena or any such nonsense," said Percy quickly. "I daresay, he is still pining away for this Frederica of his."

"I'm relieved to hear it," said the earl, "since I plan to marry Selena myself."

It was Percy's turn to look astonished. "What? Good God, you can't mean it, Charles! You marry Melford's sister?"

Heathfield nodded. "I'm in deadly earnest, Percy." A resolute expression appeared on his face. "I will marry her," he said.

"Even if it means having Melford for a brother-in-law?" asked Percy.

The earl smiled. "Even so, Percy." Percy shook his head, thinking that his poor cousin must really be in love to contemplate such an awful fate.

25

When Melford returned home that evening, he and Selena seemed to settle on a chilly truce toward each other. Although Henrietta was quite relieved that the two of them hadn't resumed their quarrel, she was finding the silences and cold looks her husband and sister-in-law exchanged during dinner quite upsetting.

The strain of family discord took its toll on Henrietta and the following morning she stayed in her room, complaining of a headache. Melford and Selena sat at the breakfast table alone, scarcely uttering a word to each other. As soon as the meal was over, the duke went off to his library while Selena made her way to the drawing room.

Taking up her needlework, Selena frowned as she stitched the outlines of a rose on fabric. She was still quite aggravated with her brother and was cataloging her grievances against him when a maid appeared in the room.

Selena looked up from her embroidery and regarded the servant questioningly. The servant bobbed in a curtsy. "Begging your pardon, my lady, but there is a gentleman to see you."

Selena's pulse quickened at the thought that Heathfield was there to call upon her. Fearing that she was blushing, she attempted to speak in a calm voice. "Who is it, Mary?"

The maid paused dramatically for a second and then said in a rather awed voice, "It is Mr. Henry Travers, my lady. The poet."

Selena had a difficult time not showing her disappointment. Henry Travers? Why would he be wanting to see her at such an early hour? She hesitated for a moment, on the verge of sending the poet on his way. However, her curiosity got the better of her and she decided to see him. "Very well, Mary, show Mr. Travers in." The maid gave another curtsy and scampered out of the room. She returned shortly with the gentleman behind her.

"Mr. Travers, my lady," said the maid, who wished that she could stay in the room to witness the meeting between Selena and the poet. Mary found the handsome, dark-haired Travers a very romantic figure and she was quite envious of Selena. She had no doubt that the poet very much admired her ladyship. It was obvious by the way he rushed into the room, hurrying to the sofa where Selena sat. Sighing, the maid retreated from the drawing room, closing the door gently behind her.

"My dear Lady Selena!" said Travers, taking the hand that Selena had extended to him and holding it much longer than custom dictated. When he finally released Selena's hand, he continued to stare down at her with an intent expression in his dark eyes.

Selena was somewhat disturbed by Travers's effusive greeting. However, she managed to smile and civilly suggest that he take a seat. To her dismay, the poet promptly took the place next to her on the sofa.

Dressed in his usual careless style, Travers pushed an unruly dark lock from his prominent brow as he continued to gaze at her. "You are about early this morning, sir," said Selena.

"Yes," said the poet, "I was up all night. I was unable to sleep. I couldn't wait to bring this to you." He reached inside his coat pocket and produced a small maroon-colored volume. Travers smiled at her. "You see I've had it next to my heart."

Selena, who was now wishing that she had never allowed the poet to be admitted to the house, looked down at the book. She noted the name Travers in gilt letters on the cover. "Oh, it is a book of your poems."

"Yes, it has just been published," said Travers. "And it is my best work. I do not doubt, my dear lady, that this is the work that will put me in the pantheon of the immortals."

Selena had a difficult time not bursting into laughter at this remark, but she managed to control herself. "I'm glad you find it a success, sir," she said.

Travers smiled and, opening the book with a flourish, he pushed it toward her. "You must read the dedication," he said.

Selena felt some trepidation as she read the words printed on the page before her. The dedication read "To my divine muse, Lady S." Looking up, she found the poet's intense gaze once more upon her. "You see, I've dedicated it to you, Lady Selena. It is you who have inspired my genius!"

"Really, sir," began Selena, but Travers had taken back the book and was quickly flipping the pages.

"I must read you 'The Summer of Aphrodite,' " he said, and finding the poem, he began to recite it in his loud, melodious voice. Selena listened with dismay as the poet continued on and on with lines that described Aphrodite's beauty in embarrassing detail. Ending the poem with a line declaring his rapturous joy and delight with Aphrodite, Travers looked expectantly over at Selena. When she did not speak, he smiled. "I see you are overcome, Lady Selena." He paused dramatically and murmured. "My Aphrodite!"

To Selena's horror, the poet then snatched up her hand and pressed a fervent kiss upon it. It was at that precise moment that the door swung open. Both Selena and Travers looked up to find Melford staring at them with a shocked expression.

"Good God!" cried the duke, "what the devil is going on here?"

Travers quickly sprang up from the sofa. "Your grace," he said, bowing. "I was just reading one of my poems to Lady Selena."

"I didn't see you reading anything," growled the duke.

Travers smiled a trifle uneasily. He picked up the small volume for Melford to see it. "It is my newly published work. I have dedicated the volume to Lady Selena."

"What?" Melford gave the poet a horrified look. "You had the audacity to dedicate your drivel to my sister?"

Travers's face reddened. "Drivel?" he sputtered furiously.

"Please, James," said Selena, but the duke silenced her with a furious look.

"I suggest you leave my house, sir," said the duke.

Travers brushed back his unruly lock again and cast a tragic look at Selena. Then, without another word, he left the room. As soon as he left, Melford exploded again. "Great God in heaven, Selena, have you lost all sense of propriety? First you tarnish your reputation with Heathfield and now I find you with that debauched poet Travers!"

Selena frowned. "I don't need another one of your lectures, James."

"Oh? Well, I think you do. And now this damned Travers has dedicated his poetry to you? What will the scandalmongers make of that?"

"I don't care one fig what anyone thinks," said Selena roundly.

"That is painfully clear," said Melford. "You have no thought about embarrassing the family again."

Selena got up from the couch. "I shall spare you any further mortification, brother. I will have my maid pack and will return to Melford Castle."

James frowned, remembering his wife's words about Selena's going back to Northumberland alone. "There is no need for that," he said, speaking in a more reasonable tone. "But I do think it wise that we leave town for a time. I thought we could go to Gateswood Lodge."

"I have no intention of going anywhere with you!" cried Selena angrily. "I will return to Melford Castle tomorrow!" And with those furious words, she hurried past her brother and out of the room.

26

Henrietta was still in bed when her husband came into her room, his face looking quite grim. Sitting up, she eyed him with a worried expression.

Melford walked over to her and, leaning over, kissed her on the forehead. "Are you feeling any better, my dear?" he asked solicitously.

Henrietta nodded. "Yes, my headache seems much improved," she said. The duke seemed relieved by this since he felt it gave him license to relate what had just occurred with Selena and Travers.

After telling his wife the story in some detail, Melford shook his head. "I don't know what has got into my sister, Henrietta. Selena has always been so sensible."

"I'm certain that she wouldn't do anything foolish, my dear."

"What do you mean? She's already been doing foolish things, arranging trysts with Heathfield and then letting that damnable poet take liberties with her. How could she have even admitted Travers into the house?"

Henrietta patted his hand and then she pushed her covers aside. "I shall get up and talk to her."

The duke seemed encouraged. "Yes, that would be helpful. You must convince her to come to Gateswood Lodge with us. She can't be trusted to go to Melford Castle alone."

Although Henrietta was not at all sure she could convince her sister-in-law of anything, she got dressed and then made her way to Selena's room. There she found Selena and her maid busily packing.

"Oh, Selena," said Henrietta, "you can't run off like this."

"I'm not running off, Henrietta," said Selena as she continued sorting through her things. "I'm just returning home. Since James has never been overly fond of Melford Castle, I'm certain he won't mind if I remain there."

"But you must come to Gateswood Lodge with us," protested Henrietta. "It is very lovely there this time of year. And we won't be completely without society. Why, James said that Count von Gessler has just gone out to his estate, which is very near to ours. He is such a charming man and we will doubtless see a good deal of him there."

Although Henrietta didn't realize it, this was hardly an inducement for Selena to wish to go with them. "I'm sorry, Henrietta," she said, "but I'm determined to go back to Northumberland."

Henrietta watched in silent frustration for a time as her sister-in-law went on with her preparations to leave.

"Excuse me, my lady," said the lady's maid, holding a length of blue silk in her arms, "but did you wish me to pack this?"

Selena looked at the material the maid was holding up. Remembering Princess Frederica, she shook her head. "No, Betty, I intended to give that to someone. Please wrap it in paper." She turned to her sister-in-law. "I shall take this to Princess Frederica before I go. If my brother will allow me to leave the house."

"Don't be silly, Selena. Of course you may call on the princess."

"Will you accompany me?"

The duchess, who was beginning to fear that her headache was becoming worse again, shook her head. "No, but do give the princess my regards, Selena. And I shall have William bring the carriage around for you." She paused. "Oh, I do wish you would change your mind about going to Gateswood Lodge, my dear." However, when her sister-in-law showed no sign of doing so, Henrietta left her to her packing.

It was some time later when Selena thought once again of Princess Frederica. She very much regretted that her acquaintance with that lady was to be of such a short duration. But it was impossible for her to stay any longer with her brother. And it was probably for the best that she get away from Heathfield as well.

A short time later Selena was on her way to call at the Mac-Neils' residence. When she arrived there, she was ushered into the small drawing room where she found Princess Frederica sitting alone. "Lady Selena," said the princess, smiling with pleasure. "How very good of you to call."

Selena smiled in return and took a seat near her. "I wanted to see you before I left town."

Frederica's face fell. "What? You are leaving?"

Selena nodded. "I'm returning to my home in Northumberland."

The princess looked puzzled. "Northumberland?"

"It is at the northern edge of England," explained Selena.

"Oh," said Frederica, quite downcast. "I'm so very sorry to hear you are going so far away, Lady Selena."

Taking up the package in her lap, Selena handed it over to the princess. "I wanted to give you a present before I left."

"A present?" said Frederica, looking at the package in surprise. Her face brightened a little. "Oh, how very kind of you." Tearing away the brown paper, she stared down at the blue silk material. "Oh, it is so beautiful!" She turned back to Selena. "Thank you so very much, Lady Selena!"

Selena smiled. "I thought it would suit you."

Frederica looked down at the material again. "Oh, I do wish you weren't going away. Perhaps you could visit me at Cambridge. Is that near where you will be?"

Selena shook her head. "I fear not."

"Oh," said the princess, clearly disappointed. She then changed the subject. "I don't imagine you've seen Maximilian?"

"No, I'm afraid I haven't."

The princess sighed. "I do wish I could see him. I mean, see him from afar, for I know we must never meet."

"It seems so unfair that you must be kept apart," said Selena sympathetically.

"Yes, perhaps so." She sighed again. "But we must both do our duty for our poor country." Frederica frowned, her hazel eyes glinting in anger. "It is all because of that villain, Karl Joseph von Gessler. It is because of him that my country is so poor. And to think that his son lives in England, and his daughter flaunts the greatest treasure of Brunconia. When I think of her wearing the swan necklace, I am furious. Rudolf von Gessler is a traitor and a spy."

"A spy?" said Selena.

The princess nodded. "He is an agent for the Prussian court. It is said that he has spied for France as well. Indeed, I do not think he would be welcome in England if your government knew the extent of his intrigues."

Selena's eyes widened. "But hasn't our government been informed about him?"

Frederica shrugged resignedly. "Unfortunately, we have no evidence against the count," said Frederica. "He is as clever as he is unscrupulous."

Selena appeared thoughtful, wondering if what Frederica said were true. Certainly the Brunconians had reason to think the worst of von Gessler and spread rumors about him. But if it were true, Count von Gessler was utterly despicable.

"If I were a man," said Frederica, "I would find evidence against this Rudolf von Gessler. I would prove that he is what we say he is. Then perhaps some of what his family has stolen might be returned to Brunconia."

"Yes, that would be wonderful," said Selena. They talked for a while longer and then Selena took her leave. As she rode back to Melford House, she reflected about Count von Gessler and his family. She knew that he was very rich and lived in a princely fashion. Now he was in the country enjoying his fine house and renowned art collection.

Selena looked thoughtful. Could it be true that he was a spy? Well, she would not be surprised. After all, she had never liked the count. There was something oily and insincere about him.

She thought of how Henrietta had urged her to accompany them to Gateswood Lodge, saying they would be near von Gessler's estate as if that were a great attraction. Staring out the carriage window, Selena suddenly had an idea. Perhaps she should go with her brother and sister-in-law to Gateswood Lodge. There she would probably see a good deal of von Gessler.

Perhaps if she encouraged him, she might learn something that might be useful to Princess Frederica. After all, he had seemed rather interested in her and he was always eager to impress her. As the carriage made its way along the busy street, she resolved to go to Gateswood Lodge.

27

Melford and his wife were quite surprised when Selena returned from the MacNeil's and announced that she would be happy to accompany them to Gateswood Lodge. Although he was rather perplexed by his sister's sudden change of heart, Melford made plans to depart for Sussex the very next day. Despite Henrietta's request that they delay their departure, the duke was adamant. The sooner he got his sister away from Heathfield the better, he thought.

And so the following morning, the duke's large traveling coach made its way out of the city. Selena was kept occupied with her niece and nephew. Excited about the trip to the country, Sophie and Harold chattered happily as they rode along.

Since Gateswood Lodge was not very far from London, it was scarcely more than five hours later when the carriage pulled into the lane that led up to the duke's country residence. Selena, who had never before been to the house, was quite impressed by the lovely countryside around it. With its rolling green hills and meadows of wildflowers, Melford's property appeared extremely picturesque.

Selena was also pleased with the house. It was a large rambling Elizabethan structure with ancient oak trees shading its park. The duke, happy to see how much Selena liked Gateswood Lodge, was eager to take her on a tour of the house and grounds.

By the next day, the family had comfortably settled in. Little Harold seemed especially ecstatic to be back in the country with its allure of cows and pigs. Indeed, the only family member who did not seem pleased to be at Gateswood Lodge was the duchess, who couldn't help regret leaving town at such an inconvenient time.

That afternoon Henrietta sat with her husband and Selena in the drawing room thinking about the social engagements she was missing and how dull it was in the country. The duchess was, therefore, glad when a servant entered the room to announce that Count von Gessler had arrived to pay them a visit. "How lovely. Do show him in at once," she said.

While in the past the idea of seeing von Gessler wouldn't have interested Selena in the least, she was now quite eager to see him. Thinking that he was an agent of Prussia who probably spied for the French as well certainly made him a far more interesting person in her eyes.

The count strode into the drawing room and then bowed low to the duke and the two ladies. "Your grace," he said, with a smile. "I was delighted with the news that you and the duchess were here." He looked over at Selena. "And that you have brought the charming Lady Selena. What great good fortune for me having to be away from town."

Selena smiled brightly at him. "How do you do, Count?" she said.

Von Gessler was very encouraged by her smile. In the past, the duke's sister had seemed coolly indifferent to him. He smiled warmly at her. "Very well indeed, Lady Selena."

"Do sit down, von Gessler," said the duke, and the count took a seat near Selena. He remained for some time chatting with them about paintings and news from town. Although Selena didn't join in the conversation very much, von Gessler was aware that she seemed to be listening to him with great interest. And when he had announced that he must take his leave, he thought he detected a look of disappointment on her lovely face.

Von Gessler couldn't help but be pleased by her apparent change in attitude toward him. Before leaving, the count invited them to see his gardens the following day at his estate, Lindenhurst. The duchess, pleased at the prospect of some diversion, readily accepted his invitation. The count also observed that Selena seemed pleased at the prospect of visiting Lindenhurst. As he returned to his home, von Gessler sat back in his carriage seat, reflecting that perhaps it was still possible to win the duke's sister for his bride.

While the count mulled over the possibility of obtaining Selena's hand in marriage, Heathfield's thoughts ran along a similar vein. Since his meeting with Melford, he knew that it would be virtually impossible to overcome the duke's opposition to the marriage.

As he pondered the matter that afternoon in his library, Heathfield grew exceedingly frustrated. What was he to do? It seemed the only option was elopement. He must convince Selena to marry him over the objections of her brother.

The earl frowned. He didn't like the idea of an elopement, but if that was the only way, it would have to do. Of course, he reflected, perhaps he might still try to talk some sense into Melford. It was unlikely that anyone as thick-skulled as the duke would ever change his mind, but Heathfield supposed he had to try again. Resolving to call at Melford House, the earl ordered his carriage.

When the butler answered the door at the ducal residence, he informed Heathfield that the duke and duchess weren't at home. "Then I should like to see Lady Selena," said the earl.

"I am sorry, my lord, but the family has left town."

"Left town? Where have they gone?"

"I fear I am not at liberty to say."

While Heathfield had an urge to grab the servant by his lapels and force the information from him, he only stalked off. He imagined that it wouldn't be hard to find out where the duke and duchess had gone. The comings and goings of such august personages were always discussed in Society and the earl had numerous acquaintances who could be depended upon to know what was happening in town. If Selena had indeed left town, the earl was sure he would have no trouble finding out where she had gone.

As he climbed into his carriage, Heathfield frowned. He didn't doubt that Melford had taken his sister out of London to keep her away from him. Well, his strategy wouldn't work, thought the earl, resolving to see Selena no matter where she had gone.

The next afternoon, Selena put on one of her most attractive dresses for her outing to the count's estate. Attired in a modish dress of pea-green silk, a matching green pelisse, and stylish new bonnet, Selena looked exceptionally lovely as she stepped down from the carriage on their arrival at Lindenhurst.

Von Gessler's house, a magnificent stone building of recent vintage, was a source of great pride to the count and he eagerly escorted his guests on the promised tour of his gardens. As they walked along in the bright sunlight, the duke took his wife's arm. This enabled the count to proffer his arm to Selena. Strolling out amid the impressive stretch of green lawn and colorful flowers, von Gessler's company expressed great delight at the splendor of the landscaped grounds.

After walking about for some time, they retreated back to the house where von Gessler's servants brought in a sumptuous tea. Since his guests hadn't been in the house before, the count then took them on an extensive tour.

As usual, Melford was primarily interested in the paintings that the count had displayed throughout the residence. When they came to the long picture gallery, the duke stared at each painting for a considerable length of time, with Henrietta standing patiently at his side.

As Melford and his wife lingered behind, the count continued through the long hallway with Selena. Von Gessler was quite pleased at how Selena seemed to be hanging onto his every word. She really was quite lovely, he thought, eyeing the rounded curves of her figure with approval.

Selena, aware of the count's admiring gaze, turned and smiled coquettishly at him. "I have been worried about you, Count. That business of the duel with Prince Maximilian. I do hope it has been settled. I cannot bear the thought of bloodshed."

Von Gessler shrugged. "Business matters called me here. If Maximilian still wishes to pursue this ridiculous affair, he may find me here. Thus far, I have heard nothing from him."

"I am so glad, sir," said Selena, "but I do hope you won't entertain the idea of going through with the duel whatever the prince might say to you. By all accounts he is a dangerous hothead."

The count nodded, pleased to hear the remark. He decided to write to one of his friends in London. Certainly His Royal Highness should be informed that Lady Selena Paget had called the Brunconian a "dangerous hothead."

"I am flattered that you are concerned for me, dear lady, but there is no need." He smiled. "And permit me to say that you look very beautiful."

"You are very kind, sir," said Selena, turning her dazzling smile upon him, causing the count's hopes to rise even more. "I must tell you how much I love Lindenhurst," she said. "Everything is so beautiful here. You have wonderful taste." She stopped to study a small painting and then turned back to him. "I daresay, it must be a family trait. Your sister Lady Blackstone has such a lovely house. And she dresses so very well."

Von Gessler, not entirely pleased at having the conversation focused on his sister instead of himself, nonetheless, managed to smile. "Yes, Theresa is always at the height of fashion."

"Oh, yes," said Selena. "She always outshines everyone. Yes, she is very beautiful. I remember how she looked when we last visited her salon. She was wearing the most exquisite gown. And I shan't soon forget the necklace she was wearing. It was really quite remarkable. It was in the shape of a swan. Indeed, I was green with envy."

"Yes, the necklace is a family heirloom."

"That is what Lady Blackstone said." Selena smiled again. "Your sister said you allowed her to wear it."

"I occasionally let her wear it, but I confess I don't want her to grow too fond of it." He paused and regarded her with a meaningful expression. "It is to be given to my wife when I marry."

"Any lady would love to own such a necklace," said Selena.

Greatly encouraged by this remark, von Gessler smiled brightly. "Perhaps you would like to see the necklace. I have it here."

Selena glanced up quickly, surprised at her good fortune. "Oh, I would like that very much."

He nodded. Looking around, he saw that the duke and duchess were still at the far end of the gallery, staring at a painting. "Come with me. It's in here in the library." Taking Selena's arm, he hastened her through a doorway into a spacious room lined on two sides with bookshelves.

Selena noted a vast fireplace where a fire burned brightly. Glancing around the room, she saw that the walls that were not filled with books were decorated with a collection of swords and other weapons, giving the room a fierce, masculine quality. Von Gessler made his way to a massive desk that stood near the center of the room. He reached under it where there was apparently some sort of hidden drawer. Retrieving a key, he went over to a large cherry cabinet and flung open the doors to reveal a safe.

The count put the key into the lock and opened it. Reaching inside, he took out a large gilt box. Taking out the box, he opened it to reveal the necklace. "Oh, it is beautiful," she said.

Von Gessler smiled. "There are many other wonderful pieces. I don't have them here, of course. They are in Berlin, where my principal residence is. Have you ever thought of visiting Prussia, Lady Selena?"

Selena looked up from the necklace. "Oh, I've always wanted to travel. You must tell me all about Berlin. By all accounts it is a fascinating city."

Pleased by this response, the count smiled again. Then, hearing the duke's voice just outside the door, he put the necklace back into the safe. As he did so, she saw that there were bundles of papers stacked inside. "I'm certain that the duchess would love to see the necklace again," said Selena.

"I only wished for you to see it, Lady Selena," he said, fixing a meaningful gaze upon her. The count closed the door of the safe and locked it. Then he went to the desk and replaced the key.

"I suppose we must rejoin the others," said Selena, trying to sound disappointed at such a prospect. The count nodded, and offering her his arm, he escorted her out of the room.

28

On returning from her visit to von Gessler's house, Selena took a walk on the grounds with Fluff and Sophie. When she returned to the house, she placed Sophie into the care of Nanny Walters and then went to the drawing room.

She found her brother there alone reading a sporting magazine. "What a lovely day," she said. "Where is Hetty?"

"She is discussing menus with Cook," said his grace. Melford was pleased to see his sister in such good spirits. Perhaps she wasn't in love with Heathfield. Now that they were in the country, she didn't seem to be pining for him.

"Sophie and I had a splendid walk. And Fluff seems to adore Gateswood Lodge." Smiling at the little spaniel, who had followed her into the room, she sat down upon the sofa. Fluff lay down at her feet. "I was quite impressed with the Count von Gessler's house. And his gardens were magnificent."

The duke nodded. "Yes, the gardens were beautiful."

"And all those splendid paintings. The count must be very rich."

"Rich as a nabob," said the duke. "You seemed to get on with him very well this afternoon. I didn't think you liked him."

"Well, I never really disliked him," said Selena. "Yes, Lindenhurst is really splendid. I should like a house like that one day."

A slight frown came to the duke's face. Surely Selena wasn't developing an interest in von Gessler. Although he liked the count very much, the duke could hardly be pleased at the thought of his sister marrying a foreigner.

Melford hoped that his sister wasn't forming an attachment to still another unsuitable man. At that moment Henrietta entered the room and they began talking of something else.

Selena awakened early the next morning. Rising from her bed, she went to the window and looked out at the dew-covered expanse of lawn that stretched out from the house. The sun was shining brightly and it looked as if it would be another lovely day.

As she did with increasing frequency, Selena found herself thinking of Heathfield, wondering what he was doing at that moment and whether he was thinking about her. Turning from the window, she frowned. There were doubtlessly many other ladies in London that would make him forget all about her. No, she must try to keep from thinking about him.

Deciding to get dressed, Selena went to her wardrobe and selected clothes suitable for a morning walk. Exercise would do her good, she thought, and Fluff always enjoyed an excursion.

When she went downstairs with the spaniel following behind her, she was surprised to find Hetty there. "Why, you are an early riser," said Selena.

"It is hard to sleep in the country," said the duchess. "All those noisy birds."

Selena laughed. "And it is so very quiet in town?"

"Well, city noises don't seem to bother me. They are more natural than all that twittering and chirping."

"I prefer the birds, my dear," said Selena, smiling at her sister-in-law. "Fluff and I are off for a walk. Why don't you come, too?"

"No, thank you," said the duchess. "You know I'm not a great walker. I shall stay here and attend to some letters. But we have already had a note from the count."

"So early?"

"He sent a messenger with it. He's invited us to dinner this evening. Isn't that good of him?"

"Yes, that will be very nice," said Selena. They exchanged a few more words, and then Selena set off for her walk.

As she strolled along the gravel drive that led from the house, she thought of von Gessler. So they were to have dinner with him? Selena was pleased. Perhaps she could ask to see the necklace again.

A thoughtful expression came to her face as she walked along. Suddenly she had a thought. Perhaps she could steal back the necklace! She knew where it was and they were going to Lindenhurst that evening. Perhaps the opportunity would present itself that she could get to the library.

She shook her head. What an absurd idea. Indeed, it was utterly laughable. Still, as she walked along, she considered how wonderful it would be to return the necklace to the Brunconian royal family. Princess Frederica viewed it as some sort of talisman. Perhaps if the necklace were returned, luck would be restored to Brunconia.

Deep in thought, Selena continued walking. She passed a meadow dotted with blue and white wildflowers. When she had gone some distance, she looked down the lane, noting that a horseman was coming toward her. Moving over to one side to get out of the way, she turned her gaze back to the approaching rider. Suddenly, a look of astonishment appeared on her face as she recognized the rider as the Earl of Heathfield.

Seeing her, Heathfield urged his horse forward. He was as surprised as Selena was to meet her there. Having expected to encounter all sorts of difficulties in trying to see her at Gateswood Lodge, he could scarcely believe his good fortune. There she was! And alone!

Pulling up his mount alongside of her, the earl jumped down from his horse. "Selena!" he said. "What an amazing stroke of luck to find you here. I'd imagined I would have to storm the walls of the ducal residence to see you."

Selena regarded him with an amazed look, her heart racing. "But what are you doing here?"

"I came to find you," he said simply. Then, without a further word, he grabbed Selena into his arms and crushed his lips against hers. Although she knew she should protest, Selena returned his kiss with the fervor of suppressed ardor. When their lips finally parted, Heathfield smiled down at her. "My darling, Selena," he said, "I hope this means that you will marry me."

Selena, who was still a bit dazed from finding herself in Heathfield's arms, was momentarily dumbfounded.

Interpreting her silence for reluctance, he continued, "I do love you, Selena. I don't believe I've ever loved anyone until now. And upon my honor I will do all I can to make you happy. Your brother thinks me a scoundrel and I confess that I haven't lived like a monk, but I swear I want you and you alone. I promise I will be a true and faithful husband."

Having recovered her composure by this time, Selena smiled at him. "I shall hold you to that promise, my lord, for I love you and I couldn't bear the idea of your loving anyone else."

"Then you will marry me?"

"Yes, of course."

This reply caused his lordship to let out an exclamation of delight and once again he covered Selena's mouth with his own. As his lordship's kisses grew increasingly fervent, Selena's senses reeled. She responded with a passion that delighted the earl, yet she did not forget herself so much as to fail to suddenly recollect that she was not yet a married woman and that they were standing on a path in clear view of anyone who might happen by.

Summoning up all the self-control she could muster, she pushed him away. "We mustn't lose our heads, Heathfield."

"I have lost mine completely, my darling," said the earl. "But you're right. We must be married as soon as possible."

This remark seemed to bring Selena back to reality. "But what about my brother? You know how opposed he is to you. When he heard the rumor that we were secretly engaged, he nearly had a fit of apoplexy. He still believes you started the rumor and that you want to marry me only to wound him."

"I don't know what I can say to convince him otherwise," said his lordship, sobered by the thought of Melford. "But I did ask Maximilian about the rumor. It seems my cousin Percy thought Max was becoming too interested in you and forgetting Princess Charlotte. He told him that I was engaged to you so he would not abandon his pursuit of Her Royal Highness."

Selena eyed him in surprise. "Interested in me? But I thought he was in love with Frederica!"

"Yes, he *is* in love with her. Quite desperately, in fact. It seems that you remind him of her."

"I remind him of her?" said Selena.

Heathfield grinned. "That is what he said. I cannot see any resemblance myself. But who could fault any man for finding a resemblance in you to the woman he loves?"

"Such flummery!" said Selena, blushing a little but enjoying the flattery.

Tucking her arm in his, the earl smiled again. "I feel very sorry for Max."

"Yes," said Selena, pressing Heathfield's arm. "And poor Frederica. She is such a sweet girl and she is very much in love with him. It's a wretched business. But, my dear Heathfield, I must tell you about von Gessler."

"Von Gessler? I'd rather talk about us."

"But it is important. Yesterday we visited him at his estate. It is scarcely two miles away."

"Maximilian would think that is accurst bad luck."

"He might not think so if I were able to get back the Swan of Brunconia."

"The what?"

"The Swan of Brunc025. It was stolen from the Brunconian royal family by the count's father. Lady Blackstone was wearing it. Princess Frederica said that it's very important to Brunc023. According to Princess Frederica, when the necklace was stolen, the luck of Brunc023 went with it."

"The luck of Brunc023?"

"Yes, and Count von Gessler has the necklace hidden in his library. He showed it to me. There is a large desk in the library with some sort of hidden drawer or compartment underneath it. I saw von Gessler reach under it and get a key. And then he went to a large cabinet and unlocked the safe inside it. I saw a good many papers inside as well. I wouldn't be surprised if there is some incriminating evidence among those papers. Princess Frederica told me the count is a spy, an agent for both Prussia and France."

"A spy?" said the earl with a laugh. "And for both countries? Then he is an enterprising fellow. Come, Selena, it seems ridiculous."

"I don't think it's ridiculous at all," said Selena. "If only I could have seen the papers in the safe." She looked up at him. "We are dining at the count's residence this evening. If I could get to the library, I think I might be able to get the swan necklace back."

"What!" exclaimed the earl. "You'd steal it?"

"Why, yes. Why not? It belongs to the royal family of Brunc023. I know that from a book Professor MacNeil showed me."

"My dear Selena, I can't believe you're serious."

"Of course I'm serious. The necklace must be restored to Brunc023."

"You must forget all about this ridiculous scheme," said the earl.

"I don't see that it's ridiculous," replied Selena. "When Hetty and I leave the gentlemen to their port, I'd have an excellent opportunity. And if someone finds me in the library, I'll only say I'm looking at the count's books."

"A lady doesn't sneak about in strange houses trying to steal things from safes," said his lordship. "It could be dangerous."

"I suppose not," said Selena frowning. "It is more a man's job I suppose." She fastened her green eyes upon him. "Perhaps you could find your way in the house when we are at dinner. The servants will be distracted. You could steal the necklace!"

"I?" exclaimed the earl with a laugh. "My love, I wish to oblige you every way I can, but do not ask me to become a thief."

"One isn't a thief if he takes back something that the other person has stolen."

"Selena, it is completely out of the question. Even if I wished to help you, there would be no way on earth I could do it."

"But why not? Surely things are stolen every day and criminals are probably no more clever than you and I."

Heathfield laughed. "I shall hear no more about it. Indeed, we have enough to worry about with your brother. I should rather concentrate on how we may change his mind so that he'll accept me for a brother-in-law."

Selena smiled. "Knowing my dear brother as I do, I should think stealing the jewels a far easier matter." They both laughed and then the earl could not resist kissing her once more.

29

When the earl returned to the village inn where he had taken a room upon his arrival in Sussex, he was in exceedingly good spirits. He could scarcely believe that he had already seen Selena. And to make his happiness complete, she had declared her love for him and agreed to be his wife.

As he dismounted, one of the inn's servants hurried to take his horse. He walked into the public room of the inn, eager for something to eat. He was met by the proprietor, an amiable man who was very pleased to find a gentleman of quality at his establishment. "Did you enjoy your ride, sir?"

"Very much," said his lordship.

"We do have some beautiful views hereabouts," he said.

"I haven't seen any lovelier," said Heathfield, thinking of Selena.

"Might I get you anything, Mr. Smith?"

"I'd like something to eat," returned the earl, who, not wishing to create a stir, had given his name as Mr. Charles Smith.

The innkeeper hastened to comply. In a short time, a cold luncheon was laid before the earl, who ate heartily.

"Do you require anything else, sir?" said the innkeeper after his guest had nearly completed his repast.

"No, nothing at all. And I must say that your roast beef was excellent."

"Thank you, sir. Thank you very much," said the innkeeper.

At that moment a tall, rough-looking man entered the inn. "I'll have a pint of stout, innkeeper," he demanded in a loud voice.

"When I'm done here," said Finch.

"I'll have it now!" shouted the man.

The innkeeper muttered under his breath. "Excuse me, sir," he said, turning away from Heathfield and going to fetch the man's brew.

The earl watched the disagreeable newcomer drain his mug. The man then tossed a coin on the table and left.

"Ill-mannered ruffian," said the innkeeper, coming over to Heathfield's table once again. "You mustn't think we have that sort here in the village. He's not from here."

"You've seen him before?"

"Aye, sir. He's here from time to time. He goes to see the foreign gentleman that's taken Lindenhurst."

"Hardly a proper visitor for a gentleman," said the earl.

"Indeed, sir," said Finch. "But there's many odd visitors at Lindenhurst, foreigners and Englishmen both. If you want my opinion, sir, I believe this Count von Gessler, for that is his name, is up to no good. My sister's girl Peg is in service there and she says there is many a time when some such man comes to Lindenhurst. Some have given her such a fright for they most often come to the servants' entrance, looking like cutthroats. No matter when they appear, the count always receives them in his library. And when one of these persons is speaking with Count von Gessler, no servants may come into the room. Don't you think that very odd, sir?"

"Very odd, indeed," replied Heathfield.

"And Peg has told me that visitors come very late at night, only stay a short time, and off they go. It's said he's a smuggler."

Although Finch would have liked to have talked longer about Count von Gessler, the arrival of other customers made him take his leave of the earl. Heathfield sat mulling over what he had said.

He didn't doubt that von Gessler could be a smuggler, and he didn't like the idea of Selena's going there. Remembering that she had said she'd like to steal the Brunconian necklace, he frowned. Surely she wouldn't do anything as rash as that.

After sitting for a time, he grew increasingly uneasy. What if Selena hadn't given up the idea? What if von Gessler found her in the library unlocking his safe? Summoning the innkeeper, Heathfield asked for pen and ink. He then began to write a note to Selena.

The servant who handed Selena his lordship's communication did so very discreetly. She was quite surprised to see that the note was from the earl and that, in addition to proclaiming that he loved her very much, he stated that he was worried she hadn't given up her idea of trying to get the necklace back. On no account, he cautioned, was she to attempt anything so foolish as what she had suggested. If anyone must attempt such a risky enterprise, he wrote, he would be the one.

Selena was delighted by this note. She was certain that he would succeed and that the necklace would soon be restored to its rightful owners.

Deciding to make certain that von Gessler was well occupied at dinner, Selena dressed in one of her most attractive gowns, an extremely low-cut creation of ivory silk that revealed her considerable charms to good advantage. When they arrived at Lindenhurst, Selena was pleased to see that von Gessler seemed quite taken with her appearance. She smiled her most dazzling smile at him and seemed to hang on his every word.

While the duke was glad to see his sister being so pleasant to von Gessler, he didn't like the fact that the count seemed so enamored of her. He noted how von Gessler's eyes seemed rather fixated on his sister's décolletage. Of course, thought the duke, one could hardly blame him, considering Selena's dress and the unseemly cleavage it revealed. Although such gowns were in fashion, Melford thought his sister might show a bit more decorum.

During dinner Selena outdid herself being charming to von Gessler. She was gratified to see that the count seemed totally enthralled by her interest and flattery.

While Henrietta found her sister-in-law's behavior toward von Gessler rather perplexing, she was glad to see that Selena appeared to be enjoying herself. After dinner, the two ladies adjourned to the drawing room to allow the gentlemen to enjoy their port and masculine conversation.

Noting a striking marble-topped table, the duchess began to discuss the furniture and how cleverly von Gessler had decorated the room. After a time, the duchess remarked. "I believe Count von Gessler has a *tendre* for you, my dear. And I must say you seem to have changed your opinion of him. I never thought you liked him."

"Well, I know that James is fond of him so I decided I should be civil," said Selena.

"Well, I don't think James would ever approve of him as a husband for you. The fact remains that he is a foreigner."

"Yes, of course," said Selena, "but I have no interest in the count whatsoever, I assure you."

"I'm glad of it," said Henrietta. "James certainly loves his pictures." The duchess glanced at the pictures hanging in the drawing room. "There are several in the gallery that James would love to own."

"There are some lovely ones here to be sure," replied Selena, "I wonder when the gentlemen will join us."

"It may be some time if they're talking of art."

She had scarcely said these words when the drawing room opened and in walked Melford. Selena was surprised to see that he was alone. "Where is the count, James?" she asked.

"Oh, a servant said someone had been waiting in the library for him. Very odd time to receive callers, but von Gessler said he wouldn't be but a minute."

"He went to the library!" cried Selena, quite startled.

"Why, what is the matter?" said the duchess.

Selena rose from her place on the sofa. "I must see him. Yes, I must do so at once." She hurried from the room without another word. The duke and duchess, very much surprised, exchanged a glance and then followed after her.

Heathfield had arrived at Lindenhurst very late. Remembering what the innkeeper had said, the earl had gone to the servants' entrance. He had adopted a mysterious and rather menacing demeanor, saying he wished to see the count. When he had been informed that von Gessler had guests for dinner, Heathfield had said that he would wait for him in the library and that no one was to disturb von Gessler on his account.

The earl had been relieved that none of the servants seemed overly concerned. He had been shown to the library where the fire blazed in the enormous hearth. There was a lamp lit on the desk as well so that the room wasn't completely dark.

After being certain that he was alone, Heathfield had gone to the desk. It had taken him a good long time to find the key. Indeed, the earl had begun to think he was never going to discover the hidden drawer Selena had mentioned when his hand had finally felt a small metal latch.

Things had gone more smoothly once he had the key. Going to the cabinet, he had easily found the safe inside, and he had had no trouble unlocking it.

Although the earl was no stranger to fine jewelry, he had been unprepared for the magnificence of the diamonds on the swan necklace. After staring at it for a moment, he tucked it carefully into his coat pocket.

Then he had taken out the papers, closed the cabinet, and had brought them over to the desk. Unfolding them, he quickly paged through a number of documents.

Von Gessler restrained himself from whistling a merry tune as he proceeded from the dining room to the library. He was in the best of moods. There was no mistaking Lady Selena's interest in him. Why, she was almost throwing herself at him, he thought. Yes, the evening was going exceptionally well. And while he didn't like being interrupted by this visitor, he knew it wouldn't take long and he would soon be able to join his guests once again.

Opening the doors to the library, the count stepped inside. He saw a tall man standing over the desk looking at papers. "Yes?" he said brusquely.

So intent was Heathfield on the papers that he hadn't heard the doors open. He looked up in surprise.

"Who are you!" demanded the count. "What are you doing?"

With admirable aplomb the earl folded up the papers and stuffed them inside his coat. "Why, good evening, von Gessler, I'm sorry to intrude on you when you have guests. I shall call another time."

"Who are you?" repeated the count. Then he seemed to recognize him. "You are the Earl of Heathfield!"

"At your service," said his lordship with an ironical bow.

Glancing over at the cabinet, von Gessler's face grew ashen as he noted that the doors appeared to be slightly ajar. He turned back to the earl with a horrified look. "I demand to know what you are doing here? I will have those papers, Heathfield."

"No, I prefer to keep them."

"Give them to me!"

"No, I will not," replied the earl.

Von Gessler reached up and pulled a saber from the wall. Brandishing it before him, he walked toward the earl. "Give me those papers."

"Come, come, von Gessler, don't do anything you'll regret."

"You cannot believe I will allow you to take those papers from this room. I shall kill you first."

"Kill me?" said the earl as if the idea were inconceivable. "And how will you explain murdering a peer of the realm?"

"Who can be blamed for killing a common thief?" said the count, coming nearer.

Heathfield glanced from his adversary to the door, wondering what to do. Could he make a run for it? There were other weapons hanging on the wall. Should he try to grab one and fight the count? Von Gessler stepped closer, his menacing weapon gleaming in the firelight.

Jumping away from the desk, the earl quickly snatched another sword from the wall. "Very, well, count. I shall enjoy having the opportunity to teach you a lesson. You're a cheat and a traitor. When the truth is known about you, I won't be surprised if you hang."

Von Gessler needed no further provocation. He ran at the earl, striking hard with his saber. His lordship parried the blow and there was the clang of steel upon steel.

The count jumped back, then delivered another sword thrust. Again Heathfield parried it skillfully. At that moment Selena entered the room and uttered a cry. The duke and duchess followed behind.

"What in God's name is going on!" cried Melford. Then recognizing the earl, he gasped. "Heathfield!"

Henrietta screamed as von Gessler renewed his blows with increased vigor. The earl defended himself, and then after one particularly violent thrust, riposted quickly, catching the count off balance and knocking his sword from his hand. Heathfield closed in on his now weaponless adversary, placing the point of his saber against his chest. "I swear I'll have no qualms about killing you," said the earl, his face reddened with fury and exertion.

"Are you insane, Heathfield?" cried Melford. "Henrietta, run for the count's servants."

The duchess, however, was frozen in her tracks.

"I won't kill him," said the earl, still pressing the point of his sword against von Gessler. Taking the papers from his coat, he tossed them to the duke. "Look at these, Melford. Here is evidence of what your friend the count has been doing. He has been selling secrets to a variety of buyers. And there is ample evidence there that he has been spying for the French."

"Good God!" cried the duke.

"But what is even more amusing is that he has been selling forgeries of artworks. You'll find a letter from one of his confederates in Milan. And if you don't read Italian, there is a document from a master forger in Paris that will interest you."

Melford regarded the earl in considerable astonishment for a moment before picking up the papers and beginning to glance through them. "What are you going to do?" said von Gessler.

"I'm going to deliver you to the appropriate authorities," said the earl. "Put your hands behind your back." When the count hesitated, his lordship pushed the point of the sword against his chest. "Do as I say!"

Von Gessler put his hands behind his back. Untying his neck-cloth, the earl unwrapped it from around his neck and then bound the count's hands with it.

After glancing through a few pages, the duke frowned. It appeared to be true. Von Gessler was the worst sort of blackguard. He looked over at the earl. "You're right, Heathfield."

The earl nodded. "Now let us escort our friend out of here. Your carriage is waiting, is it not, Melford?"

The duke nodded and Heathfield grasped von Gessler firmly by the arm and led him out of the room. Melford and the ladies carefully picked up all of the incriminating papers before following after the earl.

30

Von Gessler was taken to the magistrate, who was very sur- prised to hear that such a nefarious character had been liv- ing in their midst. The duke had been very much shaken to realize that a man he had trusted was such a villain. And while Melford had found it appalling to think that the count had been in the pay of both Prussia and France, it had been even more shocking to find that he had been in the business of selling art forgeries.

The duke had been so disturbed at von Gessler's treachery that he hadn't been able to become very upset about the idea that Heathfield had come to Sussex to find Selena. After all, he had had to admit that the earl had cut a very dashing figure when fighting von Gessler. One couldn't deny that he had courage, the duke had concluded.

The following day, when Heathfield appeared at Gateswood Lodge, Melford was quite civil to him. Selena, who had spent the morning begging her brother to reconsider his opinion of the earl, had been rather frustrated that Melford seemed disinclined to do so. Thus, when the two men went off for a serious confer- ence in the billiard room, Selena felt rather nervous.

However, when they emerged, she could tell by Heathfield's face that the interview had been a success. "Yes, I have given my permission," said Melford rather grudgingly.

"Oh, James!" Selena embraced her brother and then Henrietta, who was very pleased that her sister-in-law would be joining the ranks of married ladies.

Later on, Sophie was very pleased to observe Heathfield and her aunt walking together past the huge oak trees. Watching from the nursery window, Sophie was delighted to see the earl take her aunt into his arms and kiss her, a fact she eagerly reported to her mother and everyone else in the household who would listen.

*   *   *

Attired in her new gown, Princess Frederica viewed her reflection with pleasure. The dress fashioned from the blue silk Selena had given her looked stunning. "Oh, you look so beautiful, my dear!" cried Mrs. MacNeil, coming into the room.

"Thank you, Tommie," said the princess, turning first one way and then the other. "It was silly having it made. I don't think I'll wear it anywhere. Still, it is wonderful to have such a dress."

"Yes, it is," said Mrs. MacNeil. "And don't worry, I'm sure you'll have occasion to wear it."

"I beg your pardon, madam," said a maid, entering the room. "There are two ladies to see you. The Duchess of Melford and Lady Selena Paget."

"What!" cried Frederica. "I thought that Lady Selena had gone to the country."

"She must have returned," said Mrs. MacNeil. "How wonderful for her to call. And the duchess as well! You must show them your gown. Lady Selena will be so pleased to see what has become of her blue silk."

"Oh, yes," said Frederica, eager to do so.

The two ladies went to the drawing room where they found Selena and Henrietta waiting for them. They both curtsied to Frederica.

"Duchess and Lady Selena," said Frederica. "I thought you had gone to Northumberland."

"We actually went to Sussex," said Selena, smiling brightly at Frederica. "That dress is marvelous."

"Yes, it is," said Henrietta. "Indeed, that color is perfect for you, Princess Frederica."

Mrs. MacNeil invited her guests to be seated. "You are very kind to call on us. It is so good to see you. Did you enjoy your time in Sussex?"

"Yes, we did," said Selena. "I know that you both will be interested to hear all about it. But first, I have something for Princess Frederica." Selena, who had been holding an ornate box, handed it to the princess.

"Not another gift?" said Frederica. "Really, you have done enough in giving me the silk."

"Well, it really isn't a gift, but I imagine you will be glad to see it. Do open the box."

"Very well." Frederica opened the lid of the box. When she saw what was inside she was speechless.

It was Mrs. MacNeil who spoke. "It is the Swan of Brunconia!" she cried.

After staring down at the necklace with an astonished expression, she turned to look at Selena. "How is this possible?"

"You may thank the Earl of Heathfield," said Selena. "He obtained it from Count von Gessler."

"Obtained it?" said Frederica. "But how?"

"Well, I shall tell you that in a moment," said Selena with a smile. "But first, there is someone waiting to see you." Rising from her chair she went to the drawing room door and opened it. "Do come in, gentlemen," she said. The Earl of Heathfield entered the room first. He smiled at the ladies and bowed to them. "I'm sure you remember the Earl of Heathfield," continued Selena.

"Yes, of course," said Frederica, very much surprised to see him.

"And here is a gentleman well known to your highness," said Selena. "Do come in, sir." Maximilian walked into the drawing room, causing Frederica to gasp. "Prince Maximilian of Brunconia," announced Selena.

"Maximilian!" cried Frederica, rising to her feet.

"My dearest Frederica!" exclaimed the prince, hurrying over to her and enfolding her into his embrace.

Frederica hugged him tightly, tears coming to her eyes. Then she pulled away. "I did not want you to see me. Truly I did not. It is really too cruel to see each other."

"*Nein, nein, liebchen,*" said Maximilian. "There is no reason that we should not meet."

"But what of Princess Charlotte?" said Frederica.

Heathfield stepped forward. "I fear, your highness, that Maximilian has no chance of marrying her. I've heard that she has decided to choose Prince Leopold of Belgium."

"It is you I shall marry," said Maximilian, his voice filled with emotion.

"But that isn't possible," cried Frederica. "I have no money!"

"But I don't need to find a rich wife anymore," said Maximilian.

"What!" cried Frederica. "That cannot be!"

"It's true," said Selena. "You see, your highness, in addition to obtaining the Swan of Brunconia, Lord Heathfield discovered a number of documents in von Gessler's possession. They were evidence proving what you said about him."

"But that is wonderful!" said Frederica. "But what has that to do with Maximilian's not needing a rich wife?"

"Do explain it, Cousin Heathfield," said Maximilian, smiling at the earl.

"The charges against our friend the count were very serious," said the earl. "In order to save his life, he agreed to give our government much useful information as well as a considerable amount of his ill-gotten wealth. Most of it is in England. Some of the other crown jewels of Brunconia as well as a large amount of Brunconian gold have been recovered. It will be restored to Brunconia."

"Yes, and that is not all the good news," said Maximilian. "My cousin is arranging for engineers to come to Brunconia to see how mines may be started. Heathfield will provide the capital for us to get started. And so there is no reason why we shouldn't get married."

"Oh, Maximilian!" cried Frederica, allowing herself to be once again taken into Maximilian's arms.

While the duchess and Mrs. MacNeil congratulated the happy couple, Heathfield took Selena's hand and led her from the room into the hallway.

"What are you doing, Heathfield?"

"We'll only be gone a moment," he said, placing his arms around her. "I wanted to kiss you."

She smiled up at him. "I shan't object," she said raising her lips to his and kissing him passionately. "You are truly wonderful."

"It is you who are wonderful, my darling," said his lordship, kissing her again.

"But I wasn't the one to fight von Gessler and obtain the necklace and the papers. And you are the one to risk your capital on Brunconian mines."

"It will be your capital as well when you are my wife," said the earl. "And I'll take care not to bankrupt us, in any case. And besides, it isn't a risky venture."

"Brunconian mines not a risky venture?"

He shook his head. "Not when the luck of Brunconia has been restored with the swan necklace."

She smiled. "Yes, I suppose you're right." And she kissed him happily.

Epilogue

Six months later there was great happiness in Brunconia when Prince Maximilian wed Princess Frederica. Present at the wedding in the cathedral of the Brunconian capital city were the Earl and Countess of Heathfield, Mr. and Mrs. John MacNeil, and Mr. Percy Hastings.

While Percy had harbored some disappointment that his cousin would never be consort to the Queen of England, he was somewhat mollified to see how gloriously happy his cousin and Frederica were on their wedding day. Percy had had some misgivings about coming to Brunconia, but he found the country's rugged beauty very appealing. He enjoyed meeting his other Brunconian relations, who made a great fuss over him, and he also appreciated the warm welcome given him and Heathfield and Selena by the common people of Brunconia.

The wedding feast lasted long into the night and there were fireworks and dancing in the streets. The earl and his countess stayed very long at the festivities before finally retiring to their rooms at the palace.

When Heathfield had Selena to himself, they stood by the window of their bedchamber with their arms entwined watching the fireworks. "Isn't it splendid?" said Selena. "And didn't Frederica look lovely?"

"Almost as lovely as you, my darling," said his lordship, pulling her close.

"And she wore the Swan of Brunconia," said Selena.

"Yes," said the earl, nuzzling her neck. "And so luck has returned to Brunconia." He smiled. "And I am the luckiest man in the world."

Selena didn't dispute this fact, but leaned up to kiss her lord and husband.